LETTERS IN MISSISSIPPI

GINA MOROSEY

○○ | Nerd Squad Revolution

OO | Nerd Squad Revolution

For Jonathan James Tracy —
If it weren't for him, this story would never have found the roots it
needed to grow.

"I will never forget how the sun shone brightly over the Mississippi River. As kids, we taught each other to swim there by throwing ourselves in. That's how you learn. You just swim."

WARREN LANDRY

As I leaned forward with my thumb sticking out into the I-65 traffic, I'd decided I was going to die.

"Promise you won't tell Leah where I'm going," I shouted into the cell phone pressed against my ear.

My thumb had almost frozen solid, and I was about five more rejections away from accepting my fate as a roadside cryptid when some beat-up PT Cruiser finally slowed down. I knew it was my ride when it came to a stop about twenty yards down the shoulder.

"Promise you won't fucking kill yourself," my little brother, Trevor, demanded on the other end.

It had been thirty minutes of nothing but vehicles zooming by, the wind almost blowing me back into the steep ditch behind me. I figured everyone had watched enough serial killer hitchhiker movies to know better than to pick up a guy with a guitar case on his back and whatever bludgeoning tool might be stashed inside. One driver had stuck his hand out the passenger window and flipped me the bird. Another passenger tossed an empty beer bottle at me, and I had about half a second to decide if it was a free drink or a hate crime. It barely missed my face, so I guess it was just character development.

On the bright side, all the other vehicles politely ignored me.

I hurried to where the PT Cruiser had come to a full stop before responding to my smart-ass brother.

"Kill myself and *get* myself killed are two very different things," I said. "One's a happy ending. The other's just bad luck."

"Piss off, Braden."

"Love you, too."

I snapped my flip phone in two and tossed it.

I watched the pieces tumble down the ditch, finally sinking into the shallow stream of water.

No more texts. No more guilt. Just me and the road.

Cars sped past, whipping cold morning wind that felt good against my nervous neck sweat. Late May mornings could still be chilly in Indiana, and I'd forgotten my jacket in my hurry out of the house. I patted my back pocket to make sure my pen and notepad hadn't fallen out during my life-threatening interstate hike.

I slid the strap of my guitar case off my shoulder and knocked on the passenger window.

Whoever it was, they better not have known me. I couldn't get caught. Not now. Not ever.

I bent down and peeked through the half-open window. The driver reminded me of a gray-haired Willem Dafoe.

"I can take you as far as Louisville," he shouted, his clear tenor voice cutting through the rumble of the interstate.

I nodded, and without overthinking it, opened the passenger door, hopped in, and settled my guitar securely between my knees.

I'm not going to lie . . . part of me wondered if this dude was a serial killer, a rapist, or just a guy who really committed to the aesthetic. The 70s porn 'stache, the tight blue jeans. If he had a mullet, I would've rolled out of the car like an action hero and never looked at Willem Dafoe the same way again.

He pressed the gas pedal as soon as I shut the door. I glanced at the back seat and spotted an open case of Diet Mountain Dew cans resting in the middle. Around me, there wasn't much to notice except a broken tape measure on the floor and an open

Styrofoam cup of coffee in the center console, which splashed when the guy jerked into the right lane.

I was glad I wasn't traveling with much, just enough cash for food and a motel for a week until I got on my feet. Bringing my credit card would've left a trail, and I wasn't in any position for anyone to find me, especially Leah.

It was just me, some cash in my wallet, my guitar, a baggie of depressing depression pills, and a small notepad and pen in my jeans pocket.

I turned to check this dude out. Not in a "lover boy, gay Spiderman" kind of way, more like a "I'm not about to let him pull a revolver on me" kind of way. I'd guess he was around fifty, but I didn't think his gray hair was from old age. He was probably one of those rare types who always had grayish hair, like Taylor Hicks from *American Idol*. I'd always wished for something like that. Not gray hair, but something that set me apart from the crowd.

"Got any plans in Louisville?" he asked, like he really didn't give a shit. Guess that was the socially acceptable thing to do. Make small talk about stuff that didn't really matter. So, I answered him.

"Going to play some music." I rested my hand on top of my guitar. "Hopefully find a gig and make some good tips."

He glanced over me a few quick times before saying, "Play guitar . . . you look like you're barely out of college."

Damn. I liked that one. Never been told I looked older than I was.

"I'm eighteen," I said. "Got the whole summer to figure that out."

He sort of grumbled as he veered into the fast lane. I know . . . spoiled rich kid with all the time in the world to figure out who he is and what he wants. But what most people didn't know was that I'd spent eighteen years drowning in someone else's idea of who I was supposed to be, like a Sims character with free will turned off. Sometimes it felt like my head just bobbed above the water long enough to take a breath, catch a glimpse of the life I wanted. But before I could see any clearer, I'd sink back into the deep end.

I didn't *look* rich, though. Grandpa Norris' brown shoes were a size too big, but they were comfortable. My mom would get frustrated that I never wore the shoes she bought me for Christmas, but hey, when I liked something . . . I liked it. Just like my favorite Beatles shirt I was wearing. And the yellow tie with red polka dots? Damn, Leah loved that dorky tie, how I'd just throw it around my neck because I didn't know how to tie it properly. I wore it over most of my shirts because it made people laugh. If anything set me apart from the crowd, it was that tie.

I would've given anything to bring Leah along with me. I slid my fingers down the sides of my tie, staring at the red polka dots.

I looked up, watching the trees pass by the passenger window, like a sweet goodbye to the life I'd known. It pulled my thoughts back to The Tree.

The Tree.

A place where my friends and I hung out and ate lunch every day at school. A place that pulled us out of life's chaos, giving us space to dream and just . . . . be. I remembered lying beside Leah, staring at the evening sky. Holding her hand, admiring her content expression, wondering what beautiful things she might be thinking about. She was a dreamer, so much of what I wanted to be. Being around Leah had a stronger effect than swallowing prescription pills just to pretend I wasn't depressed for a day.

As Willem Dafoe drove, I shifted my attention from the passing trees, patting Susie, my acoustic guitar, gently between my knees. She was a light brown Collings, but naming her Colleen felt too cliché. I'd wanted to name her after Dr. Seuss, but "Seuss" seemed too butch for a guitar as pretty as she was, so I chose something more melodic. *Susie.* She rhymed, told one-of-a-kind stories, and was about to teach me more about myself than I ever expected . . . I hoped, anyway.

"Is that Dr. Seuss?" I remembered Leah asking when I took her to The Tree for the first time.

I read *And to Think That I Saw It on Mulberry Street* to her as we sat at The Tree. I loved that story ever since Grandpa Norris first read it to me when I was little. It was the saddest story I'd ever heard, but it also gave me immense hope. The endless possibilities behind one character's eyes. The dreams someone could have, only to be pushed back into the imagination when the threat of judgment loomed. How is it that I, too, dimmed my light the moment I walked inside my own home?

"Are you going to finish it?" Leah had asked when I stopped at the final page.

I'd always pretended the final page didn't exist

"I don't like the ending," I responded, lost in thought for a moment. "I think I'm going to change it."

That same night, lying under The Tree, she promised me she wouldn't lose sight of the forest for the trees. I made no such promise. However, I did vow to myself that I wouldn't fuck up her life, too, and I made Trevor promise not to tell her where I was going. My little brother—fourteen years old with the loyalty of a mafia member—wasn't even going to tell our parents. What he didn't know, though, was that I hadn't told him the full truth.

I was planning on killing myself.

I glanced briefly at Willem Dafoe beside me. I supposed it was my turn to say something. He probably thought I was a coddled trust fund baby who didn't give a damn about anything, too cool to care. The truth was, I did care, just about the important things. And a trust fund? Not that I knew of. My dad owned the Gregory Auto Shops in Tipton County, Indiana, and he made me earn every penny of my savings from all those after-school and weekend shifts.

"You, uh . . ." Why the hell was I so awkward? "What's your name?"

He kept his eyes on the road, kind of a serious guy.

"Paul," he said. "And you?"

"Bra—" I stopped myself. I wasn't used to this runaway life. I'd only run away once before when I was fifteen. Took a bus all the way to Alabama and stayed with Grandpa Norris until my parents dragged me back home.

I didn't care if people knew my name, but I was still too close to home.

"Blake," I said, trying to sound confident. Not my best work. I could've gone with something cooler like Sebastian, Phoenix, or Axel. Instead, I sounded like a guy who sold insurance.

Blake could be cool, too. Blake, the guitarist. Blake, the guy who played gigs down south until Epic Records offered him a once-in-a-lifetime record deal. Blake, who was too cool for a record deal, turned it down and went solo to follow his dream, staying true to himself. I kind of liked Blake.

"How long you been playin'?" Paul asked.

"I took lessons all my life but haven't had much time to really play around . . . to see what I've got." I realized I probably shouldn't talk too much, but by the time anyone found out I was gone, I'd never see this guy again. Hell, it was better than my psychologist, who kept everything I said in her red journal of dumbness.

"I've written a handful of songs," I continued. "I want to write more. Maybe I'll get inspired somewhere and it'll all pour out."

"Don't have any restaurants where you live? Bars? Schools where you can play?"

"Not possible when my parents have my leash so tight, I can barely breathe to sing a note."

Paul pressed his lips together in a frown that said he knew exactly what I meant.

"No better place to find your soul than down south," he said.

I nodded and cleared my throat. I didn't know why I always got so nervous around people, yet at the same time, I couldn't shut up.

"That's why my grandpa moved down there. He said it's the heart of every good artist whether that be a painter, musician, writer . . . anyone who has a splash of color in their spirit."

"Oh? Guess I better get down there myself."

"You work in Louisville?" I asked, feeling a little more comfortable, allowing myself to look at him longer. He cleared his throat and gripped the steering wheel tighter with one hand, his other resting in his lap. Paul was a cool name, too. Pauls didn't play by the rules. They were too cool for school and didn't even bother answering people's questions.

"You stayin' with your grandpa then?" he asked.

"Not at first. He doesn't live in Louisville."

"What're you going to do then? Sleep on the streets?"

"I'll probably hop around a few hotels until I can make enough tips."

"And your folks?"

I couldn't tell him I'd left home. Even though I was eighteen, my parents would flip. But if they really knew me, they'd get it . . . I was never coming home again.

"They know I'll be visiting my grandpa," I lied. "They love family."

I dragged the word *love* through my head, knowing it wasn't true. Grandpa Norris wasn't the only family member they'd stopped talking to. I had an aunt down in Memphis . . . Sibby. I barely remembered her, but I remembered enough. The last time I saw her, she was in our kitchen with my mom, whipping up a puff pastry dessert. I was sprawled out in the living room, glued to a classic rock special on MTV. The clinking of dishes drifted through the house, and soon, the warm scent of fresh-baked crust and berries filled the air. After a few glasses of wine, their giggles sounded like chipmunks overdosing on estrogen. I never understood why they stopped talking. I liked Sibby. She'd sneak me a candy bar with a wink every time she visited, even though my parents hardly ever let us have sweets. I'd take it, hide in my room, and scarf it down, thinking how cool she was for breaking the rules. I wondered what she was up to now. I was planning to pay her a visit, especially if she would make me one of those pastries . . . and tell me why she and my mom had cut ties.

"Spill it, kid," Paul said.

His voice pulled me back to the present.

"Silence says a lot," he said, not even glancing at me. "I had rough parents, too. Mine perfected the art of emotional neglect with a side of 'you'll understand when you're older.' Guess what? I'm still waiting."

I watched him, wondering if I'd accidentally said my thoughts out loud. I stretched my arms out, keeping one hand firmly on Susie. I stretched a lot when I was nervous.

"Mine are the opposite," I said. "They're too good at the parenting shit. They go overboard to the point where I don't even want to get out of bed in the morning because I don't like who I am . . . who they want me to be."

Paul grunted. "Ain't nothin' like a potent shot of pressure to push someone overboard."

"The opposite happened to my dad. My grandpa was too loose with him, let him try too many things, didn't set up the right parameters for him. My dad's type . . . needs parameters. Otherwise, they fall hard into drugs or alcohol."

"Which one hit him?"

"Alcohol. I'd never seen him take a drink, but he told me it all happened before I was born. He's been sober since. My grandpa though . . . he drank a lot when my dad was a kid. It's not like I don't understand my dad; it's just one extreme to the other. Where's the middle way? And my mom lost her mind after my brother was diagnosed with diabetes. At least she finally had something to fixate on. She'd tried everything else. Turns out, stress and guilt also make a potent cocktail."

"Tough luck."

"Yeah." I rolled my neck in a slow circle, then turned my gaze to the passing trees outside the window.

I could never look at a tree the same way again after meeting Leah. She wasn't like my other friends. Back in middle school, she was the kind of girl my friends and I used to laugh about with mismatched thrift store clothes, stringy hair, quiet... easy to target. And that worn-out unicorn shirt she always wore, secretly, I liked it. My friends and I could be assholes, so I understood why she didn't like me much when we officially met this year during *The Miracle Worker* auditions.

I glanced over at Paul to make sure I hadn't said anything out loud, but he was still focused on the road ahead. I didn't want him asking about Leah. The less he knew about me, the better, especially in case anyone came looking for me after I disappeared.

I'd driven to the high school earlier that morning. I'd already made my decision. I was leaving town and never coming back. So, I'd written Leah a letter explaining why I was leaving and that it wasn't her fault. I jammed about ten grand of my savings into the envelope for her. Enough for college, or whatever she wanted. It was crazy to bury ten grand at The Tree, but Leah was the only one who knew about the letters. I trusted her to find it.

I buried it in a Ziplock bag, and when I did, I uncovered a letter that she had previously buried. My heart pounded as I glanced around. It was Sunday. No one in sight. As much as I longed to see her, a wave of relief washed over me. The last thing I needed was to see those glistening brown eyes begging me to stay.

In her letter, she basically said that she wasn't going to go to college because she needed to stay here with me. As much as it meant to me, I couldn't let her do that. She was meant for bigger things. For *her* life.

Not for this. Not for me.

I read her words over and over, each one sinking in, and still I had to let her go. I wasn't about to let her sacrifice her future just because I couldn't figure mine out.

Leah had big dreams. Well, maybe not big to the world, but for Leah Roy, they were everything. College. A simple life. Happiness. That's what she wanted, and somehow, in the chaos of it all, I could see how beautiful and important those dreams were.

People always said we needed these massive goals. That to succeed in life, we had to be constantly climbing the ladder, breaking records, shattering ceilings. If we weren't chasing something bigger than ourselves, we were failing.

But Leah wasn't failing. She was living. And I couldn't help but think that maybe *we* had it wrong. What happened to just being in the moment? To enjoying life without worrying about what you hadn't achieved yet? Maybe her dreams weren't about conquering the world. Maybe they were about conquering *her* world.

She didn't want to be Warren Buffet. She just wanted to be Leah Roy.

And me? I just wanted to be Braden Gregory. I didn't know who he was yet, but I was damn sure going to die trying to figure him out.

"How long you gonna be hotel hoppin'?"

I snapped back to reality at Paul's question. For a second, I'd forgotten where I was, floating in my mind like a balloon caught between the clouds and the earth. I shifted uncomfortably in my seat, trying to steady myself. It was strange. Talking about it made everything feel more . . . real.

"I don't know," I said, glancing at the road ahead. "Until I figure things out, I guess. Not really in any rush."

I let my hand slide from Susie, forcing it to rest naturally on my knee. I wasn't sure why I always ended up gripping Susie like my lifeline. It wasn't like she was going anywhere. But when I was alone, or when my thoughts spiraled, having something to hold onto—something real—made the chaos in my head feel just a little more manageable.

Paul chuckled again, the sound more guttural this time, like he had spent years accumulating dust in his chest. He kept his eyes on the road, the occasional flick of his hand tightening around the steering wheel as if the car, too, was something he was trying to hold together.

My stomach growled. I'd skipped breakfast in my dash out the back door. The thought of cheeseburgers, the kind you could only get from some greasy diner off the side of a highway, sounded like heaven. The kind that came with soggy fries that never quite matched the picture on the menu. I hadn't eaten much lately. Lost about ten pounds over the last month.

Ever since my fuck-up, food didn't seem as important. Sucking down a whole bottle of antidepressants in the back of my minivan didn't fix anything, and it didn't kill me either. All it did was hurt people. Leah, Trevor, my friends, my parents, even the people at the hospital who probably looked at me like "Great, another one." It was easier to numb myself with pills, at least until I realized it wasn't doing a damn thing. Just making me feel worse and causing more damage than I could handle.

And then, there was the spiral. The mental one that started every time I felt that emptiness inside, that sinking feeling like I was being swallowed whole by everything I hadn't been able to face. You know where everything goes dark and you can't see past the next minute, let alone a future worth sticking around for.

I was getting sick of spirals. Sick of being constantly caught in one, spinning around and around with no way out. The thing about spirals is you always think you're on the edge of something. Hope, relief, freedom. And then the next curve drops you right back into the abyss.

Every part of me wished Leah never had to find me like that. Seizing in the back seat of my van, like some kind of electrocuted idiot. I could almost laugh at how I must've looked. What a handsome devil I was—foamy drool stuck to my face, dripping delicately down my neck like a before shot for a "Don't Do Drugs" ad, but with way more style. My eyes rolled back like I'd seen the light and decided, "Nah, not today." If my obituary had been written, I hope they'd at least have the decency to Photoshop my dignity back in.

I remember hearing Leah's voice. Her frantic screams echoing in my head, as if they were coming from a deep well. She was probably yelling my name, though I couldn't be sure. Everything sounded muffled, like I was underwater. The paramedics were shouting orders, moving me, pulling me out of the van, but I couldn't process any of it. I just felt the cold creep in, cold from my skin, from the numbness in my veins.

Then, the world went black.

I woke up on a hospital bed. It wasn't a sudden shift back into consciousness, but more like coming to, piece by piece, and realizing I was trapped in some miserable, surreal version of my life.

As I was freezing down to my bones, all I could do was lie there, shivering under the hospital sheets. The air in the room felt so damn sterile, I could smell it. That clinical scent that burned my nostrils.

And then I saw her.

My mom sat next to me, squeezing a wet tissue in her hand. I could tell she had been crying, even before I saw the traces of makeup smeared on the tissue she held tightly. She didn't look at me right away. She just stared at the ball of wet tissue in her hand, rubbing it between her fingers, like maybe it could somehow clean up the mess I'd made of everything. It took me a second to realize what I was seeing. Her face was red, her eyes swollen. I wanted to apologize, to tell her that I hadn't meant to put her through this.

But the words wouldn't come.

She squeezed the tissue tighter when she noticed I was awake, as if the act of squeezing it could stop all the hurt. All the hurt I'd caused, all the worry. When she finally looked at me, there was nothing but silence. That silence was worse than the shouting I'd heard from the paramedics. It made me feel like I'd been lost and no one had found me.

"Braden," my mom whispered, her voice trembling in that way that could shatter any semblance of strength. I could barely keep my eyes open, but I could hear the worry in her voice. She would've called for my dad, but he wasn't there. It was just her.

I so wished Trevor would've been there. He wouldn't have made it such a big deal. He'd be leaning back in the recliner, spinning the release handle, probably bugging me to get my lazy ass out of bed and go piss in a real toilet instead of lying there like a vegetable. But my mom? She had a way of turning every situation into this suffocating thing. And I get it, I do. She wasn't sure if I was going to make it out of this. I wasn't sure either. But at the moment, I just wanted her to lighten up, to not look at me like I was already a ghost.

I didn't respond to her. I rolled around to my other side and pretended to be asleep. All I could think about was Leah, hoping I didn't scare her off. I knew it was coming though. It was just a matter of time and fuck ups. Visioning her smile made me calm in that hospital bed, even if I knew a consequential shitstorm awaited me.

Paul drove under the speed limit. We passed the billboard for the folk music fair in Greenstown, the tune of "You Can Call Me Al" by Paul Simon popped into my head. The song seemed to match my feelings for Leah in some strange way. It was playful, lighthearted, but with a certain melancholy undertone, kind of like me and her.

I remembered teasing her about not knowing Paul Simon during *The Miracle Worker* auditions. It had been a silly way to flirt, but it was all part of the chase. Leah wasn't one of those girls you could just flatter with a smoldering look and expect her to fall at your feet. She wasn't the typical "say the word and I'm yours" type. She made you work for it, made you prove yourself, and I hated how much I *liked* that about her.

I followed her around like a nerd at a bookstore until she finally gave me her number, but only because I cut the bullshit and got real. I just looked her in the eyes and said, "Just so you know, I wasn't comparing you to Paul Simon's height. He has the voice of an angel." The second I saw the warmth in her eyes and that smile —the kind that made the whole world feel lighter—I knew there was no going back. She wasn't just some girl I had a crush on. She was *Leah*, and that meant I was already in too deep.

We'd been driving for maybe five minutes when Paul veered from the fast lane into the right lane on our way to Louisville. Being on my own carried a mix of responsibility and excitement, knowing I had the freedom to do whatever I wanted. The possibilities stretched before me, and I wasn't sure what to do first. Should I stop at a Waffle House and scarf down a huge breakfast? Should I try booking a gig somewhere? Or maybe I should just set down a hat and start strumming Susie on the sidewalk?

Shit. My Chaplin hat.

Ever since I gave Leah my bowler hat, I'd been living with this strange sense of being both exposed and more myself. Like my oversized brown shoes, the Chaplin hat had belonged to Grandpa Norris. It was something I always wore, a quiet reminder that I could be myself whenever I was ready. All I had to do was take it off. Grandpa Norris never tried to be anyone other than who he was. He was a force, like Chuck Norris, the kind of guy who commanded respect without ever demanding it. That's why Leah and I started calling him Grandpa Norris.

I'd have to get another hat . . . but which one? Maybe a fedora, like *The Blues Brothers*? Yeah, I liked *The Blues Brothers*.

When the next exit came up, Paul eased off the gas. I glanced at his fuel gauge . . . only half empty.

"Pit stop?" I asked.

Paul raised an eyebrow without saying a word. Watching him

in silence made me stretch my arms, and the back of my neck broke out in a nervous sweat.

I wasn't familiar with this exit since my dad never opened any Gregory Auto Shops south of Tipton County.

Paul took the exit and slowed down, carefully steering the car off the street. I held Susie steady as the uneven grass jolted us up and down. A flat tire? Engine trouble? I glanced in the side mirror. No cars behind us, just an empty road. Ahead, only a stretch of woods where he brought the car to a stop.

I remember this movie.

Paul jerked the gear stick into park and flicked on the right blinker. Turning to me, he said, "All right. Hand it over."

My chest tightened. "My guitar?"

"No," he said, thrusting out his hand. "Your cash."

My skin turned to ice, and within a nanosecond, my thoughts shifted from "he's joking" to "oh shit, this is how I die. Murdered in a PT Cruiser." I let out a chuckle. Not the laughing kind, but the kind that slips out when you're about to shit your britches.

"You want my cash?" I asked.

"Kid, unlike you, I don't have the whole summer to figure shit out. Fork it over."

My dad always said a wallet wasn't worth more than my life.

But my dad underestimated his stubborn-ass son. "I'm not giving you my money, asshole."

I know this next part sounds like a scene from one of those killer movies, but it wasn't. It was real life.

My instincts kicked in, and I threw my hands up as Paul pulled a handgun from the side of his car door, aiming it straight at my chest. I was having an "action movie" moment, but instead of doing some cool, slow-motion roll to dodge the bullet, I just looked like a deer caught in headlights . . . minus the grace. In another nanosecond, my thoughts shifted from "this dude is a badass motherfucker" to "he's dead serious so just give him the money, you stubborn piece of shit."

In a low, steady voice, I said, "All I have is enough to keep me going for a while."

"Give it up."

"It's all I have. It's only three hundred dollars."

I could hear my dad's voice booming in my head, yelling at me to hand over my wallet to this son of a bitch.

He squinted at me, probably calculating whether I was worth the bullet. What he didn't know was that, by then, I had nothing left to lose. I'd already lost my friends, my family, Leah . . . so why not lose my mind, too?

Russian roulette with Willem Dafoe? Let's play.

We locked eyes in what felt like the coldest moment of my life, the car's rumble a steady reminder that this standoff couldn't last forever. That's what happens when someone feels like they have nothing to lose. I'd already let go of everything. I'd even tried ending my own life. This time, I wasn't going to fail.

The next thing happened faster than a blink. Paul struck me across the face with the side of the gun, the force slamming my head against the car window.

I grunted, clutching my nose as warm blood trickled over my lips. When I opened my eyes, stars spun against a haze of black fuzz, swallowing my vision.

That son of a bitch.

My hands stayed glued to my throbbing nose as Paul rifled through my pockets.

My wallet.

He got it.

Paul leaned over me and shoved the passenger door open. His voice was a low hiss in my ear. "This is the real world, kid. Welcome to it."

With a tight fist, he landed another blow, this time right under my eye. My body lurched backward, tumbling out of the car and onto the grass, but not before I grabbed Susie. She came down hard on my stomach. I doubled over with a guttural groan, blood pouring from my nose. The last thing I heard was the screech of the PT Cruiser speeding off into the distance.

Maybe I was crazy, but out of all the wild things I could've thought about then, the only image that came to mind was Leah in her unicorn shirt.

CHAPTER 2:
Goatee Hillman

"Hey, you all right, man?" a muffled voice asked above me, sounding like it was coming from inside a fish tank. For a second, I seriously thought I might be underwater. My nose felt like someone had set it on fire, with the flames spreading to the back of my head and down my neck. Cold raindrops pelted my face like they were auditioning for some kind of weather torture Olympics.

I groaned and cracked one eye open, raising a shaky hand to shield my vision from the relentless downpour. My view was blurry, but I could make out the outline of a guy standing over me.

My first thought?

Paul.

But it wasn't.

It was some younger, dark-haired dude staring at me while his expression screamed, *"Am I about to be an accomplice to something?"*

I considered explaining myself, but it wasn't worth it. Instead, I rolled onto my side with a groan that sounded like a dying walrus.

It's not too late to go back home, I thought, pressing my hand to my throbbing face. I wouldn't go home to stay, just to grab some cash and get out of there. Paul's stunt had left me broke, but I had a little emergency cash hidden at home, enough for a gas station sandwich and some dignity.

Assuming I hadn't been unconscious for days, I told myself, squinting at the gray, drizzly sky. If it was still morning, my parents and Trevor should still be at the cabin. Hopefully, I could sneak in and out. If I could just stand up without collapsing, that'd be a great start.

"Should I call someone?" dude asked.

I couldn't get caught, not this close to home. The last thing I needed was some nosy neighbor recognizing me, or worse, calling my parents. Then again, with the state I was in, I could've passed as a washed-up rock star who'd lost a fight with a bottle of whiskey and a couple of bad decisions.

"Naw, I'm good," I grunted, pushing myself to my feet like a baby deer on a bender.

Susie.

The memory hit me like Paul's fist . . . gripping my guitar as he threw me out of his car. I'd latched onto her for dear life. Literally.

I spotted her lying a few feet away. I winced as I slung the strap over my shoulder—the one spot on my body that wasn't screaming in agony—and started walking away.

"Thanks anyway," I muttered, throwing up a halfhearted wave without looking back.

I kept glancing over my shoulder to make sure he wasn't dialing 911 or lingering like some Good Samaritan with too much time on his hands. Thankfully, he hopped into his car and drove off, leaving me alone with my throbbing face, sore body, and my piss poor plan.

Once he was gone, I let out a huge sigh and crouched down, hands on my knees, trying to catch my breath.

"What the fuck?" I mumbled to myself.

Blake would've spun some bullshit about a tour gone wrong. But I wasn't Blake. I was Braden—Tipton County's least interesting runaway—and my house wasn't getting any closer while I sulked.

The rain hammered down as I ran, each drop a sting against my skin. The cold eased the heat from my bruises, but the weight of Susie on my back was feeling like a hundred-pound regret.

I'd been running for thirty minutes by the time my soaked sneakers felt like they were shrinking, or maybe my feet were swelling.

The rain eased up as Tipton came into view. The same string of hotels, the Starbucks, the McDonald's, all mocking me with their clean, dry interiors and judgmental fluorescent lights.

Luckily, it was a quiet Sunday morning, and the streets weren't packed with people who might recognize me. My parents had connections all over town, which meant a lot of folks knew me, too. None of them knew *this* version of me, though, the one lugging a guitar with a face that looked like I'd lost a fight with Rocky Balboa.

I stuck to my plan, head low, walking out of the woods and down the short hill to the main road. Crossing at the red light was the final challenge. I waited at the crosswalk, keeping my face turned away from the cars. When the light turned red, I strolled across like it was any other day.

When I made it to the other side, I let out a breath so long it was like I'd been holding it since kindergarten. Almost there. I spotted the Home Inn where Leah's mom worked. For half a second, I considered asking her for help, but then remembered the Dear John letter I'd left Leah that morning. No way was I crawling back into her life looking like a dollar store punching bag.

So, I kept walking.

No glances, no detours, no regrets . . . well, except for the whole existing-on-earth thing.

I cut through the side parking lot of the last hotel to sneak a look at my house from the back, just in case one of my neighbors was sitting on their porch. Mr. Pritchard had a habit of sipping sweet tea and staring into people's souls like he was the neighborhood's unpaid security guard. No way was I risking that.

When I reached the bushes that separated the hotels from my neighborhood, I crouched lower than a contestant on *Survivor*. The buzzing of the interstate seemed louder than ever, like it knew I was trying to focus and decided to mock me. I trudged through the bushes and trees, passing the neighbor's yard before mine. I peeked out from behind the last tree and let out another breath. No cars in the back driveway. The coast was clear.

I crept past the garage like a ninja on his worst day and tiptoed to the back door. Then, just as I reached for the handle, the kitchen light flipped on.

I flattened myself against the house like a pancake, heart pounding like I'd just been caught robbing a bank.

"What should I take out of the freezer for dinner tonight?" my mom asked from inside.

I couldn't make out my dad's reply, but the tone said, *whatever doesn't involve me having to cook.*

Great. Perfect. Wonderful. The one day they decide to park in the *front* driveway.

I squeezed my eyes shut, silently debating my next move. My options were limited, and by limited, I mean nonexistent. Grandpa Norris would've been my go-to, but he lived miles away. My friends? Loyal, sure, but dragging them into this mess felt cruel.

Then there was Mr. Hillman. My school counselor, drama teacher, and the guy who once told me, "If you're ever in trouble, call me." That was probably just his teacherly obligation talking, but Hillman seemed like he actually meant it.

Too bad he lived on the other side of town. Too bad I'd smashed my phone in half like an idiot. Too bad I was standing here pressed against my own house, debating whether I'd make it to Hillman's without collapsing in a heap or getting caught.

Oh, what a time to be alive.

I swallowed some air and nearly choked. Maybe I was in over my head. The smart and sane thing would've been to pretend this whole misadventure never happened. I could climb through my bedroom window like a cat burglar or stroll into the house and claim I'd gone for a morning jog. Sure, my parents would think it was weird. I wasn't exactly known for my athleticism, but it was still salvageable.

No.

I had a plan.

I had a vision.

I adjusted Susie's strap snugly around my shoulder and took one last look at my house. A regular middle-class home in a regular middle-class neighborhood. My dad never flaunted his success, while my mom lived for appearances. Forced smiles and fake laughs so staged, they could've been used as stock images.

I turned and walked away, staying laser-focused on my plan. Hillman's house was on the outskirts of town, where suburbia awkwardly flirted with the countryside. His tan stone house was a lot like mine, except surrounded by open fields that made you wonder if he'd wanted the rural life but chickened out at the last second.

I cut through the woods, knowing it was the shorter route even if it felt like a sadistic foot spa. My shoes squelched in the mud, my toes rebelling. Halfway there, I made a silent promise that if Hillman wasn't home, I might strangle him. Lovingly, of course. With deep gratitude for making me walk this far.

Most students saw him before school hours for their therapy sessions, but I was too mortified to admit I needed help in daylight. So, Hillman let me schedule mine after evening play rehearsals. He'd been my go-to for months now, better than my psychologist.

Hillman was quiet, relatable. He cared. After my overdose, he was the only teacher who visited me in the hospital, handing me a copy of *Death of a Salesman* and just saying, "Glad you decided against it."

My muscles burned as I trudged through the woods, and Susie had officially transformed into a three-hundred-pound deadweight strapped to my back. Every step felt like walking on a waterbed, the ground turning into mush from all the rain. I'd been soaked for over an hour, and it was no longer refreshing. It was a personal vendetta by Mother Nature.

Passing the back roads by the high school, I crouched behind some bushes, feeling like a fugitive. Cars drove by, headlights slicing through the drizzle. I hoped Leah would understand the letter I'd left her.

This trip sucked without her. This trip sucked, period. I couldn't imagine it getting worse. Then again, I wasn't about to tempt fate. Paul had already proved his uncanny ability to ruin my day, and I wouldn't put it past him to pop out of nowhere like a cartoon villain.

Hillman's house was still a ten-minute walk away. My legs protested every step and my soaked shoes squished louder than my thoughts. Wrestling practice felt like a distant memory, replaced by too many hotdogs and Dr Peppers consumed during concession stand duty at games. I'd lost most of the weight after everything went down, but now I was just skinny and embarrassingly out of shape.

This whole walking thing had to count as cardio, right? A silver lining, maybe.

At least I knew where Hillman lived. I'd been to his house a couple of times to drop off theatre props when he teamed up with Mr. Steele, our choir director. They'd built the set for *Beauty and the Beast* together. I still remembered Hillman answering the door, brown paint smeared on his white shirt, jazz music playing in the background. He'd seemed so laid-back, like a guy who had life figured out. Or at least had good taste in music.

The rain finally let up to a drizzle. The country road was quiet now, with barely any traffic to dodge. As I neared Hillman's house, I silently thanked him for living in a peaceful area but not so far into the boondocks that I'd need a survival guide to find him.

When I reached the edge of his driveway, I bent over with my hands on my knees, wheezing like I'd just run a marathon. My legs felt like they'd been replaced with overcooked spaghetti.

"Please be home," I muttered, staring at his closed garage door like it held all the answers to my problems.

What was I doing? My plan was a mess. Humiliating. Grandpa's shoes, soaked and wrecked, and no money to speak of. I questioned every decision I'd ever made.

But I couldn't turn back now.

I straightened up, puffed out my chest, and sucked in a deep, brave breath. Just as I stepped onto the driveway, the front door swung open.

Hillman stepped out, arms crossed, his face unreadable except for a faint furrow in his brow.

"Braden," he said, his tone somewhere between a question and a statement.

I gave a halfhearted shrug, water dripping from my nose onto the cement. After a pause, he motioned me inside without another word. My sore legs limped toward him, every muscle in my body screaming in protest.

I trudged past him into the mudroom and stopped just inside. He shut the door behind me with a click, then stood there, arms folded, like a disappointed dad who didn't need to say anything to make you feel like crap.

"Well, this is better than visiting you in the hospital," he said.

"Yeah, I prefer this, too."

He pointed to the bench along the wall. I slumped onto it, shrugging Susie off my back. Hillman took her gently, like she was a person, and leaned her against the wall. He said nothing, but his eyes scanned me, taking in every bruise that must have been there, every soaked inch of my existence.

As I leaned down to wrestle with my shoes, a groan escaped my throat. These weren't just shoes, they were suction-cupped prisons. I yanked at the right one until it finally gave up with a sad squelch. My foot hit the floor like a dead fish.

I peeled off the left shoe, dropping it next to its twin. Slumping against the wall, I closed my eyes, ignoring the urge to collapse.

"I just wanted to—" I began before Hillman interrupted.

"Stop."

I opened my eyes. Hillman's hand was raised, palm out, like he was putting up an invisible barrier between us.

"I don't need to hear more," he said, his voice calm but firm. "Give me your shoes."

I handed over my soggy shoes, grateful Hillman didn't make me shuffle across the room like a dying penguin. He took them silently, vanishing down the hallway without a glance back. Classic Hillman. Stoic, efficient, withholding anything that might make me feel less like a wreck.

As I sat there in the mudroom, dripping water and self-pity, I scanned my surroundings. Hillman's place looked exactly as expected. Bachelor pad meets sophistication. A couple bedrooms, taupe carpet in the living room, a couch that probably doubled as his bed on long night of grading papers, and a Van Gogh print on the wall.

I wondered if he was dating anyone. Not that I was invested or anything, but Hillman's facial hair told its own saga. Every time he tried dating, he'd show up at school with a goatee, like some badge of misplaced confidence. No goatee today.

Students used to tease him about needing a good woman to "put a little sparkle in his eyes" or maybe just give him something to do other than referee the drama club or listen to hormonal teens complain about their mediocre lives.

When my friends tossed out comments like that, I'd watch Hillman's reaction. His face was like a brick wall: unreadable, steady. I always thought Hillman seemed pretty damn content, even if he was the only black teacher at Tipton High. It must've been a bit uncomfortable, sure. But then again, sometimes I felt uncomfortable just being the only *Braden Gregory* in the room.

There was a difference, though, between content and happy. Happy was a fleeting, surface-level thing, like biting into a chocolate bar when you're craving it. Content was different. Content was deep, a kind of peace with the way life was, even if it wasn't perfect. And that was the kind of peace I saw in Hillman, a quiet sort of self-assurance that I desperately wanted for myself.

Hillman came back with a change of clothes, handing them to me with casual ease.

"Here," he said, his voice low. "Bathroom's around the corner on the left. Give me your wet clothes, and I'll toss them in the dryer."

The bathroom smelled of musky aftershave, clean but not overdone. I stepped in, feeling the pins and needles shoot up my legs as my feet slowly warmed.

Afterward, Hillman took my wet clothes to dry while I sat at his kitchen table with a fresh cup of coffee and a couple of slices of toast, still warm. He didn't say anything. I didn't either.

Showing up at a teacher's house wasn't exactly on my bucket list, but I'd crossed that line today because I was *desperately* out of options. Teachers expected me to have it together. They knew my parents, or at least knew of them. There was an unspoken standard to meet, a pedestal meant for the son my parents *wished* they had.

Screw standards and pedestals. Standards and pedestals could kiss my ass. I just wish I would've realized that way sooner. Maybe I wouldn't have succumbed to this soul sucking black hole called depression. Maybe I wouldn't have had to run away from home and fall into this humiliating mess in the first place.

"You need some kind of a plan." Hillman's voice was calm. He was still facing the counter, his back to me.

"You got a plan?" Hillman asked.

"Loosely," I said, trying to sound like I wasn't completely winging it.

He sighed. "A loose plan isn't a plan, Braden. It's just a hopeful disaster."

A hopeful disaster? Harsh, but fair. It was about as solid as my eighth-grade science project, otherwise known as 'How Fast Can a Volcano Explode If You Misread the Instructions?'

Hillman turned and handed me two crisp fifty-dollar bills.

"You don't have to give me—"

Hillman pressed the cash into my hand. "What's the plan, Braden? Where will you go? Where will you stay?"

"Thanks," I said, taking the cash. "Not sure yet."

He pointed at my face. I glanced at my blurry reflection in the microwave door. The rain had washed away most of the blood, leaving only a red nose and a purple bruise beneath my eye.

I spent a while blow-drying my shoes. Hillman handed me my clothes when they were dry, the fabric warm against my skin. Changing out of his clothes felt like shedding someone else's life, the musky aftershave lingering like an unwelcome reminder. I tied my yellow-and-red polka dot tie loosely around my neck. Because nothing screams "competent runaway" like dressing like a malfunctioning clown. Hillman tried to hand me one of his jackets, but I waved it off. I didn't need his scent lingering on me, reminding me of him every time I turned my head. I needed to stay focused.

"I'll take you to the bus station in Fort Valley," he said, grabbing his keys from the counter. "After that, you're on your own."

I nodded. No promises, no fanfare, just the cold reality that whatever happened next, I had to figure it out myself.

We left his house and climbed into his ridiculously clean green car. I slouched low in the seat, keeping my head down at the red lights, hoping nobody would recognize me, at least not until we were far enough from Tipton County. Fort Valley was only twenty minutes away, but the bus station there felt like a small portal out of my life. Straight to Louisville, and then who knows where.

I'd taken buses before. Hell, I even ran away to Alabama when I was fifteen, but this time, I'd dared myself to hitchhike. Big mistake. If I ever saw Paul again, I'd owe him a thank you for being a colossal pain in my ass, making me realize that buses are *way* safer than hitchhiking. Lesson learned.

The clock read 11:26 a.m. I hoped Leah made it to The Tree to dig up my letter. The last real letter from me, the one where I wasn't hiding behind my grandpa's voice. Funny how writing as him had been freeing in a way, but writing that letter as myself? That tore me open. And not in the sad, pitiful way. More like a door slamming open, revealing a thousand possibilities, a thousand roads that I could walk down.

I wondered what Leah was thinking as she read it. Did she understand? Did she even know it was me the whole time? Why couldn't I just tell her straight out?

I stuffed the fifty-dollar bills into Susie's pocket and placed my hand on her.

Hillman glanced at me as he stopped in front of the station.

"You know my number if you need anything." His voice was steady. "Learn from your mistakes, Braden. And be careful."

I nodded. The bus station loomed ahead, its entrance like an invitation. A step forward. A leap.

"Thanks a lot, Mr. Hillman." I reached for the car door and opened it.

"And Braden," he said, his voice strong.

I turned back, feeling his gaze like a heavy hand on my shoulder.

"I don't want to see you again in my driveway until you've figured it out."

His words hung in the air between us, and for a second, the world paused.

I wanted to tell him I didn't need a Plan B, that he'd never see me again.

I didn't say a word, just gave him a small nod and pushed the door open, stepping out into the gray morning. Gratitude settled gently on my face, like a quiet smile from within. I closed the door. He lifted his hand in a silent goodbye and then drove off, his car fading into the distance. I closed my eyes, trying to erase his image and the fact I'd never see him again.

I avoided the rain puddles like the plague as I walked to the ticket counter, moving on autopilot, my chest tight with the full force of what was happening. This was it, right? The bus, the ticket. Everything else was just noise.

The horn of the next bus to Louisville blared, cutting through the quiet buzz of the station. I quickened my step and rushed to buy my $21.95 ticket to freedom. I exchanged a crisp fifty for a pile of crumpled change and stuffed it into Susie's pocket.

I boarded the bus, scanning the aisle for an empty seat. The bus was about two-thirds full, so I found a spot somewhere in the middle, by the window. I sank into the seat, letting the hum of the engine settle around me.

For the first time in days, I didn't feel like I was suffocating.

I had no idea what was next, but for now, that was okay.

I sighed and closed my eyes, the rumble of the bus soothing for a moment. I was thankful for having a friend like Hillman. He'd been a lifeline in this sea of chaos, even if I hadn't quite figured out what I was supposed to do next.

I reached into my back pocket, pulling out my pen and notepad. The bus doors hissed shut, and the intercom screeched to life with the bus driver's voice announcing a straight shot to Louisville with no stops for the next forty-five minutes.

As the wheels began to turn, I placed Susie across my lap, using her as a desk. I leaned forward slightly, the pen pressed against the clean page in my notepad.

I'd always known what I wanted to say to her. I'd tried, sure. But my words never landed. Dinner conversations at home often revolved around my mom's insufferable chatter.

"I had the sweetest time with Madeleine's husband after church," she'd say, and I'd respond, mid-bite, "Yeah, I bet you did. He seemed real into confession last Sunday."

A few cryptic, sarcastic remarks from me were always enough

to spark heated arguments. My dad would slam his fork onto the table, his chair scraping violently against the floor, and he'd shoot up, glaring at both my mom and me like we were some inconvenient problem. Trevor would sink lower into his seat, eyes bouncing between us, praying to be anywhere else. My dad would storm off, no words, just the deafening silence of a slammed door, leaving me to sit there, still holding my fork, wondering if I should finish my meal or brace for the second coming of Christ.

But the thing was . . . I *knew* my mom loved me. Her love wasn't always easy to see, but it came in small, tangible actions. A warm hug when I walked in the door, an endless stream of questions about how my day went. Her attempts to protect us from other people's judgment, even if it felt like smothering sometimes.

She loved me. But I couldn't shake the feeling she never really understood how much she had hurt me.

I pressed the pen to the paper, finally letting the words spill out, like I'd been dying to say for so long. The letter was my chance to put it all out there without the interruption of dinner conversations or angry silences.

It was the only real thing I could give her now.

Dear Mom,

You always said that growing up with your parents was a dream, and you wanted to give that dream to your kids. Dad didn't have the same upbringing as you, so he didn't know how to give us that life you wanted. You could've just shown him how instead of doing what you did.

I won't pretend like I understand everything, but I hope you understand my choice for once . . . my choice to leave. If being your son means I have to be protected by your wings, then mom . . . I have to be someone else for a while. Your wings got me as far as their span, now it's time to let me go.

This isn't to hurt you. This isn't out of spite. This is for me, something just for me. You of all people should understand that.

Love,
Braden

CHAPTER 3:
Hoosier Best Friend?

I dozed off for thirty minutes, the rhythmic motion of the bus lulling me to sleep. I woke to the bus window vibrating against my head. I straightened up to squint at the clock.

12:34 p.m.

I rubbed my eyes, trying to shake off the grogginess. Trees blurred past outside the window. Something was calming about the motion, a reminder that I was finally moving away from the clusterfuck of a morning I had.

Relief flooded through me. Paul was gone, out of my life, and I didn't have to think about him anymore. Although I did feel a tiny bit bad for whoever the next sucker was that he'd sink his claws into.

I had a little cash. Then what? Busk? Wash dishes? Hope for a miracle?

I glanced around the bus, eyes skimming over passengers lost in books or cell phones. I peeked over my seat at the full rows.

Guess a lot of these folks work in Louisville.

I started to turn when a woman a few seats away caught my eye. She was staring right at me. I tensed, jerking my hand up in a quick, awkward wave before turning back, cursing myself.

I sank lower, hoping I hadn't made a bigger idiot of myself. The last thing I needed right now was to attract any kind of attention.

Her stare prickled the hairs on my arms. When I glanced over my shoulder, there she was, locked onto me like a heat-seeking missile.

Oh, great. A female Paul.

Except this time, she'd have to pry the cash from my cold, dead hands or shoot me. No way was I letting another one of those weirdos get close.

Across the aisle, an older man was dozing against the window, his eyes closed. Meanwhile, Creepy Paul 2.0—let's call her *Female Paul*—slid out of her seat and parked herself next to him. She had that kind of shiny, too-perfect black hair that looked like she spent hours in front of a mirror. Her skin was pale enough to glow.

"I know you," she sang, a little too excited for my liking. "Oh, goodness gracious," she said, leaning in and grimacing as she stared at my face.

Great, here comes the unsolicited concern. What's next? Is she going to offer me an essential oils starter kit?

"What in the world happened?" she asked.

Oh, you mean the gorgeous bruise Paul left me?

I shrugged, giving her my best half-smirk. "I like to think of it as a temporary tattoo."

She stared, unsure how to respond. Fine by me. I was definitely *not* looking for another conversation.

"You're Trish's boy," she said.

You've got to be shitting me.

"I used to teach Sunday school at church with your mom," she continued, oblivious to my discomfort. "You'd come in with your dad and brother. I knew I recognized you."

"Sorry, my name's Blake," I said, trying to smooth it over with my fake name and get the fuck out of there.

That's not convincing enough.

I added, "I'm heading to a meeting at Vox Talent Agency."

When her mouth curved downward, I could practically hear the gears turning in her head. She was probably wondering how she could've gotten that wrong. She examined me, narrowing her eyes, as if I were some misplaced store item she couldn't return. How embarrassing for her.

But I didn't have time for sympathy. I had to end this now.

"Blake? Trish isn't your mom?" she asked, her voice a little too loud for comfort. "I could've sworn . . ."

I raised my eyebrows and gave a half-smile, trying to sound casual. "Nope."

I still felt like an asshole for embarrassing her, even though she was technically right. I had no clue who this lady was, but my mom knew a lot of women who looked just like her.

"Well, sorry about that," she muttered, her voice turning awkward. "You look a lot like him."

"Guess I just have one of those faces."

Her expression wavered between disappointment and skepticism, and then she got up and retreated to her seat, defeated. I could practically hear her wondering if she'd just messed up her "church lady gossip" for the day.

I exhaled, glaring out the window to block out the fear.

Shit, that's one person who'll talk to my mom the second she hears I'm gone.

Time to get off this bus. I pushed myself out of my seat and made my way to the front.

"Hey, any chance you can drop me off sooner?" I asked the bus driver, trying to keep it casual, but my eyes darted over my shoulder to make sure *she* wasn't listening.

"The only stop is the bus station," he replied, barely looking up. "But if it's an emergency, I can."

I leaned in a little closer. "Well, it's an emergency."

His eyes bounced between me and the road, probably debating whether I was about to pass out or shit my pants. Fine by me. If faking a medical crisis got me off this bus, I'd clutch my stomach and groan like I was in a Pepto-Bismol commercial.

"Alrighty then," he muttered, clearly not thrilled about the detour. "I'll take you to Churchill Downs. It's about five minutes sooner than the bus station."

I hurried back to my seat, but before I sat down, I noticed the lady studying me, this time with pure doubt. It wouldn't be long before she figured out I was bullshitting her, but I'd be long gone by then.

I grabbed Susie and made my way to the front before the bus came to a stop. As soon as the doors hissed open, I raced down the steps. I slid Susie's strap over my shoulder and power-walked along the sidewalk, humming a tune to calm myself. When I heard the bus doors close, I looked over my stiff shoulder. Everybody else remained on the bus, including Female Paul, so I continued walking as if I really had a talent agency appointment. Shoulders back, chin up. Pure method acting. At this rate, I deserved an Oscar for Most Committed Liar Under Pressure.

I hurried down the sidewalk, my pace quickening as the bus rolled away behind me. The sun broke through the clouds, casting its warm glow over the historic Churchill Downs. The building loomed against the sky, with the Kentucky Derby Museum nearby, its entrances marked by CASH ADMISSION signs.

I passed under the shadows of grand arches, my eyes drawn to the large statue in the center. A jockey and horse frozen in mid-stride, muscles taut, ready to burst into motion. The flawless craftsmanship captured the folds in the jockey's uniform, the taut reins, the horse's determined expression. At the base of the statue, a gold plaque read:

BARBARO

April 29, 2003 – January 29, 2007

I stopped walking. The name hit me with a rush of memories. My dad, eyes glued to the TV screen, shouting at the race as if Barbaro's victory had been his own. I remembered that day, our shop buzzing with excitement, the radio in the corner blasting updates, the clink of tools drowned out by the roar of the crowd.

When Barbaro was injured, the whole place fell silent. It felt like a part of us had been broken too.

I shook off the memory, yet it clung to me. History had a way of doing that. Making you feel small, yet strangely connected to the past.

I took a slow breath and turned, heading for the entrance. The doors swung open, revealing a wide, open hall with photographs of Derby winners lining the walls. The place had a scent to it. Wood, polish, and the faint trace of whiskey in the air, like it carried the stories of a hundred years.

Churchill Downs was a place of legends, where history lived in the dirt beneath your feet, the air filled with the smell of horses and anticipation.

The calm of Churchill Downs felt like a distant memory to the race-day chaos it normally hosted, but there were still enough people milling about back by the sidewalk for me to feel both invisible and exposed at the same time. I glanced at the bulletin announcing the Memorial Day Racing Program tomorrow at 12:45 p.m., then looked around at the emptiness. The place had its own rhythm, even without the horses galloping and the crowds screaming. I could almost hear the echo of past races, like ghosts cheering in the wind.

I walked back toward the Barbaro statue and stopped in front of it. I had enough cash left for a cheap motel, but I needed to save it. I couldn't fall back into the comfort of hiding away in a room. If I couldn't do this now—right here, in front of strangers who might just glance at me and keep walking—then I'd never be able to. That was the deal I had to make with myself.

So, I took off my shoes and planted them in front of me like I was setting up for something real. Kneeling down before the Barbaro statue, I felt a strange connection to that horse. Barbaro, who lived fast, burned bright, and then got taken out too soon. Basically, the rockstar life minus the drugs and hotel room destruction. A symbol of both triumph and tragedy. I was still figuring out which one of those I was going to be.

I pulled Susie from her case, her familiar weight grounding me. My fingers hovered over the strings. The last time I really played was two years ago at The Tree. That day I'd been missing my grandpa, his absence like a hole in the world I couldn't fill. My whole life, he was the only one who understood me. But that day, playing "Let It Be" felt like sending a message to him. It had soothed me back then, so why wouldn't it now?

I cleared my throat and strummed. The notes rang out, like an old friend. Music had always been my escape, my voice when words failed. The vibrations from Susie's body blended into me.

My grandpa didn't care what people thought. He sneaked books out of the library, no checkout required. Once gave a Jehovah's Witness a ride just to spend an hour trying to convert *him* instead. He blasted "Stranglehold" by Ted Nugent at my grandma's funeral just to see who could keep a straight face. Basically, if brave was a person, it was Grandpa Norris.

I sang, though my vocals cracked like a preteen at a school talent show. But it was something.

One couple passed by, bobbing their heads to the beat, and for a second, I thought, *Maybe I'm not completely invisible.*

My nerves relaxed as I finished "Let It Be." No one stopped to listen, but I noticed a few thumbs up as people walked by. I took the opportunity to toss a nickel in my shoes, pretending it wasn't a sad little joke. Who would stop for a street musician who wasn't even worth five cents?

I moved into "Fast Car" by Tracy Chapman, the easy and flowing strings fitting the mood somehow, even if the reality of where I was felt anything but.

I looked like a total loser, shoeless, my shoes in front of me like sad beggars waiting for tips. If they had little signs, they'd read: "Will work for socks." I imagined wearing Grandpa's old Chaplin hat, channeling his courage. Grandpa Norris wouldn't let anxiety win. No way.

Over the next half hour, about twenty people walked by, most of them rushing past like they had somewhere important to be. Not one coin landed in my poor shoes. But then there was this one guy, leaning against a black light post, just watching me. I glanced at him, then quickly looked away. Not my team, if you know what I mean.

Not that the thought hadn't crossed my mind before. Freshman year, Scotty dared me to shove one of his enemas up my ass before wrestling practice. I told him I wasn't scared, so I did it. Worst decision of my life. I was sweating so bad by the second round, the ref kept asking if I needed medical attention. Never. Again. Plus, I almost redefined "public restroom" when I pinned my opponent, bolted across the gym floor, and barely made it to the locker room toilet in time.

I stared at my piss poor empty shoes. By now, my nerves had settled enough to play without my knees shaking like an unsteady washing machine. But this guy, he had me glancing over my shoulder every other second.

I strummed an Eddie Vedder tune from *Into the Wild*, thinking I was venturing into my own kind of wild. Free, alive . . . and scared shitless. Judging by my empty shoes, I was headed straight for my own wilderness if I didn't make some cash soon.

The guy was still leaning against the fence, looking like he was genuinely digging my playing. One leg propped up, one arm crossed, the other messing with a mangled piece of metal, maybe a paperclip, in his mouth. He had a sly smile, like he knew something I didn't. Honestly, he could've passed for a young, skinner Eddie Vedder.

He looked like he was in his early twenties, but it was hard to tell under that mess of shoulder-length hair, tangled like he'd declared war on hairbrushes. I kind of respected it, though. My light brown hair was due for its monthly haircut. I cared too much, always feeling like eyes were on me. But most people were too wrapped up in their own issues to notice.

As I finished the Eddie Vedder song, he gave me a chill wave, like we'd been friends for years. I nodded back, propping Susie against my leg while slipping my shoes back on. Churchill Downs wasn't exactly bustling with offseason tips, and this dude had me twitchy. I tied my laces while keeping my eyes on Susie, just in case Grunge Eddie decided to punch me in the face.

Shit. He's walking over.

"Sweet jams," he said, his voice way higher than expected. "You from around here?"

He knew I wasn't from around here. The polka-dot tie, the busted face, and I was playing guitar at an empty Churchill Downs on a Sunday.

I stood up. He towered over me, but his kind eyes had this disarming gentleness. No hidden agendas, no reason to think I'd need to protect myself.

"A little further south," I lied.

"Oh yeah?" He swiveled the paperclip to the other side of his mouth. "I'm not really from anywhere. My uncle raised me in Minneapolis, but I've been everywhere since I dropped out of high school."

I busied myself putting Susie in her case. He looked like someone who needed money, and Susie was the only thing I owned worth anything.

"Nice to meet you," I said, zipping up the case and turning to walk away.

But Grunge Eddie wasn't done.

"Where down south?" he asked, catching up.

"Alabama," I said, walking faster.

"Alabama, Alabama, Alabama . . ." He repeated it like it was a foreign word. "Ah, 'Sweet Home Alabama'! Can you play it?"

I glanced at him. His eyes were bluer than the sky above us, wide with genuine excitement, like he really cared whether I could play "Sweet Home Alabama."

"I'm not that advanced," I admitted.

"Well, you can learn, right? I play music, too. Me and my girl, Kristie. We're playing at Old Time Boomer's tonight at ten if you wanna check us out."

I didn't answer right away. Maybe Grunge Eddie wasn't here to rob me in broad daylight.

"Old Time Boomer's sounds like a nursing home," I said.

He laughed, finally taking the paperclip out of his mouth. His knotted hair fell into his face as he kept pace beside me.

"It's actually a pretty rad bar down on Fourth Street. You gotta be good to get a gig there. Me and Kristie gave them our demo a couple years back. They hired us that same night. We play here every time we pass through. Not staying long, though. We're heading to Tennessee soon."

Tennessee.

Every real musician knew Memphis was where it all began. Elvis Presley, Aretha Franklin, Johnny Cash, Jeff Buckley . . . they all had a story in Memphis.

And I found myself wanting a story, too.

My feet slowed as we neared a small crowd waiting at the crosswalk.

"Name's Hayden," he said, extending a hand.

I liked that his name rhymed with mine, but I couldn't tell him my real name. I shook his hand. "Blake."

"Nice to meet you, Blake."

He studied me with a crooked grin, his head tilted slightly like he was trying to figure me out. Hayden was lanky. His brown jacket looked two sizes too big, draping over a faded Twisted Sister T-shirt, and his tight ripped jeans showed a lot more knee than denim. Despite his chaotic style, his kind eyes carried a warmth that made him seem harmless.

"You haven't seen Ali's house yet, have you?" he asked, his grin widening.

I frowned. "Ali?"

"Muhammad Ali," he said, leaning back so far I thought he might fall over. His voice jumped an octave, like I'd just admitted to not knowing who invented air. "His childhood home is right by here."

"Really? I didn't know he was from Louisville."

I'd always figured he was from Indiana, like me. That's where all the cool people were from. John Mellencamp, Michael Jackson, James Dean. I thought Ali had to be from some small town, staring out his bedroom window, dreaming about the big city.

"You *gotta* see it," Hayden said, like skipping it would be a crime against humanity.

What he didn't know was that if I didn't make some cash soon, I'd be sleeping under a bridge somewhere, living my own version of *Into the Wild* without the scenic Alaskan views.

"Uh . . ." I glanced around. Churchill Downs wasn't happening today. Maybe I'd have better luck after the baseball game at Cardinal Stadium, but by the time I got there, I'd be playing to pigeons.

The light turned green, and the crowd crossed. I stayed put. Playing outside Muhammad Ali's childhood home sounded . . . strange. But maybe it'd work if I picked the right songs.

"Where is it?" I asked.

The walk to Ali's house consisted of *Kristie 101*. By the time we got there, his girlfriend's name was stuck in my head like a bad pop song.

"Kristie caught the biggest catfish I've ever seen."

"Kristie's a kickball *legend*."

"Kristie's literally the nicest person you'll *ever* meet."

Hayden talked with his whole body, his arms flailing as he emphasized Kristie's greatness. He'd lean back dramatically, gesturing so wildly I kept expecting him to topple over.

"Kristie once saved a squirrel from drowning. She built it a tiny life raft out of a Pringles lid. Swear to God." His tangled hair fell into his face every time he moved, but he didn't seem to notice . . . or care.

"She's gorgeous," he said, bumping into my arm again. "You oughta see her. She's knock-you-out-of-your-socks gorgeous. You got a girl?"

I thought about Leah the whole time Hayden went on about Kristie. I didn't know if Leah ever went fishing or played kickball, but I *did* know one thing . . . Kristie couldn't possibly be the nicest person to ever walk the earth if Leah already had that title.

When Hayden asked if I had a girl, my brain short-circuited like a computer trying to run on Windows 98. I could've said no. I could've said yes. Instead, I made a noise somewhere between a cough and a duck quack. That must've screamed, *it's complicated,* because he didn't press. I was starting to like him. He seemed authentic, and he didn't smell half as bad as I'd assumed when I first saw him. That tangled mop of hair? Surprisingly non-offensive. His clothes? Faintly fresh, like linen detergent caught on the breeze.

"Kristie's back at the RV," he said as we crossed the street. "She's visiting an old friend about an hour from here. I told her I'd stay back to check out a couple of bars. Maybe snag a gig for later in the year."

"What time is your gig again?" I asked.

"Old Time Boomer's at ten. You should come check it out. Cool crowd there."

"I'm not twenty-one."

"Aww, they'll still let you in. They just won't serve you your poison."

I stayed quiet, considering my options. It wasn't like tips were rolling in today, so it couldn't hurt to check it out.

Hayden talked about his music as we strolled. I mostly listened, which I didn't mind. He wasn't the kind of guy who droned on about himself. Every story, every detail, was about someone else. His admiration for people seemed bottomless. It made me wonder if he saw everyone this way, for who they truly were, not for who they pretended to be.

"You do anything crazy as a kid?" Hayden asked.

"Naw. Normal. Nice. Safe. The typical stuff. I have a little brother who kept me entertained."

"Let me guess. He's the total opposite of you."

I chuckled. "He's different, that's for sure. He's on a better path. I hope he stays on it."

"Your path doesn't seem so bad. You're out here following your dreams. Not a lot of people have the guts to do that."

"Pink Houses" by John Mellencamp popped into my head as we stopped in front of a small pink house in a typical Louisville neighborhood. I was expecting a shrine. At least a giant glove or a boxing ring. But nope. Just a nice little house with a fresh coat of pink paint.

There was no crowd. Not even a single person loitering nearby. So much for tips.

"I doubt it's open," Hayden said, eyeing the house. "Sometimes I catch 'em, sometimes I don't. I've been here a few times. It's only been open once. Costs eight bucks."

A narrow walkway led to the porch of the freshly painted house. The concrete porch had just enough room for two chairs, tops. I stopped at the bottom of the porch steps.

Hayden walked ahead, turning back at the door. "You coming?"

"You go in," I said. "I'll wait out here."

"We didn't walk all this way just for me to visit a place I've already been," he said, shaking his head.

"I don't have much money," I admitted.

Hayden laughed. "Dude, you were begging for tips at Churchill Downs." He patted my shoulder. "I got you."

He knocked on the door.

We waited.

No answer.

I don't know why I was expecting some immaculate home. It was a simple house, uncomfortably close to the surrounding houses. I understood its discomfort as Hayden stood awkwardly close to me as we rose on our toes to peek through the door window. You could see a living room, kitchen, and maybe a couple bedrooms. As I stared through the front window, I imaged Ali wanting out even though this was a place someone could be happy in. I knew happiness was more a state of mind than the result of our environment. But I could understand Ali wanting more out of life. Growing up in such a humble home was probably what kept him kind. I believed that people who didn't forget their roots and where they came from had a better chance of staying grounded.

"Better luck next time," Hayden said. "Hey, you eat anything yet? I know this great place 'bout a five-minute walk from the Downs that has the best barbeque ribs your fingers would ever touch. On me."

He just had to say the words barbeque ribs to get my stomach burning. Damn, I was hungry, and didn't expect Hayden to cover that, too.

Hayden wasn't like Scotty. I imagined Hayden as the kind of guy that would butcher karaoke and buy a round for everyone in the bar. And for some reason I imagined Hayden as the kind of person you could talk to about anything and he would never judge you. Scotty was different. He wasn't the problem though. I was. I wanted to open up to Scotty, to tell him what I was going through at home and what I thought when I laid my head down to sleep. The farthest I ever went at being vulnerable with Scotty was stepping on the scale before our wrestling matches and him listening to me barfing a pound of weight out in the bathroom just so I wouldn't have to wrestle a heavy weight.

Scotty and I talked often. He did most of the talking, especially when things went sideways with his mom or he considered escaping to his dad in Silicon Valley. I still don't understand what kind of country-fried dumbass doesn't haul ass to Silicon Valley if given the chance, but whatever. I liked helping Scotty. I liked feeling needed. It was better than feeling like an open stab wound for other people to sprinkle salt over. I know I should've had more faith in people, especially my friends, but I'd learned to guard my heart after finding out what my mom did.

Maybe Blake didn't have to be so guarded.

"What do you think?" Hayden asked with a hopeful look. "Southern Mike's for some ribs?"

Southern Mike's was a weathered red brick building with a flickering sign that read "BEST RIBS IN TOWN." The thick wooden door creaked as we stepped inside.

The smell hit me first. Smoke, spice, and something sweet, like brown sugar, hanging thick in the air. My stomach immediately perked up, and Hayden shot me a knowing smirk. "Told you," he said, as if the scent alone had already won me over.

Inside, the place was cozy with mismatched furniture, clinking glasses, and laughter blending with the smoky scent of meat and cornbread. The walls were covered in faded concert posters, old license plates, and autographed photos of local legends. A string of Christmas lights blinked lazily around a chalkboard menu that proudly announced *FINGER-LICKIN' GOOD RIBS PLATTER: $12.99.*

Hayden led the way to a booth near the window, sliding in like he owned the joint. I hesitated for a moment, brushing a few crumbs off the vinyl seat before sitting across from him.

Shirley, the waitress, appeared and took our order. "Two rib platters, extra sauce, and two sweet teas." She smirked. "Hydrated with sugar water, sure."

Hayden leaned back, folding his arms behind his head. "You're about to eat the best ribs of your life."

I raised an eyebrow. "That's a bold claim."

He leaned forward, tapping the table for emphasis. "Blake, I don't make claims. I make promises. And I promise these ribs are gonna change your life. If they don't, you can personally slap me with a coleslaw spoon."

When the food arrived, it came on oversized metal trays lined with parchment paper. The ribs were glistening under a thick layer of sauce, their edges charred to perfection. A small mountain of golden-brown fries sat beside them, dusted with just enough seasoning to make my mouth water. There was also a side of coleslaw.

I picked up a rib and took a bite. I swear I saw my dead ancestors nodding in approval. The flavor hit first, rich and deep, like it had been kissed by the flames of an ancient pit smoker. Then came the sauce—sweet, tangy, with just the right amount of spice to make my tongue tingle. The meat practically melted in my mouth, falling off the bone with zero effort.

"Holy crap," I mumbled through a mouthful, barely able to stop myself from diving in for another bite.

Hayden laughed, pointing at me with a rib. "Told you! What'd I say? Happiness with a side of 'hell yeah.'"

"It's . . . it's incredible." I admitted, already reaching for the next rib.

The fries were crispy on the outside, fluffy on the inside, and seasoned so perfectly that I could've eaten a whole plate of them on their own. Even the coleslaw, which I usually avoided, was creamy and refreshing, balancing out the richness of the ribs.

By the time we were halfway through, Hayden's hands were coated in sauce, with a streak on his cheek that he didn't care about.

"Man," he said, leaning back and wiping his hands on a stack of napkins, "this is what life's about, you know? Good food, good music, good company. Everything else is just an illusion."

I chuckled, licking the sauce off my fingers. "You sound like a fortune cookie."

"Yeah, but a cool fortune cookie," he shot back.

We talked about sports, which turned into me listening as Hayden waxed poetic about his high school cheerleading days.

"Best decision I ever made," he declared, gesturing with his beer for emphasis. "And not for the reason you think. It wasn't about hanging with pretty girls. Though, you know, perks. Nah, it's the respect it gave me for the female species." He tilted his head, smirking like he'd just said something profound.

I raised an eyebrow. "The 'female species'?"

"I'm serious, dude! You try throwing someone into the air while they're spinning and smiling at the same time, then tell me it's not a sport. But they go through some shit." He leaned closer, his expression conspiratorial. "All I gotta do is shake it twice after pissin', you know?"

I laughed. Hayden had a way of being ridiculous and weirdly wise.

"Kristie must be something else," I said. "The way you talk about her, it's like she walks on water."

"She's everything, man. You'll see. She makes you believe in soul mates."

The way he said it, with so much conviction, made me think maybe he was right. And maybe I wanted to believe in soul mates, too.

After the meal, Hayden shot up suddenly, his face twisting in urgency. "Be right back," he said, nearly tripping over his own feet as he darted toward the bathrooms.

I shook my head, smirking as I watched him go. Leaning back in my seat, I pulled my pen and notepad out of my pocket.

> Dear Scotty,
> This is weird. I know you're not much of a reader . .
> . or a writer, so just bear with me. I wasn't a good
> friend. I wasn't much of a friend at all. I should've
> trusted you enough to know that I didn't have to keep

all this shit to myself. You would've been the first person there for me. You kicked Garrett McGordon's ass when he tackled me in the parking lot after I whooped his ass in that match. You took the blame for me when Mr. Steele was going to make me write that paper about not screwing off during rehearsals. You were one of the first people at the hospital when I had my overdose. What I mean is that the door didn't swing both ways. You always trusted me enough to tell me when shit wasn't right with you. Now it's my turn to trust you.

My family has some secrets. Trust me, all my pill skipping and mental breakdowns are nothing compared to the dirt in my family. My dad hates his dad. My dad barely talks to any of his family members. And the worst is that my mom cheated on my dad. They think going to their vacation cabin every weekend and pretending like they suddenly have all this time together will make the past disappear, but they forget about the person it affected the most.

Sorry, man. Thanks for being there for me.

Braden

Hayden strolled back, stretching his arms like he'd just finished yoga. His loose, carefree movements suggested he'd been meditating instead of whatever questionable thing he'd rushed off to handle.

Before he even said a word, his eyes caught on something outside the window. He froze mid-stretch, beaming like a kid spotting an ice cream truck.

"Well, Blake," he said, nodding toward the parking lot with the enthusiasm of someone who'd just won the lottery, "there's our ride. And my R.F.L."

"Your what?" I asked, but he was already slapping some cash onto the table and practically sprinting toward the door.

I turned to look, squinting through the blinding glare of sunlight reflecting off car windshields. There it was, rolling up at a slow, deliberate pace. A weathered Winnebago that looked more like it had been dug up from a junkyard than driven here.

When Hayden mentioned an RV earlier, I pictured a modest, roadworthy house on wheels. What pulled up instead was a glorified tin can that had seen better days . . . if it had ever had better days.

The sun baked the pavement as I stepped outside, the heat immediately prickling my skin and blurring my vision with waves of distortion. The Winnebago crawled to a stop, the engine sputtering like it was gasping for its last breath. Its faded mustard-yellow stripes stretched along its sides, interrupted by patches of rust and paint chips so severe it looked like the thing had been through a war. A giant, retro Wonder Woman "W" was plastered along its flank like a badge of honor, though the peeling edges suggested it wasn't so much a choice as a remnant of some long-forgotten era.

The windows were grimy with a film of dust that had likely been accumulating since disco was in style. Through the streaks, I caught glimpses of what looked like spatulas dangling from hooks and something resembling a dreamcatcher swaying with the vehicle's idle vibrations.

The tires were a story in themselves. Bald and cracked, practically begging for mercy. As someone who spent enough time working in my dad's shop to recognize bad rubber, I knew those tires wouldn't survive more than two decent potholes.

Hayden motioned for me to follow, his lovestruck gaze never faltering, as if this relic on wheels wasn't a deathtrap waiting to happen. Too far away to argue—and admittedly too curious—I trailed after him, figuring I'd at least meet this mythical Kristie.

The Winnebago creaked as it rocked gently in place, the engine coughing one final time before stalling out altogether. A faint smell of old grease and stale cigarettes wafted toward me, carried on the hot breeze.

"Isn't she a beauty?" Hayden called back, throwing his arms out as if he'd just introduced me to the Queen of England. I wasn't sure if he was being sarcastic or if his standards of beauty were just incredibly forgiving.

"She's . . . something," I said, stepping closer to what I was starting to think of as the automotive equivalent of a senior citizen on life support.

Glancing over at Hayden and his wide, lovestruck grin, I knew it wasn't the clunky, beat-up Winnebago making him beam like that. Nope. His goofy grin was aimed at the tiny, four-foot-nine ball of energy who burst out of the driver's seat like a firecracker. Kristie flew at Hayden with an "eek" that could've summoned every dog in Louisville, wrapping her arms around him as her feet left the ground. It was cute . . . someone so thrilled to see you, even after just a day.

Kristie bounced back down to earth, looking like a bundle of sunshine wrapped in curls. Her wild, shoulder-length hair seemed to have a mind of its own, spiraling in every direction with perfect chaos. Her petite frame was all muscle and energy, her brown skin catching the sun in a way that made her seem like she carried her own glow. She wore a cropped tie-dye tank top, ripped shorts, and mismatched sneakers—one neon pink, the other lime green. Somehow, it worked.

Her dark brown eyes sparkled with an energy that was somewhere between pure joy and a caffeine high, and she chewed gum like her life depended on it. "Hi there!" she chirped, her voice a little less squeaky than her "eek," but just as lively. She stuck out her hand, practically bouncing in place.

I awkwardly took her hand, glancing at Hayden, who was clearly enjoying my discomfort. "Uh, hey. I'm Blake," I managed, trying not to sound as socially inept as I felt.

"Kristie," she said, her gum snapping as she gave my hand a firm shake. She smelled faintly of cinnamon and sunscreen, which seemed fitting. "Nice to meetcha! Hayden said you're a guitarist. That's awesome!" She rocked back on her heels, then forward again, like she couldn't stand still for more than two seconds.

"Well, let's not just stand here!" she said, clapping her hands and spinning around in one fluid motion. "Old Time Boomer's is calling our names!" She popped her gum and skipped back to the driver's side of the Winnebago like a kid heading for recess.

Hayden held the side door open, beaming at me. "C'mon, man. You need gigs, right? We need a guitarist. Half the tips are yours if you're in."

The Winnebago's engine coughed to life, wheezing like an asthmatic dog, and the wheels, bald as a baby's scalp, lurched forward with a faint screech against the pavement. The side door swung open like a pendulum, slamming against the body with a hollow *clang*. Hayden disappeared inside, leaving me standing there in the suffocating summer heat, my Beatles shirt sticking to my back and sweat trickling down my temple like a countdown clock.

I squinted against the glaring sun, watching the Winnebago slowly wobble its way down the street, each bounce threatening to pop it apart like a rickety carnival ride. Inside, Hayden stood wedged between the green vinyl seats, gesturing wildly as he laughed with Kristie. Her voice shouting for me to come along— bright and cheerful—carried faintly over the rattling engine, a burst of uncontainable energy even from this distance.

Pressure built in my chest. I liked them. I *wanted* to like them. But this was insane. I barely knew them. What if they were the type to sell kidneys on the black market? Or worse . . . what if they were Willem Dafoe-level psychopaths? I'd seen enough sketchy setups to know this had all the makings of a true-crime podcast episode. I could already hear the dramatic voiceover: "And that was the last time Blake Knight was ever seen again . . ." And yet, something about the way Hayden laughed invited me. Light and easy, like he wasn't afraid of anything.

For a moment, I saw Scotty and me laughing our heads off about middle school Leah and her mismatched clothes. It was mean, stupid laughter, the kind that made your stomach hurt in the worst way later. Hayden wasn't laughing like that. He was laughing *with* someone, not *at* someone. That kind of laughter—the kind I'd only ever known *with Leah*—meant something. It wasn't just noise. It was trust. And maybe, just maybe, it was a chance for me to learn how to be better. To be a real friend.

Hayden glanced back and caught me watching. He didn't say anything, didn't shout, "Come on!" or make a dramatic plea. He just smiled. It wasn't pushy or smug. It was the kind of smile that said, *The door's open. It's your call.*

The wheels picked up speed, and the door swung wider. My heartbeat quickened. This was the moment to decide. The heat pressed in, but my mind felt clearer. Was I going to watch the Winnebago slip away, or take a risk, even if I could lose?

Shit.

I *had* nothing left to lose.

The Winnebago drifted farther down the parking lot, the clanging door fading into the distance.

I adjusted Susie on my back. The decision wasn't easy, but it was mine. For the first time in a long time, I wasn't running from something . . . I was running *toward* it.

My legs moved before my brain caught up. I sprinted after the lumbering van, my shoes pounding against the asphalt, my heart racing faster than the wheels. The door was still open, wide enough for an idiot like me to leap in.

And I did.

"Ever been to Tennessee?" Kristie asked, her tone light and breezy as she expertly handled the wheel.

Kristie drove like a pro, one hand on the wheel, the other drumming a beat on her thigh. The Winnebago was a chaotic mix of mismatched colors and decades-old wear, with scuffed linoleum and faded carpet underfoot. Cabinets lined the walls, with peeling laminate exposing lighter wood beneath. There was a single-burner stovetop that looked like it hadn't worked in years.

"Gatlinburg a few times," I said, leaning forward so she could hear me.

"Perfect," Hayden said. "That's where Old Time Boomer's is."

"You said Fourth Street in Louisville."

"Naw," Hayden said. "Fourth Street. In Gatlinburg."

I sat at the fold-out table, which was wobbling slightly, its surface marred with scratches and coffee rings. The curtains—one floral, one striped—swayed with each turn Kristie took. Outside, the trees blurred into a wall of green as we sped along.

The faintest whiff of sewage drifted by as Kristie rounded a sharp corner. I grimaced, realizing the bathroom door, located just past the kitchenette, had swung open again. The tiny bathroom was no bigger than a closet, with a plastic toilet and a shower curtain that hung half off its rings.

Hayden rummaged in the fridge, the shelves inside rattling as he tossed cans around. He finally grabbed a beer and lobbed it toward me.

I caught it, hesitating. "Uh . . ." Crap. Eighteen wasn't exactly the cool age I wanted to be.

"A few more years." Hayden winked and tossed me a Coke instead.

"Thanks," I said, cracking it open.

"Gatlinburg," Hayden mused, popping his beer. "Great ziplining down there."

"What?" Kristie shouted.

"Remember that ziplining we did in '05?" Hayden cupped his hands around his mouth.

Kristie turned with wide eyes. "You guys wanna go?"

Hayden didn't even hesitate. He just looked at me, letting the decision hang in the air.

What the hell was I supposed to say? Ziplining sounded like a fast track to breaking my neck. I wasn't the kind of guy who jumped off platforms for fun unless someone dared me.

"Old Time Boomer's is just a brisk drive from that ziplining place," Hayden said casually, as if we were just planning a grocery run. "Babe cakes, let's hit it up after the gig!"

"You got it!" Kristie shouted.

I stared out the window, wondering what kind of alternate reality I'd stepped into. These two were a force of nature. Relentless, loud, and impossibly full of life.

"Man, I love the adventure, don't you?" Hayden said.

I glanced at him. He leaned back, one arm draped over the back of the seat, the other holding his beer like he didn't have a care in the world.

"I do," I admitted, surprising myself.

"Tonight, Old Time Boomer's," Hayden declared, raising his beer like a toast. "Tomorrow? Memphis. What do you say?"

I looked at the tiny living space around me, with its peeling edges and cluttered charm, and thought about how far I'd already come. I liked the Winnebago. So much that I was going to start called her Winnie.

"Sounds like my kind of adventure," I said, a thrill sparking through me.

"That's what I'm talking about!"

A sudden grunting noise came from the back room, growing louder and closer. The door creaked open, and something low to the ground shuffled out. I leaned forward, squinting. Hooves? Snout? Either I was hallucinating, or Winnie had a barn section.

"That's a pig," I said slowly, just in case no one else was seeing what I was seeing.

"That's Margaret," Hayden corrected, like I'd just insulted his grandma.

It was pink, speckled with dark blotches, and built like an overstuffed football with ears. I shot up so fast I nearly smacked my head on the overhead cabinet.

Hayden scooped up the chunky intruder. At first glance, I thought she was a mutant Dalmatian dipped in pink paint, but no, definitely a pig.

"Blake, meet Margaret. Margaret, meet Blake," Hayden said, lifting her closer to me like she was a priceless treasure.

Margaret responded by snorting loudly and lunging forward to give Hayden a series of wet, sloppy kisses across his cheek. He didn't flinch. He didn't even blink.

I, on the other hand, was frozen in place.

What the hell is happening?

It wasn't that I hated animals. I just wasn't *used* to them. My family wasn't exactly the "let's get a furry (or hoofed) friend" type.

Hayden offered Margaret like a gift. "She doesn't bite. Go ahead. Give her a pat!"

I cautiously extended a hand, brushing her bristly hair. Margaret shoved her rubbery nose against my palm, leaving a smear of pig snot.

When I recoiled, wiping my hand on my jeans, Hayden burst into laughter, tears in his eyes.

Margaret, oblivious to the chaos she caused, wiggled her way out of Hayden's arms and hit the floor with a soft thud. Her little hooves made an oddly satisfying clip-clop sound on the scratched-up linoleum as she trotted over to a bowl in the corner. Without hesitation, she buried her entire face in the food, chomping loudly and snorting like she was trying to eat and communicate at the same time.

"You don't get out much, do you, Blake?" Hayden teased, still chuckling as he plopped into the booth.

"Not to places with pigs," I muttered, watching Margaret inhale her food.

"Margaret's not just a pig," Hayden said, mock-serious. "She's a teacup pig. Royalty around here."

I smirked despite myself. "Royalty. And I'm her loyal subject?"

"Damn straight," Hayden said, raising his beer in a toast.

Margaret let out a satisfied grunt.

I glanced at Susie, her worn strings gleaming under the light. Despite Margaret's slime, she felt solid and reassuring in my grip.

Hayden leaned over the tiny, battered Winnebago table and grabbed my hand like he was about to read my palm. He turned it this way and that, then dropped it.

"Yep. Those are the fingers of a guy who's never stroked a real tune in his life." He leaned back. "Don't worry, though. We'll whip you into shape. If you're gonna jam with us tonight, you need to know the vibes, just the basics. No pressure."

I tried to laugh, but my throat was dry. "You're not worried about me ruining your gig?"

"Nah, we play to make people happy, not to win Grammys. Worst-case scenario, you're terrible, and we just lean on Kristie's killer kazoo skills." He winked as Kristie hollered from the driver's seat, "Damn right!"

Hayden hopped up, crossed the cramped space, and opened a

narrow closet wedged between the kitchenette and bathroom. He pulled out a guitar that had more scratches and dents than the family car after a demolition derby.

"Let's hear what you got," he said. "What do you like to play?"

"Uh, a little of everything. Mostly Beatles."

"Yellow Submarine!" Hayden bellowed toward Kristie.

In a flash, "Yellow Submarine" burst from the glitchy speakers. Hayden didn't even look at me before starting to strum, nodding his head like a bobblehead in a breeze.

I hesitated for half a second, then lifted Susie into position. Her neck fit snugly against my palm. The chords came instinctively, and before I knew it, I was playing along. The simple progression felt like muscle memory.

When the song ended, Hayden set his guitar aside and gave me a sly smirk. "Guess I underestimated those under-callused fingertips."

"Nice job, guys!" Kristie hollered, twisting around to flash us a radiant smile.

Hayden turned back to me. "What else you got in your bag of tricks?"

"Uh, more Beatles. Some Tracy Chapman. Always wanted to play Jeff Buckley, though."

That made him pause. His grin turned into something reverent. "Ah, Jeff Buckley. Legend. Gone too soon." He lowered his gaze like he was holding a moment of silence. If he'd had a hat, he would've tipped it.

"I found him by accident," I said, strumming absently. "I meant to buy a Beck album at the record store, but someone had put Buckley in its place. I almost returned it at the counter, but something about the cover art made me keep it. Best mistake I ever made."

Hayden nodded solemnly, then abruptly slapped his thighs. "Well, I'm warmed up, Blake's a superstar, and I'm starving. Kristie!" He hollered toward the front. "How about I whip up those fried zucchinis you're crazy about, and we swing by the Cumberland River for a dip?"

Kristie gave him a thumbs-up and cranked the volume as "Lucy in the Sky with Diamonds" swirled through the camper. A slow, knowing gaze spread across Hayden's face. "See? The music's already calling."

On the drive, Hayden had cooked up a batch of breaded zucchini on Winnie's avocado-green gas stove. Hayden flipped a zucchini slice in the pan with the confidence of a man who could win "Top Chef" armed with nothing but a spatula and blind optimism. The smell alone made my mouth water, and when I took a bite? Heaven. The crisp, golden crust, seasoned just right with garlic salt, gave way to the smooth, warm freshness of zucchini beneath.

"Kristie's great-aunt's recipe from Louisiana," Hayden said proudly, tossing me another piece. "If you like that, you gotta stick around. Ever had deep-fried Twinkies?"

We rolled into a spot near the Cumberland River after two hours of what felt like the shortest drive of my life. The final stretch was all gravel and potholes, but Winnie didn't flinch. She might've been older than dirt, but that Winnebago had some fight left in her.

When we stepped out, the late afternoon sun hit us like a warm hug, though the river breeze kept it from feeling too oppressive. The air smelled faintly of brine and earth, with a hint of something sweet, maybe wildflowers blooming somewhere along the bank.

From here, the Cumberland River stretched wide and steady, a shimmering ribbon of deep green and brown. Trees lined the opposite bank, their branches dipping low as if they'd come to sip from the water. Downstream, white water crashed over boulders in bursts of energy, but where we stood, the current moved slow and steady, as if inviting us to stay awhile.

"Beautiful day for a swim," Hayden said, arms stretched out toward the sky. "How 'bout it, Blake?"

I stared at the river, at the murky water where God-knows-what was lurking beneath. I wasn't afraid of water moccasins, but if one so much as looked at me funny, I was ready to turn around and walk straight back to hell.

The smoky purr of Winnie's engine as Kristie turned her off hit me with a wave of remembrance. It smelled like old garages and long Saturdays spent working on cars with my dad. I hadn't thought about home much until that moment, but now it crept in, guilt tagging along like an unwelcome guest.

Kristie bounded out of Winnie with a bounce in her step, stopping just long enough to tug on my yellow-and-red polka dot tie. "This tie's got 'I'm here to party' vibes," she said, like it was the most groundbreaking fashion statement since the fanny pack revival. She let it go and spun around, her eyes wide as she took in the river and the sky.

Hayden leaned back against Winnie. "Told ya this was a good spot."

For a moment, I let myself get lost in it, the way the light danced on the water, the easy laughter between these two. Standing there, the Cumberland River stretching out before us, it felt like the whole world had pressed pause, just for us.

And yet, somewhere in the back of my mind, that little voice whispered. The guilt. The self-doubt. Was I doing the right thing, leaving home? Running from what I'd left behind?

The sound of Kristie's laughter caught on the wind, light and easy. For a split second, it reminded me of her.

Leah.

Her name alone unraveled me. My shoulders tensed as I tried to shove her out of my mind, but she clung to every corner of my thoughts. It felt like a betrayal—thinking of her while I was here—but I couldn't stop. Blocking her out should've been easy, like shutting a door, but Leah wasn't something you could lock away.

She was the sunlight creeping through the cracks, unavoidable and warm. That smile of hers, so impossibly bright, haunted me. And deep down, I hoped I had something to do with putting it there.

A loud laugh pulled me back. Hayden crouched by the bank, yanking off his pants and tossing them aside like we were on some deserted island. His shirt followed, revealing tattoos I hadn't noticed before. A delicate bouquet of flowers, the stems winding down his ribs, and a name inked in elegant, looping script. He caught me staring and grinned as if daring me to comment. Then he moved to Kristie. With a swift tug, he untied her halter top, and before I could process what was happening, she shrugged it off. Naked. I whipped my head to the side, heat flooding my face.

Hayden boomed. "Relax, Blake! Nothing you haven't seen before!" He smirked. "Don't worry, I'll spare you my bare ass."

In a flash, he was in his boxers, running toward the water. Kristie followed, stripping her last layer as she went. I stared hard at the ground, refusing to look up until I heard the splash of water and their giggles in the distance. Even then, unease prickled at me. Not just from their carefree nudity. It was something deeper. My mind flashed back to a memory I'd buried long ago of walking in on my parents. I was seven. I'd barged into their room, ready to ask for chips. Instead, I got an education I wasn't prepared for. Turns out, "mom and dad time" wasn't as snooze-worthy as it sounded.

Later, my mom patted my head and giggled.

"Sorry, sweetheart. The one time we forget to lock the door."

Back then, I took it as proof they loved each other.

Then came the truth, the gut-punch revelation of her affair. I'd heard them arguing one day and they caught me listening in the hallway. I wished I had heard them wrong. It wasn't just my dad she'd betrayed . . . it felt like she'd cheated on all of us. On the family. The memory churned in my stomach, thick and sour. I stared at the rippling water where Hayden and Kristie splashed and laughed, so free, so unburdened. And I wondered if I'd ever know what that felt like again before I died.

Margaret snorted at me as I ducked back into Winnie to grab Susie. Her wet nose was aimed straight for my leg, but I darted out before she could slime me. With Susie in hand, I found a spot near the shore, a patch of sun-bleached pebbles warm underfoot.

Sitting down, I stretched out my legs and let the cool water touch my feet. The sensation was intense, a jolt of cold that sent shivers up my spine. I rested Susie across my lap, but I didn't play right away. Instead, I stared out at the rippling water, watching how Hayden and Kristie's movements sent tiny waves skittering toward me.

They swam further out. Hayden's booming roar mixed with Kristie's high-pitched giggles, the sound bouncing off the trees. For a moment, I thought about yelling at them to be careful. Undertows could grab you without warning. But something about those two . . . they didn't seem like the type to worry about undertows. If the water wanted to sweep them away, they'd trust it. Let it take them somewhere better.

If I went under, it'd be because I jumped in, screaming 'YOLO!'

The sun beat down on me, warming my skin as I stared at the horizon. Maybe Buckley's spirit would find me here, like it had all those years ago when I first stumbled onto his music. Maybe his courage, his way of pouring everything into his songs, could somehow flow into me, giving me what I needed to figure out this tangled mess of a journey.

Hayden's laugh was so full and free, and I smiled along with it. Watching them, I felt it again. That spark. Whatever came next, I wanted to find out.

I pulled out my pen and notepad.

Dear Leah,

When I downed all those pills the night of our play,

the last thing that went through my mind was you.

As I was laying on the back seat of my van, all I could feel was regret only because I knew it would hurt you. I've heard people say suicide isn't about wanting to die. It's about wanting the pain to end. I'm sorry I put you through that hurt. I'm sorry I put everyone through that. I would've haunted myself if I died knowing I could've lived a life with you, but that would've been even more selfish.

If I'm being honest though, I didn't care too much about how my parents felt. I didn't think about them too much as I was going through all that at the hospital then back at the psychiatric clinic then back at home to "recover". I know that's not fair, but I was still so angry at them. They had clouded so much of my view of myself and my view of the world.

I wonder why I'm here. What am I doing here?

Rich people problems, huh . . . well, I know you understand.

I didn't want to end it in the back seat of my van. I want to go in peace, somewhere I love.

I'm at a river down south. I know the first thing you are going to think of is Jeff Buckley, but don't worry, I won't end myself by drowning. I'm starting to think I won't end myself at all if life could really be this good.

I met a couple people who I think you would really like. Just being with them is contagious to more laughter than I've heard in so many years. True, real, deep laughter that makes your stomach hurt.

I know we wanted to go on a trip together, but if I

can't take that road trip with you, I'll take it for you.

If this doesn't end in a positive way, well . . . just know that I tried. I really tried.

I love you, Leah.

Braden

Hayden ran out of the water, shaking his head like a wet dog as droplets sprayed in every direction. He was grinning like a fool, his soaked boxer shorts clinging to him in ways that were hard to ignore. The guy wasn't exactly shy, and I respected that kind of confidence.

"You coming in, or you just gonna bake out here?" he asked, catching sight of the notepad in my lap.

"Nah, I'll skip. Got a fear of bodies of water," I said, shutting the notepad.

Hayden dropped onto the ground next to me, cross-legged and dripping water onto the dry pebbles. "You don't swim? At all?"

"Not in lakes. Not in rivers. Definitely not the ocean. The whole thing feels . . . hostile."

"Hostile?" he repeated, like I'd insulted his best friend. "Or maybe it's the most welcoming thing there is. No phones, no walls, just you and the water. Floating on your back, staring at the sky. It's peace, man. The kind that sticks with you."

I let his words sink in, but all I could picture were jellyfish, sharks, and rip currents. "Yeah, well, peace doesn't come with teeth and tentacles where I'm from."

Hayden chuckled, running a hand through his dripping hair. "Fair enough. But you're missing out on something big." He nodded toward Kristie, who was still out there, slicing through the water with ease. "You know, she taught me how to let go. Not just of the shore, but of . . . everything."

I raised an eyebrow. "What do you mean?"

He leaned back on his hands, glancing at Kristie like she held all the answers. "Before her, I was the guy who needed a plan for everything. A backup plan for the backup plan. But Kristie? She's got this way of making you realize that life doesn't give a shit about your plans. You just have to take the ride."

I stared at him for a moment, surprised at how honest he was being. "Doesn't that freak you out? Not knowing what's next?"

"Sometimes," he admitted. "But I'd rather take the risk and live fully than spend my life playing it safe. You gotta trust, Blake."

Kristie walked out of the water looking like she was auditioning for the next Bond movie. Meanwhile, I was just trying not to drown in my own self-pity. She stretched her arms toward the sun and let out a satisfied sigh, as if she'd just conquered the world.

Hayden pointed. "See? That's what I'm talking about."

I shook my head, laughing a little. "You're a weird guy, Hayden."

"Maybe," he said, smirking. "But weird's where all the good stories are."

"Ah, I just love swimming," Kristie said, dropping her arms dramatically and looking at us.

Her orange halter top was soaked halfway, clinging to her skin as she sat beside Hayden. I tried not to stare at her, but her nipples poking through made it impossible to ignore my damn hormones.

Kristie tapped Hayden's thigh with her foot. "Hayden, would you mind driving the next stretch?"

"You know I'd do anything for you." He tickled her calf.

A few minutes later, we were back on the road. Kristie made me tea while Hayden took the wheel, humming along to the light '80s rock from the radio.

"Chamomile," she said, handing me the mug with a flourish. "One of my favorites. Super healing."

She slid into the seat across from me, her curiosity evident as always. "So, you got a girlfriend?"

The question hit like a sucker punch. I wanted to spill everything about Leah—the way we met, her letters, her smile—but all I could manage was a stiff, "No . . ."

Kristie raised a skeptical eyebrow, sipping her tea.

"She'll take you back, sweetheart," she said after a moment. "Sometimes people just get lost for a while. Doesn't mean they're not worth finding again."

Her words hit deeper than I wanted to admit.

I shrugged, changing the subject. "You and Hayden met in high school, right?"

Kristie set her tea down. "Chess tournament. He lived a few towns over. We locked eyes, and I knew. I was about to school this dude at chess and steal his heart in one fell swoop. He never stood a chance."

"Who won the chess game?"

"Me, obviously," she said with a cheeky grin.

I laughed. "Hayden said you guys are dropouts?"

"Yep. Not an easy choice, but my home life sucked, and at seventeen, it was either drop out or end up in foster care. When you're faced with a decision like that, you grow up fast." She glanced toward Hayden, her smile brightening. "He saved me from going down a bad road. I know it sounds crazy, but even as dropouts, we've built a good life. We don't need much. Just gas, some food, and a good song to sing. Who could ask for more?"

"That's brave," I said.

"What about you, Blake?" she asked, eyes sparkling. "What's been your favorite place to visit so far?"

I hesitated. The truth was, I hadn't been many places. Family vacations were predictable. Gatlinburg and a million Cracker Barrels. Nothing inspiring. I swear, I could've written a travel blog titled "Cracker Barrel: The Unofficial Capital of My Childhood."

"Honestly? Probably where we just were by the river," I said.

"That's sweet." Kristie eyes glowed with warmth. "Hayden tells me you like Jeff Buckley?"

I nodded, tracing the rim of my mug.

"He's kind of addicting," she said. "Hayden and I listen to him when we're lying in bed. His music's got this . . . raw fever. It gets under your skin in the best way."

I smiled, feeling a little more at ease.

"Hey, you're going to love Old Time Boomer's," she said, her enthusiasm contagious. "It's not a huge bar, but the people are amazing. You could play one chord, and they'd lose their minds. I love performing for crowds like that. They're so genuine."

She picked up her sketchpad and started drawing, her face lighting up with quiet focus. I moved up front to sit with Hayden, the soothing '80s music playing from the speakers.

The two-hour drive passed in a haze of music and chatter until we rolled into the gravel lot of Old Time Boomer's. The moon was high, casting long golden rays that glinted off the windshields of scattered pickups and cars. Winnie crunched to a halt in a free spot, her engine groaning like an old man settling into a chair. Outside, clusters of people milled around a makeshift patio, sipping beers and chatting as the M in TIME flickered sporadically, leaving the neon sign to read "Old Tie Boomer's." Still sounded like a nursing home to me.

I fiddled with my tie. My reflection in Winnie's window reminded me I needed a change of clothes, but that wasn't exactly a priority when you're sprinting out of the house like a fugitive.

Hayden bounded out first, his energy infectious, as if arriving at Boomer's was the highlight of his month. Kristie followed, looping an arm around his waist and beaming up at him.

Inside, the bar pulsed with life. The air reeked of smoke, beer, and fried food. Rope lights strung along the walls bathed everything in a soft, colorful glow, casting the room in the kind of light that made you feel you'd stepped into someone's party basement . . . if their basement had a pool table, dartboards, and a fully stocked bar.

The small stage in the corner looked like it had seen its fair share of scuffed boots and spilled beer, but it had a charm of its own. A few speakers stood on tripods, and the mic cables snaked across the floor like lazy rivers. Hayden greeted people left and right as if he were running for mayor of Boomer's, exchanging high fives, back pats, and even a couple of fist bumps.

"Manny!" Hayden called, dragging the name out like an old friend's song.

The guy fiddling with the P.A. system stood up. He was shorter than Hayden, with a balding head and an easygoing demeanor that immediately put me at ease.

"You made it!" Manny said, pulling Hayden and Kristie into quick hugs before turning to me. "And who's this?"

"This is Blake," Kristie said, wrapping her arm around my shoulders in a side hug that felt oddly reassuring. "He's a killer guitarist. You're gonna love him."

I stammered out a "Nice to meet you" as Manny hugged me, too.

"Well," Manny said, gesturing to the stage, "she's all yours. Let's see what you've got."

The room buzzed with chatter as Hayden grabbed his guitar and Kristie adjusted the mic stand. I followed suit, strapping Susie on and tuning her strings, trying to look more confident than I felt.

This wasn't Hayden and Kristie's first rodeo. They breezed through setup like pros. Meanwhile, I was running on fumes after one of the longest days of my life. Getting my ass kicked that morning, walking what felt like a million miles in pouring rain, and then hours of driving. But adrenaline had me wired. I wasn't about to pass up the chance to make some cash, play a good song on Susie, and finally feel like I belonged somewhere.

The crowd was small but lively, a mix of folks at tables, along the bar, and near the pool tables, their conversation relaxed and familiar, like longtime patrons catching up after a long week. The way they turned toward the stage with anticipation made my stomach flutter. But as I looked out at the rope-lit room, at Hayden and Kristie's easy smiles, and at Susie resting in my hands,

I felt something new. An electric charge, like the music was already waiting to escape.

I was glad I'd skipped my depression pills. They dulled my edges, blunting the intensity I needed, but tonight, I was fully awake. Right now, I felt vibrantly, fiercely alive. Like a caffeinated sloth, but still, I was alive.

Kristie popped in front of the mic, already owning the room. I glanced at Hayden, hoping he'd back me up with a guitar or bass so I didn't crash and burn solo, but he settled behind a keyboard and small drum set.

Great. All eyes on me, then.

"I see you there, Leonard!" Kristie waved to someone in the crowd as Manny flipped on the spotlights. Suddenly, I couldn't see squat except a haze of faces and Kristie's silhouette.

"Give me a tune," she whispered, her curls bouncing as she turned toward us.

Hayden raised an eyebrow at me, leaving the song choice in my hands. I froze. What if she didn't know it? What if he didn't know it? I bit the bullet and strummed the opening tune of "When I Was Young" by The Animals.

Hayden picked up the beat with a rhythm on the drums, just enough to lift the sound without overpowering it. His timing was impeccable, like salt on a sugar cookie. Unexpected but perfect.

Then Kristie opened her mouth, and the game changed. Her voice hit me like a freight train—a stunning mix of Janis Joplin's spunk and Tori Amos's soul. She didn't just know the song; she owned it. I caught myself gawking, starstruck, and had to snap back to keep playing.

We hit our groove fast. Heads started bobbing, and before long, people wandered up to drop tips into the jar at Kristie's feet. She flashed them a wink mid-song, her voice weaving Eric Burdon's lyrics into something entirely her own.

For the next track, Kristie left the stage, mic in hand, and worked the crowd. "Me and Bobby McGee" was her pick, and it fit her like a glove. She danced through the room, her movements smooth and playful, while buzzed patrons swayed beside her, beers sloshing in time to the music. I stumbled through the chords but kept going, too caught up in the moment to care.

Song after song, we kept the energy high. "American Pie," where everyone belted the chorus like it was their anthem; "Landslide," which had Kristie tearing up, nearly bringing us to a halt; and "Hurts So Good," with Hayden hammering out a beat so tight the crowd cheered.

Finally, Kristie leaned toward us, her eyes sparkling under the stage lights. "One last song," she said. "All You Need Is Love."

Relief washed over me. It was a song I could play in my sleep. I strummed the familiar chords, and Hayden joined with gentle drumming. Kristie's voice soared, and by the second chorus, the audience was singing along. The room buzzed with something intangible, something bigger than all of us.

Near the end, Hayden and I stopped playing, leaving just Kristie and the crowd carrying the melody. The clapping grew louder, hands raised in the air, everyone chanting together until the last note faded.

For a moment, silence. Then the room erupted in cheers and whistles.

Kristie bowed. "Thanks for a great night!" she shouted, waving to the crowd before turning back to us, her face flushed and beaming.

For the first time in ages, it was like gravity had finally cut me some slack. It was the same feeling I got performing in musicals or lying under The Tree, letting myself drift so deep into dreams they felt real.

"That was so much fun," Kristie said, plopping onto Hayden's lap like she'd claimed the best seat in the house. He responded with a slow, dramatic kiss that could've scored applause if anyone cared to watch.

As I packed up Susie, another guy strolled up. This guy, Chris, looked like an NSYNC member, complete with gelled hair and baggy pants. Behind him was Rodney, who radiated *The Shining* energy. Think Jack Nicholson, but less murdery.

"Chris!" Hayden called, exchanging a fist bump. "Man, it's been forever!"

Rodney's face lit up in a way that chased away his "room 237" energy. "Nice to meet you, Blake. What brings you out here?"

"Oh, you know . . . just chasing gigs," I said, trying to sound cooler than I felt.

"You got plans after this?" Chris asked, glancing between us.

Hayden and Kristie shot each other a look, their matching grins dripping with mischief. My gut dropped.

"We're going ziplining," Kristie said.

The fuck if I am!

"Take us with you," Rodney chimed in. "I could use another rush after that performance."

Fuck you, Rodney.

I plastered on a polite smile, wondering why we couldn't celebrate with something safer, like . . . pizza. Surely no zipline was even open this late. This had to be a joke.

Kristie wandered off with Chris and Rodney to chat with some older woman, leaving Hayden and me alone. He clapped a hand on my shoulder and handed me fifty bucks.

"Here," he said, like he was giving me a party favor. "The gig paid us a hundred and fifty. Your cut."

"Oh, you don't have to—"

"Take it," he interrupted, already fishing for a cigarette. "We're glad you came. I know Kristie's had a rough time lately, and having you around has been good for her."

As he lit his cigarette, I awkwardly stuffed the cash into Susie's pocket, hoping he didn't notice my baggie of depression pills slipping out before I shoved it back in.

He dug through the tip jar and handed me another wad of cash. "Your share. About a third. Not bad for your first gig."

I pocketed the money, surprised by the heft. It felt like twenty-five bucks in ones and fives. A starter fortune. "Thanks. I'm glad I came out here with you guys."

"Fun's not over yet." He exhaled a cloud of smoke.

"Yeah, about that . . . I'm not going ziplining."

"You don't have to," he said with a shrug. "But watching's boring. Just saying."

Hayden bounded off toward Kristie while I secured Susie's pocket, double-checking that my cash was safe. After Paul jacked my wallet, I wasn't taking any chances.

A few people came up to compliment my guitar skills, which felt nice. One guy asked how long I'd been playing, and for a second, I thought he'd follow up with, "How old are you, anyway?" But he just nodded, said "cool," and handed me a few bucks.

I made my way to the bathroom, where I spent a solid two minutes pissing out everything I'd held in all day, including, I hoped, my fear of being dragged into ziplining. No such luck. With my bladder empty but my dread fully intact, I rejoined Hayden, Kristie, Chris, and Rodney at the entrance.

I stayed quiet as we piled into Winnie. I still didn't believe ziplining this late at night was an actual thing, but apparently, in Gatlinburg, it was. I remember vacationing there almost every summer, but seeing it at night like this was different. The city came alive as we drove through, neon lights splashing every corner, crowds darting in and out of museums, restaurants, and souvenir shops. Hayden navigated like he had the place mapped in his brain, and before long, we pulled up to a ziplining joint lit brighter than a Vegas billboard.

Either people here were nuts, or I was the biggest chicken shit this side of Marty McFly. Ziplining could kiss my ass.

Rock music blasted from speakers hanging on wooden posts as I stared up at the lit tower where people jumped off the edge, trusting their lives to cables vanishing into the abyss. Above the chaos was a sky glittering with stars, like someone had tossed a handful of diamonds over a navy-blue blanket.

The line wasn't as long as I'd expected, but I still wasn't budging. The air smelled sickly sweet, and I spotted a funnel cake stand near the line. Rodney bought a couple to share. I was starving, and the funnel cake tasted like it had been handcrafted by a sugar-coated angel.

Leah popped into my head again. She had a habit of doing that. Usually, I didn't try to block her out, but then I'd end up zoning so hard people had to snap their fingers in my face to bring me back. So, I made an effort to stay present when Rodney talked to me.

"You play guitar pretty doggone good," he said, funnel cake crumbs clinging to the corners of his mouth like they were in it for the long haul. All I could think about was how gross that was and silently hoped my face wasn't betraying me.

Rodney had that early-balding situation going on. Poor guy. Looking at him from the front, he might've been 27, just a couple years older than Hayden. But from the back? Easy 57. His dark brown hair thinned out on the sides like someone had given up halfway through buzzing it.

And his face, long and hollow-cheeked, gave him this permanently ticked-off look, like Eminem gearing up for a diss track or Rob Thomas trying to survive Matchbox Twenty's next reunion tour. Add in the slight hunch at the top of his lanky frame, and you had Poor Old Rodney in all his glory.

"Do you play?" I asked, breaking off a piece of funnel cake before he devoured it all.

"I play video games," he said, mouth full. "I'd probably break a guitar if I ever touched one."

Thank God Susie was safely tucked away in Winnie.

I didn't know what else to say, but Rodney didn't seem to care. He was laser-focused on that funnel cake, demolishing it like he'd skipped every meal for a week. I was hungry, sure, but I wasn't desperate enough to wrestle funnel cake crumbs out of Rodney's powdered-sugar-coated fingers.

Hayden threw an arm around my shoulder, yanking me close like we were best buddies facing death together. "You're doing it!" he hollered in my ear, loud enough to scare away common sense. "It's scary as hell the first ten seconds, but then? Then you're flying."

He spread his arms like an overgrown bird, nearly smacking a worker in the face. Before I could respond, he spun Kristie around, picked her up like a sack of potatoes, and planted a dramatic kiss on her neck. She shrieked, giggling like he wasn't about to send us all to our doom.

We climbed the wobbly tower. Each step taunted my courage. Less oxygen, more hyperventilating. "Don't look down," I muttered to myself, which of course made me do the exact opposite. Big mistake. The ground was a hundred miles away, and the only thing between me and it was this rickety tower and my stupid decisions.

I was tough, right? I was a wrestler. Just not tough enough to stop shaking like a Chihuahua in a thunderstorm. And honestly, the Chihuahua probably had better survival instincts.

"Almost there!" Hayden shouted, cupping his hands like some kind of mountain goat who'd made it to the peak. He let out a howl, which echoed ominously into the night, as if making fun of me for my life choices. Meanwhile, Kristie clung to him, laughing like we weren't all about to become human zip-tied cannonballs.

And then, we were at the top.

I didn't know knees could shake like mine. It was like my body had turned into a wet noodle, but only from the waist down. I gripped the railing, scrutinizing every click of the harness like an OSHA inspector. It looked secure. Solid. Foolproof. But what if the cable snapped? Or what if I flipped upside down?

Hayden slapped my back, breaking my hyper-focused stare. "We're up next, buddy!"

Fantastic.

My knees were shaking harder now. All I had to do was make it to the other side. Just one little ride across a cable strung over a death drop. That's where the miracles happen, right? At the other side? Or so I told myself as the worker waved me over with a big, toothy grin that might as well have screamed *fresh meat*. I was about to throw myself off a cliff, and this guy's grin was as reassuring as a "Welcome to the Jungle" sign at a petting zoo.

Still.

Fuck you, Rodney.

The couple ahead of me casually stepped off the tower, zipping into the dark like it was just another weekday. Their excited screams sliced through the night air.

How could they do that? Be so free, so fearless, like gravity didn't even apply to them? Meanwhile, my stomach was trying to crawl up my throat and bail on this whole situation.

I forced myself to shuffle up to my spot, my brain desperately trying to flip the "off" switch on whatever part of me screamed, *What the hell are you doing?* There were five zipline positions, perfectly set for our group of maniacs. As the workers strapped and hooked me in, I glanced at the others. Kristie was practically vibrating with excitement, Hayden's wild expression was wider than his face, and even Rodney and Chris looked like this was their version of Disneyland.

I wanted to feel that. I really did. But all I felt was a fuzzy, static sensation creeping through my body like my brain was buffering just to stay upright.

"Whenever you're ready," the worker said, stepping back with a cheery expression that made me want to punch him.

I'm not ready! my brain screamed.

Rodney was the first to go, launching himself off the platform with a guttural "Hoot, hoot!" that was half battle cry, half mating call. Chris wasn't far behind, mimicking Rodney in a way that made me question his mental stability.

Then Hayden turned to Kristie. "Are you good for this one, Babe Cakes?" he asked.

What did he mean by *this one*? What had Kristie done—or not done—that made him check in like that? Before I could spiral down that rabbit hole, Kristie's crazy ass took three steps back, sprinted full tilt, and hurled herself off the edge like she was auditioning for an action movie. Her scream shattered the air as she disappeared into the void.

Hayden stood next to me now. "See you on the other side," he said, far too casually for someone about to fling himself into oblivion. I shuffled away just in case he decided I needed a "friendly push."

He backed up, shouted, "I'm coming, baby!" and sprinted into the night, his scream joining the symphony of madness that had already vanished into the distance.

And then it was just me.

My mind, unhelpfully, pulled up the lyrics to *Grace* by Jeff Buckley. *Wait in the fire . . . wait in the fire . . .*

Buckley had love in his life. Maybe that's why he wasn't afraid to die.

I loved Leah, but did it count if I wasn't going to be alive anymore? All I had was Susie and some leftover funnel cake. Hardly poetic, but here I was. Somehow, some way, I took that step. My hands clutched the harness straps, knuckles white, before I stepped off. A bottomless, blind leap into nowhere. For a split second, gravity grabbed me by the ankles, yanking me down. Then the harness caught, and suddenly I was flying. My body swung through the air, the wind roaring in my ears, the stars above me like a scattered map to freedom.

I screamed.

I screamed so hard I could've been cast in a horror movie. Somewhere in the world, Jamie Lee Curtis felt threatened.

In the middle of that screeching song, something cracked open inside me. Fear wasn't just leaving—it was sprinting out of my body like it owed someone money. Along with it went a cascade of memories. Climbing to the top of the jungle gym as a kid, knees shaking; the time I bombed my first guitar recital; and the night Leah stood at my back door, fire in her eyes, demanding to know why I was pulling away. All of it poured out of me, carried off into the infinite night by the howl of my terror.

The wind ripped past my ears as the zipline carried me further from the platform. My heart, initially pounding in a frantic Morse code for *GET ME THE FUCK OFF THIS THING*, settled into something strange. Fuzzy warmth unfurled in my chest. The fear dissolved into something lighter, something that felt almost . . . peaceful. And, as usual during my near-death experiences, my mind found its way back to Leah.

I started playing "All You Need Is Love" in my head. Leah was love. She would've been on the cable next to me, laughing, her fearless spirit making this whole ziplining thing look like a walk in the park. While Hayden hollered himself hoarse, I imagined Leah smiling at me, her hair whipping in the wind, shouting something like, *See? It's not so bad!*

Gliding through the open, crisp sky, my hands slipped from the harness straps. Hesitant at first, my arms spread slowly, then fully, and I was free. No fear. No resistance. Just the rush of the wind, the twinkling stars above, and the faint bouncing of everyone's screams. I was weightless, untethered, a feather drifting through the universe without a care.

This was what it meant to be alive. And for a fleeting moment, I could swear Leah was right there with me, showing me how to fly.

CHAPTER 5:
Miss Sibby

After ziplining, I had a raging hunger. We hit a gas station where I crushed three hot dogs, two Dr Peppers, and a bag of chips. It wasn't gourmet, but I didn't regret it.

Back in Winnie, Rodney, Chris, Hayden, and Kristie cracked open beers while I sipped on a Coke. They talked about laser tag and bungee jumping, but my brain had already checked out. My head bobbed like I was at a Metallica concert, only way less cool.

I wondered if I had a right to crash here, but then I remembered Margaret, snoring like an asthmatic chainsaw, and let it go.

Just as I was about to conk out mid-conversation, Kristie tapped my arm. "C'mon," she said, grabbing Susie and motioning for me to follow.

I trailed behind her as she asked if I had family nearby. My brain, now running on fumes, pulled out the truth I'd been sitting on all night. "Yeah, I've got an aunt in Memphis. Haven't seen her in years. I can't wait to see her again." I didn't mention the part where my parents cut her off when I was a kid.

Kristie smiled at me over her shoulder, a look so warm it made me feel guilty for being a tired buzzkill sack of shit. Did these people ever sleep?

"You had a long trip," she said, leading me into the world's tiniest bedroom. It was cozy, definitely her and Hayden's space judging by the caricature drawings on the wall. She pulled back the blankets on the bed and fluffed the pillows like a mom in a feel-good movie.

Margaret was snoring from a tiny dog bed in the corner, her stubby legs twitching in some dream where she was probably chasing me down for another unsolicited kiss. I eyed the too-tall bed and sighed in relief. At least she couldn't reach me here.

"I can't take your room," I mumbled, the words slurring together.

Kristie's warm look made me feel like a buzzkill. "You need this more than we do," she said, tucking Susie against the wall. "Good-night, Blake."

She left, closing the door quietly behind her, and I stood there, dumbfounded. How had I made anything better? I slid under the covers, and within minutes, I was out. Fourteen hours later, I was pretty sure I'd met the closest thing to heaven.

The morning light poured through the windshield, showing the smoke Winnie puffed out like she'd had one too many cigarettes. Kristie, with her hair pulled into a messy bun, was swerving us confidently through the interstate lanes as if Winnie were a sports car and not a dinosaur on wheels.

"On a mission to find Blake's aunt!" Kristie declared as she adjusted the radio to something bluesy, setting the mood for Memphis.

Turned out, Hayden and Kristie were regulars in Memphis, having played countless gigs there over the years. Hayden had already made a call, a hole-in-the-wall karaoke bar, and secured us an opening spot.

I sat at the table in Winnie's cramped kitchenette, staring down at a plate of eggs and potatoes that Hayden had whipped up like some kind of rock-and-roll chef. He slapped a piece of buttered toast down next to it with a flourish.

Hayden asked, "You drink coffee?"

"Black," I replied.

Hayden handed me a steaming mug, and Kristie shouted from the front seat, "Make mine weak, baby!"

"She's already had three cups," Hayden said with a smirk. "Chris and Rodney didn't leave 'til sunrise. They wanted to party, but I told them we have to find your aunt," he said as if it were the most obvious thing in the world.

I thought about how cool Hayden and Kristie were for taking the time to do this with me. A jolt of fear and thrill raced through me at the thought of finally seeing Sibby.

"I don't have her address. Just her name and that she lives in downtown Memphis. I want to surprise her."

"We'll find her," Hayden said, typing away on his phone.

Margaret trotted into the kitchen, pausing dramatically by her food bowl. She scarfed down some of the mush Hayden had set out for her, then turned to me and gave an exaggerated snort.

"Okay, I get it. I'm not your favorite." I held out my hand to her in peace.

Margaret snorted at me and turned her back, waddling off with an attitude. At this point, she had more passive-aggressive energy than an entire season of reality TV.

Hayden leaned against the counter, sipping his coffee. "We've got a few hours to kill before the gig tonight, so we'll do some digging. If Sibby McGee's in Memphis, we'll find her."

As we rumbled down the highway, I stared out the window, the landscape flattening into the Mississippi Delta. I wondered what meeting Sibby might mean. Would she have answers about my parents?

Maybe she'd know something that could help me finally make sense of it all.

Or maybe the real adventure was just beginning.

"Hah! Sibby McGee," Hayden said triumphantly, already dialing.

He dialed with practiced ease. When someone answered, Hayden immediately switched to his fake persona.

"Yes, this is Mike from downtown Fast Gas. We found a savings card for Sibby McGee and just need to confirm it's yours."

I stared at him, coffee halfway to my lips. What the hell? I've heard of shady detective work, but this felt like we were about to discover some coupon scam conspiracy.

"Yes, ma'am," Hayden continued, waving a hand at me as if to say, *Relax, I've got this.* "You've had a savings card with us for a couple of years. Maybe you signed up once to save five dollars on gas? We need to confirm your address to send it back."

The guy didn't miss a beat. As whoever was on the other end spoke, he snatched up a pen and jotted something down on a scrap of paper. "Thank you, ma'am. We'll mail it out in the next . . ." He crumpled some paper into the receiver, mumbling a few filler words before hanging up.

He turned to me like he'd just pulled off the heist of the century.

"That's how you find somebody without making them suspicious," he said, sliding the paper across the table.

"You think that was her?" I asked.

"Smoker's voice?" Hayden asked, studying me.

I shrugged. I couldn't remember her voice that well. What stuck with me was the smell of watermelon bubble gum on her breath and the way her hand felt so light on my shoulder, like it barely existed.

"How old did she sound?"

"I'd guess around forty," he said. "People always think I'm older, too," he added with a chuckle.

I stared at the slip of paper: 707 S. Wilson Ave.

"How sure are you that this is her?" I asked.

"Unless there's another Sibby McGee in downtown Memphis, I'd say we nailed it."

"And we're going there now?"

Hayden leaned back in his chair, arms crossed. "Got somewhere else to be?"

I shook my head, the slip of paper suddenly heavy in my hand. My stomach twisted, excitement and dread tangling together in a messy knot. Was I doing the right thing? Should I leave well enough alone? But nothing about this was "well enough." It was eating me alive and burnt a hole through everything I tried to build for myself. Hayden, on the other hand, seemed perfectly fine. Maybe he had a secret stash of "don't give a shit" pills.

This wasn't just about finding Sibby. This was about finding answers, about understanding the cracks in my family that had split me apart. I couldn't go to Grandpa Norris, not yet. My parents had him under surveillance, just waiting for him to report my whereabouts. He wouldn't, but I couldn't drag him further into this mess.

All I had was this address of a near-ghost of a person who might hold the key to everything I didn't know.

"Let's go meet your aunt." Hayden announced.

I watched the trees blur past, the paper clenched in my hand. Whatever waited at 707 S. Wilson Ave., was a door I had to walk through.

My stomach knotted, nerves shot at the thought of seeing Aunt Sibby after all these years. Memories of her were faded and disjointed, like trying to recall the details of a dream after waking. Would she even recognize me? Would she care that I'd shown up? Most of all, what would she say about the fallout with my parents?

I stared out the window to escape my thoughts, but the scenery in the fast-lane was just a blur of potholes and the occasional trucker giving me a thumbs-up. So much for soul-searching.

The scenery blurred into stretches of cracked asphalt, boarded-up buildings, and the occasional bright splash of color from a diner's weathered neon sign.

Meanwhile, Hayden and Kristie bantered in the front seat, their voices steady and familiar, pulling me back whenever I drifted too far, mostly because Kristie was explaining why she couldn't live without avocado toast. It was oddly comforting.

When the questions clawed at me again, I leaned into a memory of Leah. I pictured her hand resting over mine, steady and grounding, and let the sound of a John Lennon song play in my mind. The thought of her brought a bitter-sweet ache. Leah had been a grounding force for me, someone who made me want to be better. Not just for her, but for myself.

In the front seat, Hayden reached across the middle console to stroke Kristie's hand where it dangled. She glanced at him with the faintest smile, a quiet contentment passing between them like a secret they didn't need to say out loud.

I missed that.

I missed Leah.

I missed being a kid.

I missed the kind of life where money, time, and all these other adult problems didn't exist.

With a sigh, I pulled my pen and notepad from my back pocket and set them on the table in front of me. Writing had always been my way out, my way through. I wasn't sure what I wanted to say yet, but the pen felt good in my hand—steady, ready for whatever I needed to spill onto the page.

Dear Leah,

You were right. I was an entitled hot shot, but that wasn't all I was. If you had known me before, I was the kid that would've played with anyone at the playground. I would've embraced anyone, even if their teeth were crooked or they had holes all over their clothes. I didn't care about stuff like that. I cared about how they made me feel and how I could make them feel. Friends are more to me than the things that don't matter. We can't take all that fake stuff with us in the end. We can only take our growth, what we learned, our minds and everything in them. I just wanted people to like me, to like being with me. I just wanted to make people smile. I never stopped being that way, but yeah, there was a part of me that let that fake stuff get in the way. It was when I started thinking it mattered. It's a hard pressure to resist, but that's when you came into my life and reminded me that it all wasn't real. This is real. What I'm experiencing right now . . . what I experienced with you . . . that was real and it sucks because I will never have it again.

Braden

My gut twisted when Hayden shouted, "Welcome to Memphis!"

I'd been staring out the window when the sign came into view, declaring our arrival in the birthplace of legends. A magical kingdom, I thought, a place where countless lives were changed. Would it change mine?

The city sprawled ahead, its streets a mix of faded history and stubborn resilience. Downtown Memphis wasn't the shining beacon I'd imagined. It was more like an older, worn-out cousin of Gatlinburg, clinging to memories of better days. Broken windows, boarded-up storefronts, and cracked sidewalks told stories of a city that had seen its share of struggles. A knot formed in my chest as we drove through, a tangle of sadness and frustration swirling inside me. This was the home of Elvis, Johnny Cash, and B.B. King. Their legacy now lay in chipped paint and scattered trash.

But there was still life here. Tourists wandered in clusters, street performers danced and flipped on the sidewalks, and the smell of barbecue and deep-fried something wafted through the air. Music poured from open windows, weathered and soulful, filling the cracks of the city like glue holding it together. I couldn't stop smiling. It wasn't perfect, but it was real. Memphis had a heartbeat, a rhythm that pulsed with history and heartache and hope.

I thought of Sibby. Did she love this city, flaws and all? I hoped so.

Off the main streets, small, tired homes lined the block. Some had sagging porches, and others showed effort with trimmed grass. Winnie bounced over potholes.

"Home sweet home," Hayden said as we slowed in front of a light blue house on the corner.

It wasn't falling apart, but it wasn't thriving. Dusty windows and a crooked shed spoke of someone doing their best. A vase of yellow flowers sat in the window, a small burst of joy.

My stomach churned. What if my parents had already warned her?

"Want us to come with you?" Kristie asked from the front seat.

I hesitated. Yes, I thought. Please. But the past was a mess I wasn't ready to explain, the awkward, tangled stuff about my family. So, I shook my head and forced a grin. "If she drops dead from surprise, I'll wave you in."

I climbed out of Winnie, the door creaking behind me. My legs felt shaky as I walked toward the house. I wiped my sweaty palms against my jeans. Someone peeked through the blinds, and my heart jumped, nerves and excitement crashing together.

At the door, I pressed the bell with a trembling finger, the faint chime ringing inside. A moment later, a light-haired woman cracked the door open.

"Yeah?" she said, her smoker's voice low and wary.

It was her. Even through the smudged glass, I saw it—the slight creases at the corners of her eyes, the ones I remembered from when I was a kid.

"Sibby?" I asked.

She opened the door fully, stepping into view. Light brown eyes, light brown hair cut to her shoulders, tan skin that spoke of hours spent in the Memphis sun. She stared at me for a long moment, then tilted her head slightly, a flicker of recognition in her gaze.

"You remember Trish? Trish Gregory?" I asked.

"Why?"

The moment I said, "I'm her son," Sibby froze.

My smile widened, trying to break the tension, anything to fill the silence between us. For a second, I imagined she might step forward, arms outstretched, ready to pull me into a hug, but nothing happened. She just stood there, her light brown eyes boring into mine, as if she was trying to decipher something.

"You are Sibby McGee, right?" I asked.

"What're you doing here?" she asked, calm but distant.

Her question knocked the breath out of me. My nerves kicked in, and I stumbled over my words. "I just wanted to say hi," I said. "I was driving through and thought I'd see you. It's been a while."

Sibby's hand tightened on the doorframe. She glanced past me, her gaze skipping over Winnie and the street beyond, as though she couldn't bear to meet my eyes anymore. Her lips pressed into a tight line, and I thought I saw a flicker of something in her face. Regret? Sadness? Anger?

"Yes, it has," she said, but there was no warmth behind the words.

"I thought I'd say hi and maybe see if you wanted to hang out or something."

Sibby's hand trembled as she adjusted her grip. She looked at me, swallowed, and her eyes shimmered briefly.

"I have work," she said, her voice tight.

"Oh, okay," I said, nodding too quickly. "Maybe tomorrow?"

"No." She swallowed again, and when she said my name, it hit me like a warm, fleeting hug. One I didn't know I needed.

"Braden . . ."

For a moment, I thought she might change her mind, might let me in. But then her eyes hardened, and her voice turned firm, a barrier I couldn't cross.

"You need to go, okay?"

The words cut deeper than I expected. My smile faltered, then disappeared entirely. "What?"

"It's best if you go," she repeated, her voice growing shakier.

I opened my mouth to say something—anything—but no words came out.

"Go!" she said, stepping back into the house. Before I could process what was happening, the door slammed shut, and the sound of the lock clicking into place ricocheted louder than it should have.

I stared at the door, my heart pounding in my chest, waiting for something to happen. For her to open it back up, for her to say she was sorry, for her to explain. But nothing came.

When I turned back to Winnie, Hayden and Kristie stood outside, expressions weighted with sympathy. They didn't say a word. I couldn't decide if that made it better or worse.

I climbed into Winnie, sinking into the kitchen booth, silent. My thoughts spun as we pulled away, the house shrinking behind us. A dozen questions clawed at my mind. Had I done something wrong? Had my parents warned her away? Her rejection landed, and the ache spread across me, slow and stubborn, like a bruise forming after a hit.

We drove fast, heading for the gig, but it felt like I was dragging behind, stuck in that moment, replaying her words over and over again. The protective cloak I thought I'd found in hearing her say my name had been stripped away, leaving me bare and shivering in the cold reality.

The stars began popping faintly in the sky, their persistence like a quiet challenge. *Get it together, kid.* I stared at them like they had all the answers, but considering how my life was going, they probably didn't even know where the nearest gas station was.

We parked near the karaoke bar and squeezed through the alley, the smell of beer and fried food in the air. Hayden practically skipped ahead, his energy infectious, while I followed, trying to match his enthusiasm, even though I felt more like the crumpled receipt stuck to my shoe.

The moment we stepped inside, the noise of clinking glasses and laughter hit me like a cymbal crash. For a moment, I let myself pretend I was Elvis Presley stepping into the building.

Maybe it was a coping mechanism, an escape from the shitty meeting I'd just had with Sibby, or maybe I just wanted to shake off all the pressure on me. Either way, pretending to be the King of Rock 'n' Roll helped.

Inside, eyes turned our way, but I convinced myself it was because I *was* Elvis.

Hayden greeted the first person he saw, a bouncer built like a brick wall with a grin that could've powered the lights on Beale Street. I swore Hayden could make friends with a houseplant. His energy made me want to crawl into my own skin, but instead, I decided: *Nope, not tonight. Tonight, I'm grateful.*

Grateful for Hayden, whose boundless excitement could probably pull me out of a pit if I let it. Grateful for Kristie, who waved at us from a tiny table she'd just set up with her art. She adjusted her microphone, standing on tiptoes to reach, and I smiled at how tiny she looked next to it. And grateful for this dingy little bar, with its mismatched chairs and worn-out floors, for giving me somewhere to be and pretend life wasn't chewing me up.

The guy working sound handed me a stool, and I nodded my thanks as I scooted it next to Hayden's. Kristie's mic stand wobbled, and she smacked it like a misbehaving child before pulling out her sketchpad. I couldn't help but chuckle. Maybe humor wasn't in short supply tonight, either.

Hayden pulled Susie out of her case and handed her over like she was made of glass. The smooth wood rested in my hands, familiar and grounding, the strings perfectly tuned. A piece of home, even if I wasn't home anymore. I let my fingers drift over the frets, playing a quiet chord to test the sound.

Maybe I wasn't Elvis, but maybe I didn't have to be. Maybe it was enough to be Blake, the kid with a guitar, a couple of good people in his corner, and a night full of possibilities waiting to happen.

Kristie handed me a water bottle, her wink a silent promise that everything would be all right. I wanted to believe her, but she didn't know what I knew . . . that my days were numbered.

She started singing Bob Dylan's "It's All Over Now, Baby Blue." I didn't know the song, so I kept my strumming simple, letting her featherlight voice fill the space. Kristie didn't overdo it. No ego-driven theatrics, no unnecessary crescendos. She stayed true to the song, and I respected that. When people oversang, they lost the meaning, drowning the emotion with their own self-importance.

I tried to focus on being grateful. For Kristie. For Hayden. For this moment. But Sibby's voice still echoed in my mind. The sound of her door locking shut played on repeat, and no amount of Dylan's poetry could drown it out.

Hayden took over next, performing a Bee Gees' song in a voice that sounded like a frenzied parrot. The audience howled, and even I cracked a smile. It was the kind of smile that starts somewhere deep in your chest and surprises you when it finds its way out. Kristie noticed. Her eyes flicked to mine, and I caught the hint of satisfaction on her face as she tapped out a beat on her drums.

He was hilarious, mimicking them with the voice of an orgasming chipmunk, his over-the-top squeals sending laughter rippling through the room. It reminded me of the time Scotty and I did karaoke at a cast party. We'd belted out "Stayin' Alive" in those same chipmunk voices, our falsettos so ridiculous that people were practically falling out of their chairs, clutching their sides from laughing too hard.

Then Hayden gestured for me to take the mic.

Shit.

Apparently, it was my turn to butcher a classic. The crowd quieted as I stood, my steps heavy as I walked to the stage.

One song came to mind, one I'd only ever sung in my head, never out loud. I gripped Susie, my knuckles stiff as I strummed the opening chords of "House of the Rising Sun." My eyes fell shut as the first words tumbled out, lower and rougher than usual, like gravel grinding deep in my throat. I didn't have to be perfect. This song wasn't about being perfect.

Kristie joined in with her drums, her rhythm steady, grounding me. Hayden followed with his guitar, and together we built something that felt bigger than any of us. I sang with everything I had. Every note carried the frustration and fury that had been sitting inside me for years.

Why hadn't my mom just told me the truth? Why did she bury everything in secrets, in lies? Why did my parents work so hard to control my life when theirs was a disaster? I was done. Sick of the weight, sick of the silence. In that light stone house near the Tipton County interstate, I hoped—no, I *willed*—my parents to hear me yelling. But deep down, I had to face the truth . . . I'd never get the chance to yell at them again. So instead, I yelled at the audience.

They listened. They *heard* me. Better yet, they understood

because music transcended words. Music healed. And with every scream, every lyric spilling from my chest, every soaring verse, every trembling high note, and every guttural low, I felt pieces of myself knitting back together. I was healing, cracking open and mending all at once.

When the final chord rang out, I stepped back from the mic, lungs burning, throat raw. The room stayed silent for a beat, then erupted in applause—whistles, cheers, calls for an encore.

I looked up, startled by their reaction. These strangers didn't know me, but they *felt* me.

Kristie appeared beside me, her hand resting lightly on my shoulder. I met her eyes . . . calm, steady, understanding. She stepped up to the mic without a word, giving me space to breathe. I let out a shaky laugh and unscrewed the cap of my water bottle. I sat down, feeling like I'd finally shed a layer of myself I didn't need anymore.

Kristie spoke excitedly to the audience, but her words blurred in my mind as I packed up Susie. My hands trembled slightly, a mix of adrenaline and something deeper that I couldn't name. I made my way toward the front door, desperate for air, for a moment to steady myself and sort through the storm swirling inside.

Before I stepped outside, Hayden caught up with me. He handed me a water bottle and said, "You found your voice." His half-smile was brief before he walked away.

Outdoors, the night air greeted me with its humid warmth, clinging to my skin like the residue of all the emotions I'd just poured out on stage. The streets were alive, buzzing with life, but I needed distance from it all. I wandered to the quieter side of the building, where a bench sat half-hidden from the main crowd.

I collapsed onto it, Susie beside me. The moon hung low, and the sound of the city rumbled in the background. I wondered if Leah was looking at it too. Maybe I wasn't ready for Memphis, or any of this.

Kristie's voice floated faintly through the night, covering

"Time After Time" by Cyndi Lauper. Her voice felt like a tether pulling me back from my thoughts. Part of me wished I'd stayed inside, cheering them on, pretending things were okay. But another part of me knew it wasn't that simple. My old life—my parents, Trevor, even the version of me that existed back then—felt impossibly far away. The memories tugged at me, filled with regret and longing. I wondered if running away had been a mistake, but even that thought wasn't enough to make me change my mind.

I exhaled, running my hand over Susie's smooth neck, when I noticed someone approaching from my left. The steady rhythm of her steps caught my attention first. She moved slowly, her denim jacket catching the faint glow of the streetlights. Her shoulder-length hair framed a thin face that carried a hint of weariness, though it was her eyes, locked on me with quiet determination, that froze me in place.

Sibby approached. I stood, gripping Susie like she could shield me. My legs itched to run, but I stayed put.

"Braden, wait," Sibby called, urgency in her voice.

I paused, feeling the toll of the night on my shoulders.

"I'll tell you if you want to know."

The words hit me like a punch, leaving me shaking my head slightly, caught in the grip of indecision.

"I didn't expect anything from you," I said, voice breaking. "Just wanted to say hi."

"Hi," Sibby replied.

It stopped me, a strange satisfaction flickering. I wasn't built for rejection, not giving it or taking it.

With a sigh, I turned back and sat beside her on the bench, resting Susie between my knees.

She looked at me, hesitating. "You've grown up." Her gaze flicked to my black eye. "Aside from that, you look good."

Her voice had this husky warmth to it, the kind that made you want to protect her.

"It's been what . . . ten years?" I asked, even though I knew the answer.

"Eleven," she said quietly.

"Why'd you stop coming around?"

Her hands fidgeted in her lap. "I thought you just wanted to say hi."

"You didn't track *me* down just to say hi. How did you even know where I was?"

She looked down. "When I slammed the door . . . I regretted it instantly. But you were gone when I came back out to apologize. So, I followed you here."

"You've been watching me here?"

"I just . . . I didn't want to lose the chance to talk to you."

She shifted closer. "Your voice is incredible, Braden. I hoped you'd sing another song."

I glanced at her, not sure what to make of the praise. Then she placed her hand over mine. Warm, familiar, and heartbreakingly nostalgic.

"I'm sorry," she whispered. "I was scared. I didn't think I'd ever see you again."

I wanted to believe her, but something didn't sit right. "Why?"

Her lips pressed together like she was holding back a dam of words. "You probably have questions about the fight, why I stopped talking to your parents. But . . . it's not my place to tell you."

"Not your place?" My voice rose despite myself. "It's my family. Nobody tells me anything. I have a right to know."

"Have you asked your parents?" she countered, almost too quickly.

"Does a duck shit white?" I snapped.

She laughed, a genuine, short laugh that softened the edges of the moment. Against my better judgment, I laughed too, even if it was hollow.

"They're fine, by the way," I muttered. "Still controlling as hell, though."

"Is that why you left?" she asked, studying me like she was piecing together a puzzle.

I didn't answer, but she nudged me, her voice dipping into something almost playful. "Come on, Braden. I ran away twice when I was your age. Slept by the river once after my parents had this huge fight. The other time . . . well, never mind." She shook her head. "Point is, I get it."

Her casual tone grated on me. "You don't get it. Not really."

She sighed, leaning back. "I'm not saying you have to talk to them, but at least let them know you're okay. Send a postcard or something."

"I don't want them to know where I am."

"Then send it anonymously." She shrugged. "You don't have to forgive them, but don't let them think you're dead. That's cruel."

Her words stung because they were true. I looked down at Susie, my fingers brushing over the case.

"I didn't have much family growing up," I said, trying to steady myself. "You were the only one who ever came around. So what happened between you and my parents?"

She hesitated, her lips trembling. "There was . . . a situation. Something I knew about."

"Don't worry. I know my mom cheated on my dad."

Sibby's eyes widened, and she stood abruptly, pacing a few steps away. "Braden . . ."

"Just tell me the truth," I pressed. "I'm not a kid anymore. I can take it."

She turned, her expression a mix of sorrow and fear. "Your dad had the affair, not your mom."

My breath hitched. "What?"

"Your mom slapped me when I told her. I was young, stupid . . . thought I was doing the right thing."

"My dad?" My voice cracked, disbelieving. "Why should I believe you?"

She sighed. "I wouldn't lie to you. What would I gain?"

"What would you gain?" I snapped. "To ruin my relationship with them? Or just for attention? I don't know. I don't even know you anymore."

Her face fell, and for a moment, I thought she might cry. "I don't expect you to trust me. But you've spent years blaming your mom for something she didn't do, haven't you?"

The words sliced through me. She might have been right, and I hated her for it. "How do I know you're not just making this up?"

"You don't," she said. "The only way you'll know is if you ask them. But I think you already know the truth. You've felt it for a long time, haven't you?"

Her question hung in the air.

"I'm sorry, Braden," she said. "I wish I could undo the past, but I can't."

"You don't have to worry about me," I said, standing and slinging Susie over my shoulder.

She didn't stop me this time, but her words still followed. "But I am."

I paused, glancing down at her as she sat back on the bench. Slowly, she reached for my hand, pulling it toward her like she was trying to anchor me. "Where are you staying? Do you have money? A vehicle? Do you even have a plan?"

I shrugged, my face still guarded. "I don't even know what I'm doing tomorrow, honestly. And you know what? I like it that way."

Her lips quirked into a sad sort of smile.

"Stay with me for a while," Sibby said. "I don't have much, but I have a house and an extra bedroom."

I shook my head. "I've got friends."

"The ones in the camper?" She raised an eyebrow, a small

laugh escaping. "Whoever's driving definitely doesn't have much love for stop signs."

That got a small laugh out of me too.

Her expression softened. "They're welcome too. I mean it. We could have a little vacation, go see the sights. I can't remember the last time I used my vacation days."

I stayed silent, turning her offer over in my mind like a shiny new toy I wasn't allowed to touch.

"Well . . ." She released my hand reluctantly. "You have my address. Apparently."

Sibby stood, a fragile hope in her eyes as she hesitated. "Should I wait here?"

I glanced toward Hayden, who was leaning against the karaoke bar's entrance, cigarette in hand, laughing at something with a couple of locals. "No," I said. "You don't have to wait."

Her shoulders fell just a little, but she nodded like she'd expected it. "Okay. If you show up, that'd be amazing. If not . . . I'll understand." She paused, biting her lip before adding, "Just promise me you'll call, all right? I'd like to have a relationship with you, Braden. I always have."

I stood there as she stepped closer, wrapping me in a hug so tight it felt like she was trying to hold all the broken pieces of us together.

As she pulled back and turned to leave, I called out after her. "Hey, wait."

She stopped mid-step and looked back, her expression a mix of curiosity and caution.

"Why'd you turn me away? Back there, when I first showed up. Why did you do that?"

She stared at me for a long moment, and it didn't feel awkward or invasive. It felt like she was seeing something in me, something even I couldn't figure out. Her gaze lingered until she finally sighed.

"Because seeing you reminded me of all the good I can do," she said, her voice quiet. "I just have a hard time believing I can."

I blinked, unsure if I really understood her. My chest tightened, a tug I couldn't ignore, and for a second I hesitated, wondering if I should just let her walk away. But something in her —her quiet strength, the way her eyes held me—pulled me forward.

Before I could say anything, she turned and walked away, her hands running through her hair as her face tilted toward the glowing city lights. And just like that, I knew . . . I had to go back with her.

CHAPTER 6:
Me And Sibby McGee

I woke up in a bed that wasn't mine but felt oddly familiar. The quilt, scented with lavender dryer sheets, reminded me of home. Sunlight streamed through the window, filling the room with a golden glow. I rubbed the sleep from my eyes and surveyed my surroundings.

Sibby didn't have much, but she made the room feel inviting. Despite the busted drywall and peeling wallpaper, it was clean, with dust-free surfaces and neat furniture. An old lamp sat next to the bed, its bulb likely dead. My freshly washed clothes were folded beside it, a small but thoughtful touch.

Wearing one of Sibby's oversized shirts and sweatpants had been necessary, but I was grateful to get my own clothes back. It was a small step toward reclaiming myself.

Last night, when I knocked on her door, Sibby pulled me into a tight hug. Her embrace felt like a shield against everything I'd been carrying. She led me through her modest house, full of personality, with scuffed floors, flea market furniture, and the faint smell of cinnamon candles.

Hayden and Kristie had promised to stick around town for a few days, just in case I needed anything. Before leaving, Hayden handed me more cash in case I got stuck. It was more than kind; it was something a big brother would do.

The thought hit me . . . Hayden had stepped into a role I never knew I needed. And yet, had I ever been as good a brother to Trevor? The guilt gnawed at me, forcing me to face the uncomfortable truth.

I changed into my clothes and wandered over to the window. The view was oddly charming. Each house had its own character. Some with sagging porches, others with stubbornly bright paint. The cracked sidewalks showed their age, but it didn't bother me. Not much did when I felt good. Seeing my aunt and knowing she was just as happy to see me was enough to make this new place feel safe.

Her words from last night echoed in my mind. Seeing me reminded her of the good she could still do. What did she mean by that? What had happened between her and my parents to make her feel estranged? There were stories buried there, ones I wasn't sure I was ready to unearth, but I knew I had to try.

Maybe, just maybe, I could do something to help her. Fix something broken between her and my parents. The idea had gnawed at me all night, refusing to let go. And then another thought crept in, uninvited but persistent. Maybe I could do one last good thing before I went through with my plan to end myself.

Susie leaned against the wall where I'd left her, my cash still safely tucked into the case pocket. Sibby wasn't like Paul. She didn't steal from me when I was at my lowest. That small act of trust felt like a lifeline, fragile but real.

I pulled the baggie of pills from my pocket, staring at it like it held all the answers. My stomach twisted. I wasn't ready yet. The magnitude of that truth settled over me, comforting and suffocating. I shoved the baggie back, hoping the decision to wait wouldn't kick me in the ass.

Reaching under the pillow, I retrieved my pen and notepad, the same ones I'd hidden there earlier so Sibby wouldn't stumble across them on the nightstand. The idea of her seeing my messy, unfiltered thoughts scrawled across the pages made me bite my cheek. Some things weren't meant to be shared.

I moved to the tiny desk near the bedroom window and sat down, the legs creaking under my weight. The desk was old, its surface scarred and uneven, but it gave me a place to think, a place to try to make sense of everything swirling inside my head. Outside the window, the sunlight had softened, and the neighborhood looked a little less broken. Or maybe it was just me.

Dear Trevor,

Being away from you with the thought of never seeing you again sucks. I'm sorry and I'm sorry for whatever you might go through after all this shit happens. Thanks for looking out for me. I hope I was a good brother. I hope you go on to accomplish all your dreams, which I know you will. You were always a stubborn little ass, so I'm sure you will put that to good use.

I'd say tell mom and dad hi for me, but I'm struggling to give a shit about them anymore. I'm learning a lot while I'm down here. I'm learning that mom and dad aren't the perfect people they always pretended to be and I hope they at least have the decency to be honest with you one day so you don't live in the dark and the effects of whatever secrets lie in their pillows at night.

I love you, man.

Braden

The smell of coffee and warm bread made my stomach rumble. After brushing my teeth and splashing water on my face, I wandered into the kitchen. Sibby stood at the stove, humming. When she heard me, she turned, her hair bouncing, and her energy brightened the room.

Sibby wore khaki shorts and a light blue tank top, the steady noise of the window A/C filling the space.

"Morning, Braden," she said, her voice lighter than I remembered. "How'd you sleep?"

"Much better than my own bed."

"So, what's on the agenda?" she asked, flipping some pancakes with practiced ease. The smell hit me, and I damn near lost it. I loved pancakes, but I didn't want to admit it and come off like a sugar-crazed little kid.

"I thought we could hit up Sun Studio," she said, glancing over her shoulder. "You still like The Beatles, right?"

I felt a grin tugging at the corners of my mouth, and I hoped it wasn't too obvious. The fact that she remembered something like that, after all these years, caught me off guard. "The Beatles for life," I said, reaching for the coffee pot and pouring myself a mug.

"Drink a glass of water, too," she added. "It gets pretty warm in town, so make sure you stay hydrated."

"Thanks," I said, taking a sip of coffee before settling into a chair at the small kitchen table.

She hummed a familiar tune as she worked, flipping the pancakes one last time before sliding them onto a plate. A moment later, she placed them in front of me with a bottle of maple syrup.

"You always liked pancakes," she said, beaming down at me. "So I thought I'd make you a batch."

Her words made me pause. Apparently, I was still that sugar-crazed kid in her eyes.

I wolfed down the pancakes in a performance worthy of an Olympic event. If there were an award for speed-eating, I'd definitely have at least a silver medal. Sibby didn't seem to mind. She just got up, smiling, and plopped a couple more on my plate.

"So . . . Sun Studio?" she asked, sliding back into her seat. "Oh, and I was thinking we could do a horse-and-buggy ride around town, too."

"That sounds cool," I said, my mouth already full again.

The morning drifted by in easy conversation, mostly about my parents. Sibby reminisced about her and my mom's Starbucks tradition, where they'd always order something new just for the fun of it. Her voice was soothing, like the calm after a storm, and every smile or laugh from her felt like sunlight breaking through. I couldn't stop thinking about how much better my mom's life might be if she had Sibby back in it.

When it was time to head out, we didn't even need Sibby's car. Downtown was close enough to walk to or, in this case, ride to. We climbed into a horse-drawn carriage, the white horse adorned with pink flowers and the carriage gleaming with subtle rope lights. Sibby ran her fingers along the heart-shaped fencing, admiring it. Meanwhile, I kept glancing at the horse, wondering if he was secretly judging us for not driving our own car.

I sat captivated by the steady rhythm of the horse's hooves tapping against the road. Meanwhile, the driver chatted nonstop, pointing out landmarks and sharing bits of local history with the enthusiasm of someone who truly loved their city.

We stopped as a trolley passed, the driver waving at us like we were all on some big city tour. It felt like we were extras in a badly scripted movie, but I was starting to enjoy my role as the slightly uncomfortable yet fascinated tourist. I took in the charm of the moment. The gentle sway of the carriage, the movement of life all around us, and the unexpected feeling that maybe, just maybe, today was a good day to be alive.

"And to your left here is the wax museum," the driver said, gesturing with his hand. "It recently won an award for the most realistic wax statue of Tom Hanks."

A wax Tom Hanks? I could only imagine the hours of painstaking work that went into perfecting his waxy, slightly confused expression.

The streets of Memphis, alive with roots and stories, had a way of drawing you in. I glanced at Sibby, wondering how many times she'd seen this town through the same lens. For me, though, it was new, a place I could already imagine falling in love with.

Yesterday, Memphis felt like a city that had seen better days, like a band that peaked in the '90s and was still playing gigs in the local dive bars. But now, riding through it, I reminded myself of its deep roots. Memphis wasn't Atlantic City, glitzy and polished for tourists. This was the Mississippi Delta. Shaped by hardship, resilience, and music. Blues, born here, spoke to those who poured their struggles into it. Just like me.

Memphis was a poor place, sure. There were abandoned buildings, struggling neighborhoods, and plenty of hardship. But it was also rich in all the ways that mattered. The soul of this city lived in its music, in the haunting strum of a guitar, the ache of a harmonica, and the stories woven into its lyrics.

This wasn't a simple city. It was a stage, a heartbeat, a living, breathing song. And in that moment, I realized something . . . the blues wasn't just what kept Memphis alive. It was what made Memphis unforgettable.

We passed the blue-and-white sign for The New Daisy Theatre, its vintage lettering a reminder of its heyday as a bustling movie palace in 1937 before it transformed into a music venue in the '80s. The history of this place was palpable, and I imagined the countless performances that must've awakened its walls over the decades.

The streets buzzed with life as we continued, the air thick with mouthwatering smells. Each bar and restaurant seemed to offer something unique. Sizzling cheeseburgers, crispy fried fish, everything imaginable dipped in batter and fried, and the irresistible sweetness of fresh donuts. My stomach twisted, equal parts still hungry and amazed.

The buildings were aged, their brick facades telling stories of better days. I asked the driver why they weren't being renovated. "Nashville's the place now," she said with a shrug.

The sun blazed, the heat bouncing off the pavement in waves. The horse and buggy stopped, and Sibby tipped the driver.

I paused to take in the painted portraits on the building. Jerry Lee Lewis, Johnny Cash, Carl Perkins, and, of course, Elvis Presley. The faces of legends who had stood where I was standing, their music reshaping the world.

This studio was a shrine to the birth of something bigger than any one person. A place where dreams, melodies, and a whole lot of guts.

When we arrived at the front of Sun Studio, I stopped in my tracks. I was walking on the same sidewalk that countless trailblazers had once used. A massive, yellowish guitar hung above the main door, its bold presence declaring that this was legacy. Despite its fame, the building itself had a humble charm that reminded me of downtown Tipton.

There wasn't much of a line, just a handful of people waiting for the next tour. The moment I stepped inside, it was like being transported straight to the 1950s. The walls were covered in vintage records and black-and-white photos, the floor was a classic checkered pattern, and everything was bathed in vibrant yellow, black, and white.

I stood there, the place where rock 'n' roll was born. The hairs on my arms tingled as they rose, like the air itself was charged with music that had changed the world.

We strolled past the gift shop, filled with shirts, hoodies, hats, CDs, postcards. I picked up a postcard, running my thumb over its glossy print, thinking how much my friends back home would love to see this place.

Near the small café, Sibby ordered two pops, but I was too excited to stay still. While she waited, I wandered off, my eyes darting from one incredible piece of memorabilia to the next. The walls were lined with treasures: original records, photos of legendary sessions, and items that told the story of every note recorded here.

Then there were the 45s. A section of original records sat neatly displayed.

One piece—a vibrant painting of Sun Studio—caught my eye. I would've decorated my bedroom with it if I thought I'd ever go back home.

The tour guide led us upstairs to the studio museum. Museums like this gave history a heartbeat, keeping memories alive for people eager to step into the past.

I thought I knew about Sun Studio, but the tour guide quickly proved me wrong. Memphis Recording Service. That was the original name. Sam Phillips started it as a place where anyone could walk in, pay a few bucks, and record a song. One of those hopefuls was Elvis Presley. At the time, Sam didn't even have his own label; he just recorded artists and tried to land deals. What he didn't know was that he couldn't sell the same song to two different labels. A lawsuit taught him that lesson the hard way, so he decided to start his own label. Sun Records.

In the museum, I learned even more surprises. "Rocket 88," considered the first rock 'n' roll song, was born from a damaged amplifier. An accident that created a sound everyone loved.

The tour guide led us to the WHBQ radio control room of Dewey Phillips, the legendary DJ behind Red, Hot, and Blue. He was the first to broadcast Elvis' "That's All Right" and "Blue Moon of Kentucky". Seeing Dewey's control room on display was surreal. The guide played a sample of his show. Dewey's voice flew at a mile a minute, a chaotic mix of energy and humor that made it impossible not to smile. He was a character, wild and passionate, but sharp as a tack when it came to music. If he hated a record, he'd smash it live on air, throwing the shattered pieces across the room while trashing it to his audience.

I couldn't tell if the shards on the floor were from Dewey's temper tantrums or if they'd become an avant-garde art installation. Either way, they were preserved as a testament to some serious commitment to chaos.

Sibby followed me, one arm hanging at her side while the other held an album. Her expression was content, almost like she was soaking it all in for the first time.

"Have you been here before?" I asked.

"No. I've just been focused on work."

"You like being a nurse?"

"I like helping people," she said. "It's hard, though. I work with the elderly, and it's tough to lose them."

"Well, at least you don't have to worry about them getting *really* old. One perk of that job is their expiration date."

She glared at me.

"Why not work at a hospital?" I asked. "Or somewhere you don't have to be around death as much?"

"Then who would take care of the old folks?" she asked, a determination in her voice.

I didn't have an answer. "Maybe someone who's kind of . . . numb to it?"

I glanced around, realizing the irony of where we were. The museum was full of traces of people who weren't here anymore. Most of those artists were long gone, but their spirits lingered in this place. Maybe that's why Sibby worked at the nursing home, surrounded by people whose time was limited. She could still care for them, keep their stories alive, and do what she loved.

We walked into the recording studio. The actual room. My breath caught as I saw Sam Phillips' control room through the rectangular window, separating his space from where I stood. How could so much impact be created in such a small room?

I thought about what Sam once said about "perfect imperfection." I got it now. This room birthed music made by people whose voices resonated through generations, flawed and human.

They'd changed the world. They'd changed me.

The tour guide kept firing off facts, each more fascinating than the last. I hadn't known that Sam Phillips didn't like Elvis' sound at first. When I glanced at Sibby, she gave me a wide-eyed look of surprise, her expression almost childlike.

There were X's taped on the floor marking where legends had stood. I planted my feet where Bill Black once set his upright bass. Sibby stood on the spot Elvis had claimed, and when the guide pointed it out, her jaw dropped. I laughed at her reaction.

The story deepened. Sam wasn't sold on Elvis until he, Bill, and Scotty Moore shifted gears and jammed out a different tune. That was the moment Sam finally heard the spark. He took the recording of "That's All Right" to Dewey Phillips, who played it on *Red, Hot, and Blue*.

The guide hit play on a snippet of Dewey's broadcast, and suddenly, the crackling sound filled the room. My pulse quickened. I couldn't make out half of what Dewey was saying—his words ran wild, spilling over themselves—but the energy, the sheer passion in his voice, lit me up. It was the kind of fire I hadn't felt in years, the kind I didn't know I still had.

The guide shared how Elvis' success helped Sam grow Sun Studio into an international icon, signing bigger artists, hiring more staff, and creating a place that shaped music. Carl Perkins wrote "Blue Suede Shoes" on a potato sack at 3 a.m. I always imagined these guys having magical breakthroughs where inspiration just poured out of them. But the truth? The truth was sleepless nights and potato sacks.

We stood in *the* recording room, where legends like Roy Orbison, Johnny Cash, Jerry Lee Lewis, and Carl Perkins recorded the *Million Dollar Quartet*. A photo from that day hung on the wall. Four guys looking so focused and so free.

They looked put-together too, with slicked-back hair, dress shirts, the kind of polished style I always admired. I ran a hand through my own hair, trying to picture myself like them, even mimicking their expressions when no one was watching.

The guide rattled off more names. Ringo Starr, Paul Simon,

John Mellencamp, Barbara Pittman. All of them had recorded here. I shook my head in quiet envy. How lucky they were to stand where I was now, but with music pouring out of their souls, immortalizing them.

The room was still an active studio, opening at 7 p.m. every evening. Late nights and recording sessions reminded me of lying on my bedroom floor back home, falling asleep to the crackle of my record player.

Not much had changed since 1949, the guide explained.

The guide mentioned Sam passed away in 2003, only six years ago. I stole a glance at Sibby, wondering if she had cared for him in the nursing home. She didn't say, but the thought made me realize how close we all were to history, even when we didn't know it.

The tour guide pulled out the Shure 55 vocal mic, the same one Elvis, Carl Perkins, Rufus Thomas, Johnny Cash, and B.B. King had all sung into. Just staring at it, I could almost feel the soul that must've been belted into that microphone. I glanced at Sibby. Her wide-eyed wonder made me smile, though I knew she'd probably need a crash course on all this later.

Then the guide pointed out a burn mark on the piano. Jerry Lee Lewis' cigar. I wondered if Jerry had any idea how iconic that spot would become.

The highlight of it all, though, the absolute best part, was standing where Elvis himself stood when he recorded "That's All Right".

Sibby nudged me, holding up her phone. "Let me take a picture of you."

I hesitated, my thoughts drifting to my mom. The opening lines of "That's All Right" floated through my mind. Elvis singing about love that doesn't bend to anyone else's rules. I thought about Leah, and how I'd always love her, no matter what my parents expected me to do. They liked Leah and wanted me to be happy, but their priorities had always been messed up. Then I thought about Leah and my own fucked up priorities. I had to leave town. Leah needed to be free of me and the only way to do that was to leave her for good.

"Go ahead," I finally said, forcing a smile as Sibby took the shot.

The camera flash felt like a release, lifting my thoughts for a second. Or maybe it was the energy of this place. It was over-whelming, standing where my heroes once stood, their imperfect lives bleeding into the perfection of their music.

I passed through the gift shop, wanting to grab everything, but what was the point?

I stopped, my fingers brushing over the vinyl records. Maybe I could mail something to Leah. She'd get it and feel the hope of my return, not knowing I'd never be there to listen to it with her. So, I decided against it.

Sibby lingered near the postcards, giving me space. My thoughts crept back into my head, heavier this time. I'd leave here with nothing, except the memory of a room that made me realize how much of myself I still had to figure out.

I drifted outside, leaving Sibby at the cashier. The hot fresh air felt heavier than it should. I wandered to the side of the building and paused, taking in the large photo of the Million Dollar Quartet plastered on the window. Their faces beamed, frozen in a moment of creative freedom. I envied them. That happiness felt as distant to me as the stars.

The sun gleamed off the painted Sun Studio sign on the brick, the bright yellow letters almost too cheerful for how I felt. I'd dreamed of standing here for so long, and now that I was, the expe-rience was slipping through my fingers like sand. I was here, but I wasn't.

Above the sign, the painted vinyl record blurred before my eyes, spinning faster, pulling me in until it felt like my mind was playing tricks on me. For a moment, I thought it might fly off the building and smack right into me, shattering whatever pieces of me were left.

"Braden?" Sibby's voice broke through, soft but laced with alarm.

I turned to her, or at least I tried to. The sidewalk felt unsteady beneath my feet. Her image doubled, and the world warped, a cold haze creeping into my vision.

"Braden!" Her voice was distant like she was calling to me from the other side of a canyon.

I couldn't respond. The pressure in my head swelled, and before I could steady myself, my knees buckled.

The last thing I felt was the rough scrape of brick as the side of my head collided with the wall.

Everything went black.

I came to, my back against the brick. A man from the gift shop crouched in front of me, speaking, but his voice sounded muffled. He handed me a glass of water. His words starting to come into focus as my head throbbed.

I felt like a bobblehead doll, my brain bouncing around like Blake the Bobble-Headed Buffoon. That stupid nickname struck me out of nowhere, and for some reason, it made my face burn hotter with embarrassment.

Sibby sat next to me, her expression unreadable as she pressed a cold cloth against my forehead.

"You all right?" he asked, glancing at Sibby as if seeking permission to care. I nodded weakly, my head still feeling like it wasn't entirely attached to my body.

"It gets pretty hot out here," he added.

I took a sip of the water, feeling it slide down my throat, almost painfully cold against the heat of my skin. He watched me drink, looking between me and Sibby until she gave him a small, reassuring nod.

"Need a ride to the hospital?" he asked.

I exhaled, holding the cup between my knees. "No, thanks."

When Sibby pulled the cloth away, I pressed my hand to the side of my head, half-expecting blood, but there was none. Just a pounding ache.

"You take care now," the worker said before walking off.

Sibby stayed quiet until the man was out of earshot. Then she said, "I know that didn't happen from not drinking enough water, like I told you." Disappointment weighed in her voice.

"It's not from water." I sighed, already knowing this conversation was heading somewhere I didn't want it to. "I pass out sometimes when I stop taking my pills."

Her expression tightened, and I felt like she was about to scold me. "What kind of pills?"

"Antidepressants." I said it flatly, no hesitation, no shame. What was the point in holding back anymore?

She was quiet for a long moment, her gaze drifting past me, into the sunlight. She didn't ask follow-up questions or press for details, and for a second, I thought I'd dodged the deeper conversation.

But then she hit me with it.

The question.

The question I dreaded.

The question I wished people would stop asking depressed people.

"What are you depressed about?"

I let my head drop, my chin hitting my chest.

"Yeah, I'm sure there's a "Depression Handbook" that outlines the exact criteria."

"Come on, Braden," she continued, her voice edged with

incredulity. "You have a great life. More of a life than I could ever dream to have."

Her words felt like sandpaper against my nerves. I clenched my teeth, trying to keep my temper in check. Finally, I looked at her.

"How would you know what my life is like?"

She blinked, startled by my tone. "I know because I've seen it. I know because you've got everything. A family that loves you, opportunities—"

"You don't know anything about my life," I snapped. "You don't know anything about me. We haven't spoken since I was eight years old, Sibby. Eight. It's been over ten years. You don't talk to my parents. You don't know what goes on in my head, in my house, in my life. So don't act like you do."

She opened her mouth to respond but hesitated, and then, as if she couldn't stop herself, she said, "You have no right to be depressed, Braden."

That was it. The breaking point.

I shoved myself to my feet, dizziness slamming into me as I balanced against the wall. I didn't care. I wasn't staying. I started walking away, the frustration boiling over, but I couldn't stop myself from swinging back around.

"I have *every right* to be depressed," I shouted, pointing to my chest. "Every. Right. You think depression is something you get a permission slip for? That it only hits people with hard lives or sob stories?"

People were staring now, but I didn't care.

"I am depressed," I continued, "and that's all there is to it. You don't have to understand it, but don't you dare tell me I don't have the right to feel what I feel."

I turned to leave again, my head still swimming, but Sibby's voice stopped me, cutting through the chaos in my mind.

"So you're a victim now?" she called after me, her words strong and unforgiving. "That's what you're choosing to be? That's what you're making of the life you've been given?"

I froze at the curb, the cars blurring past like distant noise. Sibby caught up, her steps purposeful.

I didn't look at her. I couldn't. But I felt her standing beside me, waiting for a response I wasn't sure I could give.

"What were you and my parents really fighting about?" I stared ahead at the blur of cars passing by. "How did you find out about my dad cheating? Was he drinking? Was it one time, two, three? Why would my mom be mad at you for telling her the truth?"

Sibby grew quiet, her shallow breaths the only sound between us. I could see her struggling, her mouth parting as though to answer, but no real words formed. Instead, she gently placed her hand on my shoulder, steering me toward the bus stop a short walk away.

We sat together on the crowded bus. I didn't want to, but I didn't want to be a complete asshole to her either.

Neither of us spoke during the ride. When we got off, she motioned silently in the direction of her house.

"Braden," she said as we walked, her voice barely above a whisper. "Just like your depression . . . there are some things in life too complicated to explain."

Like why I'm still talking to you.

I kept my eyes on the cracked sidewalk, trying to control my emotions. I thought about her words, their vagueness chafing at me, and finally replied, "Facts aren't."

Sibby slowed her steps but didn't look at me.

"What happened with my parents is fact," I said. "That's something you can tell me. Depression is different."

"Why would you want to know something like this?" she asked, her tone teetering between genuine curiosity and exhaustion. "We've moved on. People fight. Sometimes people are better off apart."

"I want to know everything."

When we reached her house, Sibby took out her keys.

We stepped inside. The house was quiet except for the low

buzz of the window A/C unit, its noise filling the space like a static tension neither of us could break. I headed to the guest room and grabbed Susie. On my way back to the front door, I stopped in the living room where Sibby stood.

She scanned me and Susie with an expression that was part confusion, part dread.

"Where are you going?" she asked.

I lowered my voice. "To find out more about my family."

She wasn't going to tell me anything more, and I didn't like being treated like I couldn't handle the truth.

She let her purse drop onto the couch and stared at it for a moment before her shoulders sagged.

"Where will you go?" she asked.

I shrugged, not wanting to give her an answer. The truth was I'd probably head to Grandpa Norris', but I wasn't about to tell her that. Not yet. For all I knew, she'd pick up the phone the second I left and tell my parents exactly where I was going. Love— if you could call whatever this was love—was a pain in the ass.

Sibby tapped her fingers against her thighs, glancing at me, then at Susie, like she was working up the courage to say something big. Her movements were nervous but purposeful, like someone deciding to take a leap and not look back.

She didn't explain right away. Instead, she grabbed her cell phone from her purse, a battered old flip phone, and began dialing. I stayed quiet, unsure of what to do, so I just listened.

"Hi, this is Sibby. Can I speak to Peggy?" Her voice was firm. There was an awkward pause before she said, "Actually, everything's not fine. I need more time off."

I watched her closely, waiting for some kind of explanation. She nodded along to whatever Peggy was saying on the other end, then added, "I wouldn't call in like this if it weren't important. Thanks, Peggy. I appreciate it."

With that, she hung up, closing the flip phone with a satisfying snap. She turned to me, and for the first time since we'd reconnected, I saw something in her eyes that hadn't been there before. Hope. It wasn't bold or overwhelming, but it was there. A quiet determination breaking through the weariness.

"Give me a couple minutes to pack," she said, moving toward her bedroom.

"For what?" I asked.

She glanced back with a grin. "Mississippi."

As soon as we backed out of the driveway, I borrowed Sibby's phone to call Hayden and Kristie. Hayden nearly lost his mind when I told him where we were headed.

"They're going to Mizz-ippi!" he yelled to Kristie, drawing out the word in a way that made me laugh. I couldn't stop smiling when he said they were coming, too.

When I hung up, Sibby's excitement practically spilled out of her gleaming face.

"Why Mississippi?" I had asked before we left, watching her gather her things. She moved like someone preparing for a long trip, flicking off lights and double-checking locks.

"Because I have family there," she said. "It's where I grew up."

Something about the way she said it made me wonder if she had questions of her own waiting for her family, questions she wasn't ready to share.

On the drive, she asked, "Your friends?" as I handed back her phone.

"Yeah. I met them on the way here. They're sort of . . ."

"Drifters?" she guessed, laughing lightly. "Just make sure you don't have anything worth stealing."

I clutched Susie tighter. "Oh, trust me, if they wanted to steal from me, they'd be seriously underwhelmed. I'm like a thrift store on its last day of business."

She glanced at the case, then at me. "Why didn't you come with much?"

I couldn't tell her the truth, that I hadn't planned on needing much. That I'd broken my phone and left most of my things behind because, for a while, I wasn't sure I'd even see another tomorrow.

"I don't need much," I said instead.

"You need new clothes," she replied, eyeing my yellow-and-red polka dot tie like it had personally insulted her. "I mean, I respect the commitment to looking like an '80s game show host, but still."

"I'll worry when people start gagging at the stench."

But that time wouldn't come. I didn't want to think about what brought me here or why.

I used to spend days in bed, crushed by guilt. I stopped eating. Stopped answering calls. Eventually, everyone stopped trying. My dad tried once. He stood by the edge of the bed and asked me to get up. I just yelled back and buried my head under the pillow.

I wasn't dumb. I knew what was happening to me. Depression had sunk its claws in deep, and it wasn't letting go. I felt like a problem no matter where I went, like a parasite clinging to people's lives. That's when I realized things had taken a darker turn. A suicidal turn.

My grandpa, though . . . somehow, he knew. We never talked about it, but he could see through me. He told me to write it all out, to let the words go somewhere besides my head.

Grandpa Norris had told me stories about how he and my grandma used to bury letters under a special tree at Tipton High, because nothing says "romance" like secret correspondence and mild trespassing. It became their secret spot. Inspired by that, I started burying my journal entries under that same tree, wrapped in Ziplock bags in case it rained. I used his name, Robert, as a pen name, pretending to be him as I wrote.

The Tree was my refuge. My friends and I ate lunch there. Sara, Rachelle, Scotty, and the rotating cast of others who passed through. They never noticed the dirt disturbed near the trunk. I wondered if Scotty would ever find one of my letters, figure out it was me, and call me out for keeping it all in.

But the first person to find one wasn't Scotty. It was Leah Roy.

It was during musical rehearsals that I saw her at The Tree, sitting cross-legged, holding one of my letters. I stopped short of the back door to the auditorium, my hands pressed against the handle, and watched. She didn't see me, but I saw her face. A mix of intrigue and concern as she read my words.

I barely knew her back then. Leah was a drama club girl; I was choir. Different worlds. But the way she looked at that letter, it was like she knew me in a way no one else ever had.

The next time I checked, my letter was gone, replaced with a new one. She'd written back, using the name "Pen Pal Tina."

I'd wait until after the buses left to bury a new letter, avoiding her. We never saw each other, not directly. But through those letters, I realized I wasn't the only one carrying something heavy. Maybe everyone had their own secrets.

I wanted to meet her. To talk to her, to be close to the person who seemed to understand me so well. That's how I ended up in drama club, auditioning for *The Miracle Worker*. It wasn't my world, but it was hers.

Leah was too focused on her script to notice me. She sat by herself, studying her script, biting her lip and muttering lines under her breath. A stray lock of hair fell into her eyes, and she tugged it back, pausing to frown at a word she stumbled over before continuing. She wasn't trying to pretend or hide the mistakes or look perfect. She just was.

And in a room full of people pretending, that was everything.

Depression was swimming in molasses . . . thick, sticky, impossible to escape. I kept my head just high enough to breathe, but barely. The pressure on your chest is constant, like some cruel personal trainer sitting on you while saying, "Breathe deeper, fuckbag!"

But I did climb out.

For a while, anyway.

Leah showed up when I least expected it, like a lifeguard I hadn't called for but desperately needed.

Here's the thing no one tells you . . . pretending to be okay is sometimes more exhausting than just admitting you're not. But I couldn't admit it. I couldn't let anyone see how bad it had gotten. So I cracked jokes, made people laugh, kept the energy up. The "Braden Show" was a hit with my friends and teachers. Five stars on Rotten Tomatoes, certified fresh. If only they knew the director had no idea what the hell he was doing. When the curtain dropped and the spotlight turned off, I swear the laughter still lingered, distant and hollow, like it was meant for someone else.

That's the thing about depression . . . it makes you feel like a hypocrite. You say all the right things to keep people from looking too closely, and then you go home and sit in silence, questioning every single thing you've ever said or done. My mom would catch me staring off sometimes, lost in my own storm clouds, and ask, "What's wrong?"

"Nothing," I'd say. Always *nothing*.

I wasn't fooling everyone, though. My teachers? Yes. My friends? Definitely. But Hillman? He saw through it. He never outright said it, but I could feel it in the way he asked questions that cut through the bullshit. He had this way of looking at me like he was daring me to be honest. Not with him, but with myself.

Still, I couldn't tell Leah. Or Scotty. They needed me to be the guy who had it all together, the one they could call at midnight with their problems. If they knew how bad things had gotten, I'd lose that. And I couldn't afford to lose that, too.

So I kept pretending although the cracks were getting harder to hide. Straight As turned into Bs and Cs, and while I didn't care much, my parents did. That was the shitty part. Was I only as good as my grades? Every critique from them felt like a punch. Every raised eyebrow from a teacher, every awkward silence with my friends, felt personal. Like the world was holding up a mirror to show me all the ways I wasn't good enough.

The worst part wasn't drowning in molasses. It was the plastic smile I wore every day. I'd laugh with my friends, crack jokes about how terrible cafeteria food was, and then go home and sit in the quiet, replaying every interaction in my head, wondering if I'd done enough. If *I* was enough.

It wasn't all bad. Some days, the sun hit just right, and I didn't want to crawl back into bed. Those days were cracks of light in a locked room, just enough to keep me hoping.

But the darkness always came back, heavier than before. And I hated myself for it.

Humor was my shield. If they were laughing, they weren't asking questions. That was enough. Until it wasn't.

It was our own Delta Blues road trip. Me and Sibby McGee, winding through the flatlands where music seemed to grow from the earth itself. Most of the houses were smaller than mine, simple and worn, but I imagined their owners were some of the happiest people in the world. The wide horizon, dark green grass whispering in the breeze. This was a place where dreams didn't just start. They endured.

Our first stop was a shrine to a legend. The birthplace of Elvis Presley. The small white house sat humbly, its simplicity striking. If walls could talk, they'd sing gospel about a boy with big dreams. Inside, almost everything remained untouched by time. A single bedroom with a modest bed and a side table perched beneath the window, a kitchen dressed with green and white checkered tablecloths, and an old chimney stove that must've kept the place warm on cold Mississippi nights.

In the kitchen sat a tiny wooden baby seat, where Elvis himself had once sat, long before he became the King, long before the world devoured him like a feast. Sibby leaned over to snap a photo, and I smiled, feeling a strange mix of awe and tenderness. It reminded me of how my mom kept little relics from my own child-hood. Old baseball trophies, school art projects, even a pair of my baby shoes. Maybe she hoped I'd make those relics matter—make something of myself worth remembering.

But this place was different. It wasn't about the things left behind. About the life lived between the walls. I could almost hear the traces of a young Elvis singing along with his mama's hymns, the early stirrings of a sound that would change music forever.

Stepping outside, I let the warm air fill my lungs. It smelled like grass and blooming flowers and something deeper.

Sibby turned to me, her eyes alight with excitement. "Think he knew?" she asked, gesturing back at the house. "That he was gonna be Elvis Presley?"

I shrugged, looking at the little white house one last time. "Maybe. Or maybe he just knew he had something in him that couldn't stay small."

And with that, we hit the road again, the flat landscape rolling out before us like the long, steady notes of a blues song.

Wade's Barber Shop was a simple white building on a sleepy corner, unassuming, like so many in Mississippi. But its legacy lived beneath the surface, a steady bassline. This was the home of Wade Walton, the "blues barber." The man had played with Ike Turner's Kings of Rhythm before they got big, but he chose to stay behind, cutting hair and tending to his little piece of the Delta.

What kind of love keeps a man rooted? Had I ever loved anything like that?

The shop had a split personality. On one side, it was a barber-shop where Wade had likely trimmed generations of hair, each snip of the scissors accompanied by the harmonica he was known to play. On the other side, a tiny venue called Blues Club hinted at late-night performances. A barber who moonlighted as a bluesman. I pictured Wade there, spinning his chair around mid-trim, pulling out his harmonica, and launching into a tune that made his customers tap their feet under the fluorescent lights.

I tried to imagine my psychologist doing the same. Maybe mid-session she'd bust out a guitar and sing, "You're not my favorite patient, but I pretend to give a shit anyway . . ."

Outside, the air was thick and unforgiving, the kind of heat that made you question your life choices like wearing jeans or existing in the South at all. The gravel beneath the picnic tables crunched underfoot as we walked, dust kicking up with every step. The sun sang its relentless song, a slow, melodic verse building into a soul-packed bridge, swelling with a desperation you could feel deep in your chest. It was the kind of heat that stripped away pretense, pulling everything hidden in the shadows to the surface . . . unspoken dreams, quiet frustrations, secret hope.

To our left, a railroad track stretched out to nowhere, like the notes of a blues guitar fading into the horizon. I imagined trains rumbling by, stirring up a brief, cooling wind, and carrying the rhythm of the Delta with them to distant cities. Wade must've heard those trains day in and day out, the steady rhythm mingling with his music and his work, a reminder of lives in motion while he chose to stay still.

That's what got to me most about Wade—how he'd chosen simplicity although he wasn't small. He could've gone on the road with Ike Turner, chased the spotlight, but he didn't. Instead, he became something else . . . a cornerstone of his community.

"Think he ever regretted it?" I asked Sibby, watching the railroad tracks shimmer in the heat.

She didn't answer right away, just tipped her head toward the shop in wonder. "It doesn't look like he did."

The houses in this area caught my eye, too. They were even

simpler than the ones we'd passed earlier. Weathered porches, their wooden planks faded and bleached by years under the southern sun. The houses seemed alive with the echoes of life from another era like children laughing, music spilling out of open windows, and the steady noise of day-to-day resilience.

Just a few minutes later, we stopped at the Riverside Hotel. I'd never heard of it before, but one look at the small brick building with its modest, old benches out front was enough to pull me in. There was something about its quiet confidence, the way it stood there like a living memory, steeped in stories that begged to be told.

I would've loved to stay. Although it wasn't big or flashy, its history had more grandeur than any five-star hotel. This was where Ike Turner and Jackie Brenston stayed while writing and rehearsing "Rocket 88" in the basement—the song often credited as the first rock and roll record. That single detail made me look at the hotel like it was sacred ground, a place where the roots of music I'd grown up loving had taken hold.

Before the Riverside was a hotel, it was the G.T. Thomas Hospital. Or at least the site associated with Bessie Smith, the Empress of the Blues, who took her last breath after a car accident while traveling to a performance.

Shit.

Performing wasn't just a passion then. It was a lifeline. Musicians risked everything, pouring their souls into the road, not for money, but because music was their purpose, their rebellion, their salvation.

I let my eyes linger on the hotel a little longer, imagining what it must've been like when it was alive with musicians coming and going, their laughter and voices carrying through the halls, harmonicas and guitars spilling notes into the night.

Now? Performing didn't seem like it came from the same place anymore. It felt like so much of it had been corrupted by money, greed, and the endless churn of a machine designed to produce hits instead of heart. Back then, music seemed to mean something more, like it was worth dying for.

The Riverside stood as a quiet reminder of that era, of those people who lived and breathed music, who gave everything to it. As we pulled away, I couldn't shake the feeling that this stop had shifted something within me, nudged loose a piece of my soul that had been buried under the noise of modern noise.

Next, we made our way to the Ground Zero Blues Club, a building so full of character it looked like it had weathered generations of foot traffic, jukebox hits, and maybe the occasional bar fight. The place wore its past proudly, like scars that told stories you just had to ask about. As we stepped onto the broad front porch, I could picture folks from decades past swinging open those front doors, cigarette smoke curling through the air, mingling with the sounds of boisterous laughter and music. It was the kind of place where the blues seeped out of the walls themselves.

Out front, a couple of battered brown leather benches sat beside a simple wooden one, looking like they'd been through a lifetime of late-night conversations and impromptu jam sessions. To the side of the entrance, a tan couch rested under a window with nicotine-stained blinds that filtered the sunlight into a warm, hazy glow. Stickers covered nearly every visible surface—advertisements, guitar logos, a cat strumming a guitar, and a few so abstract they probably only made sense to someone high. The faded brick was peppered with graffiti, some of it crude, some of it oddly poetic. I wondered if they'd left it untouched as a nod to the place's rough-around-the-edges charm.

Then there was the music. Rich, real, and playing through the air. "Cross Road Blues" wailed from the speakers, wrapping around us like a welcoming hug.

Inside, the blues surrounded us. License plates, signed guitars, vintage posters, glowing neon signs, and even a chair hung upside down, adding to the club's quirky charm. Graffiti and stickers covered the tables, chairs, and walls, each marking the presence of someone who had passed through and left a piece of themselves behind.

I wandered the tables, my finger brushing over the chaotic scrawl of names, dates, and messages:

Kristin loves JB

Bonnie Sack's waz here

Kyle fucked Ronnie in the bathroom!

There wasn't much room left to mark, but Sibby and I managed to squeeze our names onto the table where we eventually sat. She took it all in, eyes wide, mouth slightly parted like a tourist. Sibby didn't seem like a blues fan. She seemed more like a "'90s hits on the commute" type. I never asked how old she was, but she had that nostalgic touch of someone who might sing along to Pearl Jam or Sheryl Crow.

The main floor was lively, with diners scattered at tables and every pool table similarly covered in writing. Our waitress came over, and we ordered food.

As we waited, I took in the scene of the dim lighting that made everything feel a little more intimate, the clink of glasses and silverware, and the sound of conversations blending into the music.

When the food arrived, it made a statement. My *Real Deal Sammich* was a masterpiece of pulled pork piled high on a soft bun. The meat glistened with a tangy barbecue sauce that smelled like hickory and honey, sweet with just the right kick of spice. With the first bite, the pork practically melted in my mouth, each strand tender and infused with a deep flavor. It reminded me of the ribs Hayden had ordered for me. The sauce struck the perfect balance of sweet, tangy, and rich while the bun soaked up every drop without falling apart.

Sibby's Jukin Blues Burger was a sight to behold stacked high with a juicy beef patty, enough melted cheese to make a lactose-intolerant person reconsider their entire life, and caramelized onions so glossy they looked like they were about to drop a skincare routine. A spicy aioli dripped down the edges, its scent hitting my nose with a zesty heat that made my mouth water. When I stole a bite, the flavors hit like a well-rehearsed band. The savory beef, the creamy cheese, the sweet onions, and the fiery kick of the aioli all playing in harmony.

The sides were just as memorable. The fries, crisp and dusted with seasoning, packed a salty punch. Sibby's burger was paired with thick-cut sweet potato fries, their edges glistening with a light drizzle of honey. The sweetness played off the burger's spice perfectly, making it hard to resist sneaking a few from her plate.

We didn't just get food, though. We got a show. The performer, Razorblade, took the small stage at the back of the room that looked like it had seen decades of heartache and triumphs. The room fell silent when he stepped into the spotlight. His voice was filled with emotion, carrying the blues in every note. Each hook was a time machine, dragging us into a smoky juke joint of another era. The crowd clung to every word, as if he were singing their stories.

I glanced at Sibby between songs, watching the way her shoulders slowly relaxed. The music worked its magic, softening the lines of tension on her face. For a brief moment, she looked almost at peace. But I knew better. I knew the emptiness in her eyes. The kind you can't hide even when you try.

During a break, the man at the table next to us introduced himself as Bud. His voice had a storyteller's cadence, rich with years spent living and breathing the blues. He told us about the Delta Blues Museum, mentioning that visitors could even record their own song there. The idea stuck with me, and as we left and climbed into the car, I was itching to give it a try.

On the drive, Sibby slid a Muddy Waters CD into the player, her recent purchase from Sun Studio. As the gravelly opening of "Mannish Boy" filled the car, it felt like the music was flowing straight out of Clarksdale's past and into our present. I fiddled with Susie, picking at a melody that was taking shape. Words started surfacing, half-lines, half-whispers, "take you to a place . . .

nothing matters more than this . . ." I hummed the fragments, testing how they fit against the beat of Muddy's voice. The road ahead blurred into the horizon, and somewhere between the rumble of the engine and the hypnotic rhythm, a song was beginning to breathe inside me.

As we drove, a tattoo parlor caught my eye. Rustic Tattoos glowed in neon. Not the most confidence-inspiring name for a place working with needles. Unless I was in the market for a tetanus shot and a life lesson. But the idea stuck with me. Maybe it was the contrast—permanence carved into flesh that would keep moving through life.

"Can we stop there?" I asked.

Sibby frowned but swung the car around. She pulled into the gravel lot, the crunch of tires underlining her skepticism. "Are you sure? Tattoos are forever."

I shrugged and stepped out of the car. "Tattoos only last as long as we do."

The parlor smelled faintly of disinfectant and cigarettes. The counter overflowed with faded flyers, candy jars, and a flash art rack worn from a million flips. Behind the counter, a tattoo artist —her fluorescent yellow hair glowing like a beacon—haggled over pricing with a customer.

While Sibby hovered near the door, I browsed the posters lining the walls, rows of dragons, skulls, and intricate lettering catching my eye. Then I saw it. A cross.

It wasn't a simple, somber one. This cross was alive. The wood was textured with earthy tones of light and dark brown, a thorn crown resting at the top. Green vines curled around it, crowned with a single bright pink flower near the edge, as if to say, "Even pain can create beauty."

"This one," I said, tapping the poster with a finger.

The artist, who introduced herself as Marin, smiled. "Good choice."

She led us to a small room with a dental-style chair, ink bottles, needles, and a window framing the evening sky. The first buzz of the tattoo gun sent a chill through my spine.

"Where do you want it?" Marin asked, pulling on gloves.

I gestured to my upper arm near the shoulder. Sibby gave me a nod of approval. I took off my shirt as Marin prepped the area.

The first sting was sharp, a needle digging into my skin and dragging its mark across me.

"It's like a cat scratch," Marin had said. Which I now realized was a lie, unless the cat in question was possessed and out for revenge.

It started as a burn, then dulled into an ache. My skin tightened, scraped like sandpaper, but the pain would mean something.

"Hey, at least it's not your nipple," she said with a wink.

I blinked. "Is that . . . a common request?"

Marin shrugged. "You'd be surprised. People get sentimental about weird things."

I clenched my jaw through the discomfort, focusing on the buzz of the machine. Marin worked with careful precision, wiping away ink and blood as she added layers of color and detail. The thorn crown looked more pronounced now, the vines more alive.

"This cross reminds me of a church I used to go to," Marin said, her voice light despite her focus. "Started out in a warehouse for recovering addicts. They had a picture like this on the wall. I always thought it was beautiful. Hopeful, you know?"

Her words hung in the air. I thought about saying something about how I wasn't sure hope was something I could carry anymore. Instead, I sat silently, letting her paint my skin with her story. Sibby shifted slightly in her seat, her eyes lingering gently on Marin as if the story had touched her too.

By the time she finished, the sky outside had deepened to navy, pinpricks of stars scattered above the horizon. She wiped the tattoo one last time, smoothing gauze over it before handing me a small bag of ointment and instructions.

"Keep it clean, and it'll heal just fine," she said. "If you have any issues, come back and see me. Shouldn't stay sore for more than a week. Neither should your black eye." She winked.

At the counter, Marin totaled the cost. "That'll be a hundred."

Before I could protest, Sibby slid a hundred-dollar bill across the counter, along with another twenty for a tip.

I frowned. "So this is how it starts. One day it's a tattoo, next thing you know, I owe you my firstborn."

She smirked. "Nah, just a nice visit once in a while."

I stopped on the sidewalk, the warm night air brushing against my sore shoulder.

"Call it a gift," she said. "I don't get to see you often, and you like it, right?"

I sighed, knowing I couldn't argue with her. Her generosity felt like a warmth settling low in my chest, as if someone had pressed a reset button I didn't know I needed. It made me feel small in a good way, like being caught off guard by the kindness Kristie and Hayden had shown me.

Back in the car, Sibby put on Little Richard. His raspy voice filled the quiet as I strummed Susie, working on a chorus. My arm throbbed. A grounding pain. Proof I was still here, still creating, even if I didn't plan to stay.

I thought about my tattoo. The bright pink flower was a contradiction, like me. Hope etched into skin already planning to fade.

Oh, the despair and hope that lived along the Blues Trail.

And oh, how I fit in so well.

Like me, Sibby ate her fast-food burgers plain, though she chased hers with an orange Fanta. I downed my Dr Pepper in thirty seconds flat, prompting Sibby to hand me a water bottle with a look that promised she'd "skin" me if I didn't drink it. The further south you went, the warmer the weather became, clinging like a second skin.

The first thing we did was check into a small motel near the river. It wasn't some broken-down, roach-infested dump. Instead, it was quaint, with maybe twenty rooms and a flickering sign near the street. An elderly couple ran the place, and their faces lit up the moment we walked in, either because they were thrilled to see new customers or because they'd mistaken us for their long-lost grandchildren.

This time, I insisted on paying, despite Sibby's protests.

The room was simple but cozy. Two queen beds, a tiny kitchenette, and a bathroom so clean it must've been recently renovated. Sibby tossed her suitcase onto the bed closest to the bathroom and sank into it with a relieved sigh.

"Feels good to follow your heart," she murmured to the ceiling.

I nodded, setting Susie down.

The night passed with a freshness in the air that came from the nearby river. I woke rested, though my shoulder throbbed from the tattoo. Sibby, showered and looking more awake than I felt, emerged from the bathroom as I tended to my sore arm. The tattoo still burned when I rinsed it, but it was worth it. It felt like armor, like a mark of purpose, something that made me stand a little taller and move a little straighter. Worth every sting.

We left the room early, eating cereal in the motel's modest breakfast nook. Outside, the morning mist still clung to the grass, and the faint cry of a train echoed in the distance.

"What do you want to do today?" I asked between bites.

"If the world ended tomorrow, what would you do?" Sibby countered, her tone thoughtful.

The question threw me. It was a big one, something I'd already wrestled with.

"Probably kiss my girlfriend," I said.

Sibby tilted her head, her eyes lingering on me as if she were weighing my words. A small smile tugged at the corner of her lips, and for a moment I could tell she was imagining the same world-ending scenarios, her mind flipping through possibilities before settling on one.

"Let's go to the market," Sibby said, snapping me out of my thoughts.

She checked us out while I grabbed Susie.

We pulled into Perry's Market, the sun baking the gravel lot. The building sat wedged between a nail salon and a cell phone repair shop, its faded sign barely hanging on to the past. In Mississippi, old stuff never felt old. Just seasoned. Like a cast-iron skillet that's seen too much but still fries up a mean catfish.

"Well, slap my ass and call me a biscuit," drawled a voice from another aisle. "Sibby G."

Her name rolled off his tongue, smooth and familiar.

Sibby's face lit up, eyes widening before relaxing into nostalgic gratitude.

"Frederick?" she yelped.

He stretched his arms wide and strode toward her, and she

stepped right into his embrace. They hugged like the world had melted away.

When they finally pulled apart, I sized him up. If I had to guess, he was half black and probably Sibby's age. He had a rugged confidence that didn't shout but invited trust. Dark hair, a strong jaw lightened by a warm smile, and a calm, easy way of carrying himself.

"You still shooting that potato rocket at Old Man Skid Mark?" Frederick teased, his grin wide enough to cut through steel. "Or did he finally take out a restraining order on your spud-launching ass?"

Sibby swatted his arm, laughing.

He turned to me, hand out, smiling. "Frederick," he said, voice rich and warm.

"Braden," I replied, shaking his hand.

Something romantic passed between them. Unspoken history. I wondered if it still mattered.

"You here visiting?" Frederick asked.

"Yeah, visiting and spending time with my nephew."

"Well, let's get together while you're here. Maybe we'll take Braden to that seafood joint you loved so much."

"That still around?" she asked.

"Best fried shrimp in town. Mr. Mandy's boy runs it now."

"I'll call you," she said, her voice sweet.

"Good meeting you, Braden," Frederick said, shaking my hand again. He turned back to Sibby, his tone teasing. "And you . . . stay away from wild geese this time, huh?"

Sibby smacked his arm again. "You're never letting that go."

"Never," he shot back, his gaze lingering even as he walked away.

"Wild geese?" I asked.

She grabbed a loaf of bread, her smile turning wistful. "Once, when we were kids, I made the grave mistake of disrespecting a mama goose. She responded like a debt collector, chasing me halfway into the lake while Frederick and the others placed bets on whether I'd survive."

"And Frederick swam out to save you?"

Her smile simmered. "After laughing his ass off. Even though I didn't need saving, he got me back to shore."

When we made our way to checkout, Frederick was behind the counter. "You should see him, Sibby G," he said as she handed him cash.

She froze for just a second, avoiding his eyes. "We'll see," she said.

Frederick handed back her change, his tone gentler now. "It'll be worth it. You might not think so now, but trust me. It will."

Sibby didn't reply, just nodded and flashed him a faint farewell. As we left, he called out, "Y'all come back now!"

She glanced at me in the parking lot, still holding onto that sweet, faraway look. "He's the nicest guy."

"I can tell, Sibby G," I teased, nudging her arm. "He's still got a soft spot for you."

She rolled her eyes but couldn't keep the smile off her face.

The sun hung low over the Mississippi River as Sibby parked the car. The air was thick with the scent of fresh water and earth. The wind stirred the trees, their leaves rustling like whispers from long ago. Birds called overhead, water lapped at the banks, and a family's laughter drifted from down the shore. I felt it. Everything I'd been carrying, even if just a little, lift off my shoulders. The river had a way of doing that, making time feel slower, life quieter, and worries smaller. But Sibby didn't look at the water or the sky. She looked at me, her eyes full of something unspoken.

We strolled along the river for an hour, mostly in silence, letting the scenery sink in. We stopped at a shaded spot and spread out the blanket Sibby had tucked into her bag, its fabric soft against the warm ground. She unpacked the sandwiches with practiced ease—bread, bologna, cheese, pickles—and handed me a can of Dr Pepper. I took it, the fizzing drink in my hand grounding me. The river at my back reminding me that some things, like this moment, were simple, real, and worth holding onto.

"I noticed you like Dr Pepper," she said. "And I've decided to pick my battles. Hydration is clearly a lost cause."

I exhaled, taking a sip and feeling the cold fizz run down my throat.

Sibby leaned back, her hands supporting her as she tilted her head to the sky. The sunlight danced across her face, the breeze tugging at her hair. I followed her gaze out over the water, watching the way the waves folded into each other. It was peaceful, almost meditative. Until she spoke.

"I understand you better than you think, Braden," she said, her voice almost swallowed by the surrounding landscape. "I moved away when I was seventeen. My parents and I . . . we haven't spoken much since then."

The moment lost its lightness. She didn't look at me right away. I could hear the tremor in her voice, the years of distance and hurt pooling into the space between us.

"Why's that?" I asked gently, not wanting to pry but needing to understand.

Sibby's fingers traced absent circles in the dirt as she spoke, her voice quieter now, as if the words were harder to say. "They don't trust me, and I don't trust them."

"Is that what Frederick was trying to say in there?" I asked.

Her eyes flicked to mine, guarded with sadness. "My parents hated Frederick. Even after all that, he still finds it in himself to be forgiving. I wish I could do that, but I just can't."

"Forgive?"

She sighed and sank against the blanket. "My mom still emails me updates about my dad, and I hate it. It's like she's trying to guilt trip me into coming down here. If she would've just taken him to the doctor instead of trying to holistic the shit out of him, maybe he wouldn't be so far gone."

"What's wrong with him?" I asked.

"Dementia," she said.

"Shit," I muttered, the gravity of it settling in. I didn't know much about dementia, but I'd heard it was cruel. The slow fade of a person, watching them forget everything . . . every name, every face, even their own.

We sat in silence for a while, the river continuing its timeless flow, indifferent to the conversation, to the impact of her words. I couldn't imagine what she must've gone through, what it must've felt like to leave it all behind.

"My mom never mentioned you much after you left Indiana," I said. "She would tell stories about her parents once in a while, but she'd always stop, like something was too painful to say."

"Did she mention that we aren't actual sisters?" Sibby's voice was dry now, but there was a playfulness to it.

"What?" I choked slightly on my Dr Pepper, coughing as she watched me with amusement. "You're kidding."

She smirked. "Nope. We were just so inseparable that everyone assumed. Kind of like those kids in elementary school who swear they're 'married' because they held hands once."

I blinked. "My whole life is a lie."

She shrugged. "Welcome to the club."

"I always thought you guys were sisters," I said. It wasn't something I'd ever questioned. I assumed my mom had cut ties with her parents since she never talked about them. The only grandparent I talked to was my dad's dad, Grandpa Norris.

She looked out at the water, her gaze distant. "My parents liked Trish a lot. She was the daughter they wished they had. I couldn't be what they wanted me to be. In the end, I just had to leave."

"Why'd you leave?"

Sibby's eyes met mine then, and there was something tender in her expression. "Same reason you did, Braden. I needed to find myself."

I leaned back beside her, the words hanging in the air. It was Wednesday, the last official day of school back at Tipton High. I wondered what my friends were doing, if Leah was doing okay. But in this moment, by the river, those thoughts seemed irrelevant.

We sat by the river for hours, snacking, talking, and soaking it all in. The air had a rich, earthy smell that lingered with the scent of water and the occasional breeze carrying the tang of mud. Sibby told me about the boats that passed through the Mississippi. She pointed out fishing boats, their nets trailing behind like woven webs.

She explained how the barges—huge, flat-bottomed vessels—carried everything from coal to gravel, iron, and chemicals, all at the mercy of the river's depth. "They have to be careful not to get stuck in the mud, especially when the water's low," she said, watching a slow-moving barge like it had beef with her. "One time, a barge got stuck for three days. They tried everything: tugboats, digging, even some old guy yelling at it like it owed him money."

I snorted. "Did it work?"

She deadpanned, "No. But I think the old guy felt better."

I was learning, really taking it all in. "They used to have steamboats back in the day," she said. "The last one's the Steamboat Natchez, out of New Orleans. It's still running, you know? It's part of the history of this river."

As she spoke, I drifted between listening to her and tossing rocks into the river, attempting to skip them. After my third rock just plopped in and sank like a dead fish, Sibby sighed.

"Okay, you have the skipping skills of a brick," she said, standing up. "Here, let me show you."

She picked up a rock, flicked her wrist, and it bounced across the water effortlessly.

I frowned. "You could've just said I suck."

"I did. But in a more supportive way."

We laughed, and the day stretched on, but then my eyes caught a group of teenagers walking by, laughing and joking in that care-free, reckless way that only teenagers can. It was like they were on a different wavelength, one I didn't fully understand anymore.

Sibby seemed to notice the shift in my mood. "You know, Frederick and I used to come here after school sometimes," she said, her voice light, but there was something different in her eyes, like she was remembering something warm. "We'd copy each other's homework and talk about everything and nothing."

I remained silent, admiring the way she spoke about Frederick, like he was always more than a friend.

And just like that, the quiet was broken by the sudden blast of a horn.

Seconds later, I heard the gravel crunch under tires, and there she was. Winnie roared like an escaped zoo animal, hauling ass with no apologies.

CHAPTER 9:
The Landslide Won't Bring Me Down

"We're from California, but haven't lived there in like five years," Hayden said, leaning back against a tree and stretching his legs out.

"What've you been doing in the meantime?" Sibby asked, all curiosity. She'd been grilling Hayden and Kristie with questions ever since they joined us by the river, making themselves right at home with our picnic spread.

"Oh, you know . . ." Hayden glanced at Kristie. "Catching up with people. Enjoying life." He made it sound like a lifestyle choice, like "enjoying life" was a full-time job.

I chuckled. They made everything look effortless, like they could take on the world one-handed.

After a while, we decided to leave the river, mostly because the conversation had somehow morphed into an intense Fleetwood Mac debate. Sibby, with the conviction of a preacher at a revival, was two seconds away from making us take a solemn oath that "Dreams" was the superior song. Hayden and Kristie, however, were ready to die on the hill of "The Chain". It got so heated, I half-expected someone to challenge Stevie Nicks to a duel.

"I want to take you guys somewhere," Sibby said, eyes locking on me. "Follow behind?"

Hayden and Kristie gave a unanimous nod, eager to follow her lead. Sibby and I slid into her car, and I could already hear Winnie's engine revving in the background.

"Where are we going?" I asked.

Sibby shot me a glance, her face shifting into something more serious. "Braden, one of the things I avoid every time I come here is the very reason I come here." She turned the wheel, guiding us down the road. "My parents."

After ten minutes, we reached a brick building in an old town. A hair salon, market, and tax office lined one side. An odd but typical small-town mix. The other side boasted an American Legion sign, faded but proud. A glass door out front, another in back.

The small parking lot was dotted with rusty cars and old trucks. We pulled in, parked, and got out as Winnie parked across a few spaces in the back.

"I didn't call for a gig tonight, but maybe we can make it happen," Hayden said, rubbing his hands together, eyes scanning the building. Kristie shook her head, and Sibby laughed, a little nervously.

I watched her lead the way to the back door, head high, shoulders squared. I wondered if her parents were like mine. Overbearing, critical, or something else entirely. My parents, despite their flaws, were enviable. My dad worked hard to keep us afloat, and my mom held us together. I never took it for granted.

Not really.

As Sibby swung the back door open, the familiar buzz of country music hit me first. The smell of cigarette smoke followed, thick and lingering. It pulled me back to a memory of my dad hosting a card game at one of his shops. I was just a kid, sitting quietly in the corner while he and his buddies sat around a small table, cigarettes dangling from their lips, passing cards around. It was a routine I never questioned until I realized, years later, that my dad had been sober my whole life. He never touched alcohol, not even when his friends offered him a drink. Just soda cans and bottled water.

The karaoke mic crackled as we stepped inside. A Toby Keith song wrapped up, and applause filled the air. The room was filled with older folks and veterans, judging by the memorabilia that covered the walls. A few kids ran around, and there were some younger people too, about Sibby's age.

A bar sat in the middle of the room, next to a kitchen. An older woman emerged from the swinging door with a tray of cheeseburgers and fries. The grease-saturated smell of fried food fought through the haze of cigarette smoke.

Sibby moved with ease, walking around the tables, scanning the crowd like she was looking for someone. She waved at a few familiar faces.

Hayden and Kristie had already struck up a conversation with an older man, probably reminiscing about Vietnam, though by the way Hayden was talking, it seemed like he was doing most of the storytelling.

Sibby passed the dance floor as applause died down. The karaoke announcer called, "Next up, George singing 'Strokin'' by Clarence Carter."

We stood before a table full of people just as George belted out the words to "Strokin'." The old man behind the beer didn't blink when his eyes landed on Sibby. But the woman next to him nearly jumped out of her seat like she'd seen a ghost. In fact, she looked like a much older version of Sibby. She gasped, hands flying to her mouth, and both she and the old man fixed me with a long, suspicious stare. I didn't recognize either of them.

The woman rose with a slight wobble, her legs careful, like they were measuring each step. Meanwhile, the old man slouched deeper into his chair, beer still firmly in hand.

"Well I'll be damned," he muttered, shaking his head, "If it ain't my daughter comin' to visit her mom and pops."

At that, the rest of the table perked up, faces lighting up with memories. Someone raised a glass. "Hey, Sib!"

The older woman hurried over, waddling faster than her thin legs seemed capable of. Sibby's fingers twisted the edge of her shirt, a tell she probably didn't even notice. This was the family reunion she had to be at, not the one she wanted.

"My baby girl," her mom cried, pulling Sibby into a tight, lipstick-streaked hug. When she finally let go, a bright red mark bloomed on Sibby's cheek.

"Hey, Mom," Sibby muttered, her voice polite but distant. Then, with a quick glance my way and a smile that looked borrowed, she said, "Mom, this is Braden. Braden, this is my mom, Edie."

Edie turned to me, her smile so tight it could've snapped. "Hello, sweetheart." She clasped my hand in both of hers. Warm, bony, assessing. "Good to have you with us tonight. What brings you here?"

Sibby hesitated, and I caught the flicker of discomfort in her eyes. She didn't want to explain, didn't want to make things weird. So I jumped in.

"Just job shadowing," I said quickly.

"Oh," Edie replied, her gaze flicking between us, unreadable. "Well, this here's Sibby's daddy, Arthur."

She gestured to the empty chair beside Arthur, still clutching my hand with the intensity of someone trying to decide whether I was allowed into their inner circle or not. "Come, sit with us."

I slid into the empty seat.

Sibby nodded at the short, round guy. "Cooter. And Deadbolt," she added, motioning to the wiry man beside him.

Deadbolt tipped his hat. "I'm still kickin', pretty thang," he rasped, barely audible over George's smooth vocals.

Bells, the oldest of the bunch but not the oldest in spirit, yelled across the table. "Good golly, Sibby McGee. Haven't seen you since you were shittin' bricks in your diapers!" Her voice could've cut through concrete.

"It hasn't been that long," Sibby laughed.

"The hell it hasn't!" Bells barked, lighting a cigarette with practiced ease.

I raised my eyebrows. These people seemed to have a certain . . . energy to them. A lot of it.

Bells winked at me. "That's a cutie you brought with you," she said, and I felt every ounce of discomfort in my bones.

Sibby must've sensed that because, without skipping a beat, she ordered me a beer from Phyllis, the waitress.

"You got an ID, hun?" Phyllis asked, voice bored.

"He left it at home," Sibby answered for me.

"No ID, no drink," Phyllis said, with all the enthusiasm of someone who had spent *way* too many years policing teenagers with fake mustaches and suspiciously laminated driver's licenses.

Sibby barely blinked. "A tall one for me, Shirley Temple for him. And two bacon burgers with fried pickles."

"You got it," Phyllis said.

I sank into my seat as everyone else resumed their card game. Meanwhile, Edie was all tight smiles. "I'm just tickled that you came by. We've missed you, baby girl."

Sibby gave a smile that didn't quite match her eyes. "I've missed you too, Mom," she said. "You guys still have Mud?"

"Hell yeah," Arthur chimed in, slapping a card down. "Tried shooting the little bastard, but your mom damn near skins me every time I pull out the rifle. He lives to breathe another day. Take him if you want."

Sibby laughed, shaking her head. "You two never got along since the day I brought him home."

"You needed to quit bringing them smelly-ass strays home," Arthur grunted. "You probably stole half of 'em, not even realizing they had homes."

Edie shot him a look. "Hey, now, our girl's a lover. That's all there is to it."

Arthur just muttered something about Mud's greys before slapping another card on the table.

"So, you stayin' in town, sweetheart?" Edie asked.

Sibby glanced at me before answering. "Braden and I don't have set plans," she said, dropping my name with just a little extra weight.

Edie's eyes narrowed slightly, but she covered it up with another bright, fake smile. "Well, you can stay in your old room if you like."

Sibby didn't seem thrilled about the idea, but she was all business. "Thanks, mom," she said, glancing around the table.

A few minutes later, Phyllis brought our drinks and food. As she set the plates down, she muttered a quick "Jose says hi."

Sibby laughed, "Tell him hi for me. And that I saw Frederick at the store today. He must be real proud."

"I second that," Edie said.

The conversation shifted, but I couldn't stop watching Edie. Every time she spoke, her eyes would dart over to me, like she was waiting for me to say something wrong.

Mid-conversation, Arthur eyed me. "Your daddy got a college degree, son?"

The table fell quiet. Everyone paused their card game and waited for my answer.

I glanced between Arthur and Sibby, then at the drink in front of me, as if it could save me from the sudden heat on my neck.

I took a sip of my Shirley Temple and set it down. "Yes. Business degree."

Arthur didn't respond right away. He just looked at me like I'd said something that didn't quite add up.

The conversation flowed back into its usual rhythm, but I could feel Edie's eyes lingering on me, almost inspecting. I realized how much of a stranger I was here.

And that's when the story began. Edie leaned in. "When this lady was about ten years old, she'd go fishin' in the creek in our backyard . . ."

"Oh, mom, come on," Sibby protested.

"No damn it, you're my daughter and I'm gonna tell this story," Edie finally acknowledged me by actually looking at me. "We wouldn't know where she was for hours until her daddy'd go calling her name out the back door. She'd call back sayin' 'I'm fine!' Then another hour later, come hauling up a bucket from the creek. She'd say, "Caught up dinner!"

The rest of the table perked up. It was a family story, after all. Sibby seemed to shrink, even as her mom recounted embarrassing times.

I glanced at Sibby, who was blushing.

Arthur interrupted, "Only problem with them bass though . . . they'd give you cancer if you ate 'em."

And with that, the awkwardness settled in again, thick enough to cut with a knife.

Hayden wove toward our table, radiating easy confidence.

"Ladies," he greeted. "Gentlemen." He acknowledged each person with deliberate eye contact and a gaze that could disarm a bouncer. "Thanks for having us out tonight. I'm Hayden. Over there is my girl, Kristie." He gestured toward her with a casual nod. "Nice setup you've got here. What's the game?"

Without waiting for an answer, Hayden grabbed an empty chair and slid it next to Edie. Someone at the table eagerly began explaining the rules of the card game to him, and soon, they were laughing like old friends. I kept to myself mostly, watching the scene unfold as the conversation swirled around me.

Every now and then, my attention wandered to the karaoke stage. Most of the singers were drunk, belting out lyrics with wild abandon, and that's probably what made it so entertaining.

Kristie eventually joined the table, sliding into the game effortlessly. She leaned her head against Hayden's shoulder, and they looked like they belonged there . . . like they belonged anywhere together. But as I glanced across the room, I noticed Sibby's parents watching them, their expressions tinged with skepticism, their stares more toxic than the smoke in the air.

"Braden here's got a thing or two to learn about Texas Hold 'Em," Sibby said casually, but the second my name slipped out, Hayden and Kristie both locked eyes with me.

A cold shiver shot down my spine.

Fuck.

My name.

The mischievous grins they wore felt like I'd just been caught red-handed. I could almost feel the heat of their knowing stares on me, like I'd just been busted with my hand down my pants.

Before I could make sense of it, the karaoke announcer's voice boomed through the speakers, calling Hayden and Kristie to the stage.

"Sorry, team!" Hayden hollered, laying his cards down with a dramatic flourish. "The show must go on!"

They jumped up like it was the best thing that had happened all night, excited as hell, and made their way toward the karaoke stage. The music for "Stayin' Alive" by the Bee Gees started blaring, and without missing a beat, they both launched into a full-on disco routine. Kristie doing finger guns like an extra in Saturday Night Fever, Hayden spinning like a man whose only reference for dance moves was a hyper rotisserie chicken.

Watching them up there, their ridiculous dance moves and over-the-top enthusiasm, was infectious. It wasn't just comedic, it was inspiring and distracted me from my identity reveal. For a second, I almost wanted to join them. To stand up and lose myself in the joy of it all. But I couldn't shake Sibby's expression. She wasn't laughing like the rest of the crowd. Her eyes held something else. Disappointment, maybe?

When the song ended, Hayden and Kristie turned to the mic and called out to me, practically vibrating with excitement.

"Get on up here, *Braden!*"

And just like that, the name that had been my shield, my secret, my disguise was out there. They'd all heard it.

Farewell, Blake. Hello, sudden identity crisis.

It was Cyndi Lauper's "Money Changes Everything". A song I knew well enough to appreciate, but not well enough to ever try singing myself. There was no way I'd survive a Cyndi Lauper track, not without the world ending in a riot.

I stood up, turning toward Sibby.

"Come on," I said with a mix of encouragement and mischief.

Sibby froze, looking like I'd just asked her to dance on a table.

"I heard you singing in the car," I added, trying to keep the mood light. "Let's sing this together."

Arthur's voice cut through the air, gruff as always. "Sibby don't sing. Last time she tried, the neighbor's cat killed himself."

But Sibby didn't flinch. She held my gaze for a while, and I watched as something flickered behind her eyes. Then, as if a switch flipped, she stood and strode toward the stage. I followed her, not sure what to expect, but a part of me thrilled at what was about to unfold.

Sibby took the mic from Hayden and launched into Cyndi Lauper's anthem like she owned it. My jaw dropped. I had no idea what I was watching, no idea who this was. In that moment, Sibby was a star, embodying the essence of the '80s with an energy that felt like it had been buried for years.

The crowd erupted in whistles, cheers, and bodies flooding the dance floor.

I couldn't tear my eyes away. I watched, completely captivated, as she surrendered to the song with a fierce, unrelenting passion. There was something deeply personal in her voice, like she had been holding onto these feelings for far too long. Emotions that had nowhere to go but out, and this was her release. It was the kind of power I hadn't realized she had within her.

At eighteen, I thought I understood repressed emotions clawing their way out. But this was different.

When the song ended, the room exploded into cheers. I clapped with everything I had, pride and relief mixing together in a cocktail of admiration. Sibby smiled, wide, unrestrained, and full of energy, as the crowd chanted for an encore.

But she handed the mic over to the next person without hesitation, her head held high. She had done what she came to do. And for a split second, I saw her—the real her—shining in front of us, unapologetically.

The next karaoke song blared through the speakers. "Strokin'" by Clarence Carter again. An immediate test of how quickly we could all suddenly remember we had somewhere else to be.

We walked back to the table together, the air still buzzing from Sibby's performance. Her face was flushed with adrenaline and there was a pleased expression there, too, as if she was basking in the glow of what she'd just done. Kristie immediately hooked her arm through Sibby's, lavishing her with compliments, telling her she needed to join them in a gig sometime.

But when we reached the table, the mood sank fast, like all the air had been sucked out of the room.

"Well done, sweetheart," Phyllis said, her voice warm as she set down another round of drinks.

Sibby's mom, Edie, however, was a different story. She had her hands folded in front of her, looking down at the table, not even bothering to glance at us. She wasn't impressed. The faintest trace of approval escaped her lips, though it was tinged with something more critical than kind.

"I would have liked to hear one of your originals, but that was good, too," Edie said, her voice flat.

Sibby's eyes flicked toward her, and the smallest roll of her eyes escaping before she sat back down. It was like a silent protest, one she couldn't fully contain. The rest of us sat down, the table sinking into silence, and I could feel the tension creeping back in like a shadow.

"Braden is such a good musician," Sibby broke the silence, warmth in her voice. "Wait until you hear him play. Are you going to play tonight?" she turned to me, hopeful.

Before I could answer, Edie cut in, abrupt and dismissive. "We don't care for secular music."

Sibby's head whipped around to face her mother, eyes flashing with disbelief. "Mom, seriously?" Her voice was stronger now, like she was standing taller, no longer trying to shrink into the background.

I was about to step in, to say something to ease the tension, to maybe bridge the gap between their worlds. But I wasn't part of their conversation. I was just the outsider.

Sibby tried again, her tone softer now. "Braden plays all kinds of music—"

Arthur cut her off, his voice low and almost accusatory. "Not the son of some businessman." He dragged out the word "businessman" like it was a curse. "Never trust anyone in business."

I wasn't sure if I was supposed to take offense, or if this was just Arthur's standard way of welcoming people. Through deep-seated resentment and subtle threats. But his words hit like a stone, cold and heavy. I glanced at Sibby, and the disgust on her face was palpable. Her jaw clenched, and she was gripping the edge of the table like it might keep her from flying off the handle.

"Don't treat our guest like that now," Edie muttered, but she didn't look at me. She didn't even acknowledge my presence.

Arthur sneered, jabbing a finger at Sibby. "Well, Miss Lauper over here better not forget where she comes from when she makes it big. Hope she doesn't leave to find a man. Nobody wants damaged goods."

The words hit me like a slap in the face. They were mocking Sibby, and I couldn't stand it.

"Hey," I said, a little louder than I intended. "That's kind of a dick thing to say to your own daughter."

Arthur's eyes locked on mine. There was no warmth in them. Just a cold, cutting gaze stabbing into me. He leaned closer. "You damn well don't know us, son, and you don't know that woman there either." His finger jabbed the air in Sibby's direction like he was trying to punctuate his words with violence.

Before I could say anything else, Sibby stood up abruptly. Her chair scraped against the floor with an unforgiving screech, and I barely caught her before she turned and stormed off.

I hesitated for only a second before I followed her. That second was just long enough for me to realize I had *no idea* what I was supposed to say once I caught up. I spotted her just as she was reaching the back door, her pace quickening as tears welled up in her eyes. She wiped them away angrily, refusing to let them fall.

When I stepped outside, the cool air hit me.

She practically ran to her car, and I hurried to the other side, slipping into the passenger seat as she slammed the door shut. She started the engine with a twist of the key, and we were off before I could say anything.

Tears streaked her face, anger burning behind them. It was as if she was trying to fight the tears, fight the flood of emotion that was breaking through every dam she'd built. But it was all too much.

She floored it, the car jerking forward.

I turned to look out the rear window, catching a glimpse of Hayden and Kristie rushing out of the back door. Hayden pointed our way as we pulled out of the parking lot, and not too long after, Winnie followed close behind.

Sibby drove fast. I tried to focus on the road, the night settling in around us. The air inside the car grew suffocating. I glanced at her again, wanting to say something, anything, but I couldn't find the words.

The sky darkened as we turned onto a narrow road that led into a field. This cemetery felt more alive, with more green grass than gray stone. I had a feeling Sibby wasn't just here for some distant relative. This place, this moment, seemed to carry more significance than that.

Sibby parked the car and stepped out, her movements almost aggressive. "Get your guitar," she said in a regretful tone.

I grabbed Susie from the back seat, wanting to ask if everything was okay, but I didn't.

I followed her, walking beside her but feeling the growing distance between us. She marched toward the heart of the cemetery, the earth beneath her feet crunching with each step.

Then she stopped. I nearly ran into her as she came to a halt in front of a lone gravestone—tall, rectangular, and curving at the top. Curiosity pulled me closer. Then I saw the name, and my breath caught.

CHARLEY PATTON

APRIL 1891 – APRIL 28, 1934

My first thought: *Too young to die.*

My second thought: *Hypocrite.*

I stared at the gravestone, my mind spinning with the significance of this moment. This was Charley Patton, the very man who laid the foundation for the music we'd been tracing on our journey, the Delta Blues trail, now culminating in the presence of the man himself.

"Charley Patton is the father of the Delta Blues," Sibby said, her voice almost reverent as she looked at the grave. "Since I was a little girl, I always wanted to be a singer. I taught myself guitar, always dreaming of being on a stage in front of thousands of people. But something happened that turned my world upside down."

I wanted to ask, *What happened?* But the words stayed lodged in my throat, like they weren't allowed to cross the boundary of this experience. She stood there, unmoving, her eyes locked on the grave, as if her hopes and dreams lay buried beneath the stone.

"People die," she said quietly. "But their spirits last as long as we live on."

I let that sink in, the cool night air wrapping itself around the words, both comforting and haunting at the same time. I stared at the gravestone, at the inscription beneath Charley Patton's name:

"THE VOICE OF THE DELTA"

The foremost performer of early Mississippi blues whose songs became cornerstones of American music.

What a way to be remembered. Charley Patton left a mark on the world. Standing there, I felt like I was at my own crossroads . . . music, legacy, something bigger than me.

Then I heard the crunch of gravel as Winnie pulled up. Sibby turned to me, her eyes shining with sadness yet anchored by something stronger. She was determined, not defeated, but still carrying something heavy in her heart.

"I wanted to be strong for you, Braden," she whispered. "But I can't."

I didn't know what to say. Something unspoken sat between us. I opened my mouth, but the words didn't come.

"We all have our battles," she continued, her gaze never leaving mine. "Mine needs to be dealt with back in Memphis."

"Are we leaving?" I asked, my heart sinking at the thought of her walking away.

"No," she said, her voice firm. "I am. You need to stay."

It hit me then . . . what she was really giving me. The space to stand on my own. The trust that I could. It felt like a gift, one wrapped in heartbreak, because it meant letting her go. And then, in a motion that caught me completely off guard, she stepped closer, reached for my hand, and squeezed it tightly. There was nothing hurried about it. Just a calm, quiet strength in the way she held on.

"Charley was great, Braden," she whispered. "You're great, too."

Her words were a reminder of what I could become. The very

thing she had always dreamed of being. And in that moment, for the first time, I believed it.

She let go, then pulled me into a peaceful hug. I closed my eyes, letting her warmth sink into me, and for once, I didn't feel like I had to prove anything. I wasn't just a kid trying to find my way.

When she pulled away, she didn't look at me. She just turned and walked toward her car. I watched her, feeling the sting of her departure but also the realization that she was giving me something far more important than she knew . . . her belief in me.

Hayden and Kristie came over, their eyes full of confusion, but they didn't ask anything they didn't already know. They simply wanted to know if I was okay.

Sibby climbed into her car. Our eyes met through the window. I almost said it. *Don't leave.* But I didn't. Instead, I just stood there, feeling a quiet resolve growing inside me. I wasn't afraid.

Whatever came next, I was ready.

CHAPTER 10:
A Little Bit of Sage

Leah once said she didn't need to know everything to love me. Hayden and Kristie didn't press for details about what happened with Sibby. I got the sense they were similar to Leah, and I appreciated it. But I did owe them an explanation about my name. As I started to explain, though, Hayden waved me off like a fly, and Kristie burst into giggles.

"We knew Blake wasn't your real name," Hayden said, like he was in on some big secret.

Kristie chimed in between laughs, "We heard Sibby call you Braden. Honestly, we like him a lot better than Blake."

I couldn't help but laugh myself. Being Blake had worked for a while, but hearing that they preferred Braden hit me in a surprisingly good way.

I thought about Sibby, though. Every second. I reminded myself not to fall into that dark pit again. Not everyone was thinking about throwing in the towel the way I was.

But, yeah . . . I was still second-guessing myself. Mississippi, the travel, spending time with people who were the complete opposite of the ungrateful jerk I'd been. It was making me question if I was making a huge mistake by even considering leaving it all behind.

The night ended at a street food festival near Sunflower County. Kristie set up her caricature stand, drawing a few couples. The air buzzed with easy chatter as stands shut down for the night.

We turned in for the night, parking Winnie in the workers' parking lot where food trucks parked alongside semis, and everyone started winding down. Before bed, I slipped out the pen and notepad from my back pocket, seeking solitude under the stars.

The picnic tables were empty, save for a few late-night workers, and the world felt a little quieter now.

Dear Leah,

I miss you a lot. You've been on my mind every day and it's hard not to turn right around and come back to you. I'm learning a lot during my time here. By the time you get these letters, I would've hopefully gotten what I needed. Enough to leave this earth anyway.

I think a lot about our time at The Tree. When life was simpler, easier to swallow one moment at a time.

I've been thrown into a wild adventure here, Leah. You would love it. You would be proud of me, too, for not giving up too easily.

I don't want to die chasing rainbows just to escape the fog. I want to be able to see beyond it, but I've accepted that I won't. I don't know what's beyond this life or if this is even the answer. I just don't know what else to do.

You were always my way out, but that wasn't fair to put on you. You know it wasn't you, right? Please don't remember me as selfish. Please remember me as selfless. You deserve to live your life to the fullest.

I hope you do.

Braden

I woke up late the next day, the festival joy vibrating through the ground as I wandered around, trying to shake off the confusion in my mind. The place was booming with people, the sounds of laughter and conversations mixing with the jazz music that pulsed from the speakers. I finally found Hayden and Kristie at their caricature stand, taking a break while they helped their friends set up on the stage. The smell of fried food, sugar, and something sweet and smoky hung in the air like a nostalgic embrace. I realized just how much I'd miss these little moments, the way a place like this could make you forget your own troubles, if only for a while.

I followed the intoxicating blend of scents to a massive line of food stands. Kristie and Hayden sat together, digging into a shared seafood platter of crab, shrimp, and clams, all piled high like a delicious mountain. I ordered deep-fried pickles and coleslaw, savoring the rich crunch of the pickles as I sat down beside them.

After we ate, we made our way toward the giant Ferris wheel, the sound of its creaky machinery and the sound of the crowd rising around us. Usually, I would have hesitated here, maybe muttered a string of bad words under my breath, clutching the safety bar like it was a lifeline. But this time, the fear had eased, replaced by curiosity. Hayden and Kristie sat on one side, while I sat on the opposite side with a random girl Kristie had invited from the line.

She was pretty, auburn hair and freckles under her eyes, with a smile that was delicate and inviting. Her voice barely rose above the wind as she whispered in my ear, reminding me of how high we were. I looked ahead, trying to ignore the weight on my chest as I scanned the town below, bathed in the warm glow of lights flickering in the distance. It was beautiful, maybe the most beautiful thing I'd seen in weeks.

And then, out of nowhere, Hayden's voice cut through the noise. "I'm the king of the world!" he yelled, pumping his fist in the air like he was Jack Dawson at a Pearl Jam concert. Too bad he didn't realize Jack dies at the end of that movie.

For a moment, I wanted to be him. Carefree and unbothered. I admired his freedom, the way he didn't seem to have a worry in the world. But me? I had to fight every second not to drown in my own head.

Living day by day wasn't how I was raised. Scotty, the opposite of me, would probably thrive in this. If he could bring his protein bars and energy drinks, he'd fit right in.

As we ascended higher into the sky, I could feel my mind straying back to my old life. The familiarity of it. The small, mundane things I used to take for granted. The smell of coffee in the morning when my dad would wake up early, the sound of my mom and brother bickering about what to wear for school. Hell, I even missed homework. How weird was that? Drama club. Choir practice. The comfort of my old purple minivan, creaking and groaning as it carried me through the same old routine.

And then, just like that, I missed Leah. I didn't know if it was the way this girl sitting next to me looked at me, or the way the sky seemed to stretch endlessly around me, but I couldn't shake the guilt. The longing for something I wasn't sure I deserved. I wished I could just text her, call her, and make everything feel okay again. But I didn't.

The more I thought about the lies I'd told, the more it pressed down on me. The better my life got with Leah, the worse I felt about myself. And now, sitting on this Ferris wheel, I couldn't escape the crushing thought . . . *What good was I to anyone? Especially Leah?*

I pressed my hand over my shoulder. Depression was like a tattoo, I realized. A permanent reminder of all the things I wanted to forget, the mistakes I couldn't take back. You try to cover it up, but it only makes it worse. And even when you think you've healed, it's still there, etched in your mind, reminding you of every failed attempt to outrun it.

I missed Leah more than anything. The girl sitting beside me didn't help. Her innocent, hopeful eyes reminded me of everything I'd left behind because, you know, who wouldn't want to feel like a garbage can next to someone's sunshine?

Her name was Sage. Way out of my league, but for some reason, she liked me. She walked close enough that our arms brushed together, and I wondered if she knew how much I was thinking. She didn't talk much, thankfully, because I didn't shut up. I probably sounded like a record stuck on repeat, rambling about The Beatles and my weird music taste. But hey, it was something to talk about.

We hit up some of the food stands, because when you're at a street food festival, your main goal is to eat your weight in delicious food. I was feeling adventurous, so I got something called Gator Bites. Tasted like sausage. They said it was alligator. Did I want to know? Probably not. Somewhere, a gator was plotting revenge.

"You go to school around here?" I asked, chomping down on another piece of Maybe Gator.

She pointed ahead, her voice a little softer in the chaos. "At the high school just down the road. I'm a junior."

Being a junior had been one of the best years of my life. But thinking back, I wondered if everyone looked at the past through rose-colored glasses.

"You're from Indiana," she said, breaking into my thoughts. "What on earth are you doing in these parts?"

That question was a tough one. *Sucky home life, looking for myself, got knocked out of a vehicle on my first hitchhiking attempt .. . yeah, and then the whole deciding-to-kill-myself-when-it's-all-over thing.* Totally casual, right? Yeah, no. So I just went with the safe answer.

"Just visiting some old relatives."

"They live around here?"

"Yeah, but I'm not a fan of some of them. It's just the right thing to do," I added, thinking of Sibby's parents.

She gave me a knowing smile. "We can't choose everyone in our lives, can we?"

I couldn't stop smiling back. Her face had this effortless charm, and I could barely look at her without wanting to gawk like a doofus. We finished eating, and she suggested we try some home-made ice cream. She knew the folks at the stand, so we got a free serving, and I wasn't about to turn that down. We grabbed a table that had just cleared out, and as we dug in, the hot air from earlier had cooled into a perfect evening. The stars popped out, twinkling above, and the sounds of the festival swirled around us. Music, laughter, the occasional shout.

I could hear Hayden and Kristie on stage, finishing up their set. After a few songs, the singer called Hayden's name. For the first time, I really heard Hayden's voice—Eddie Vedder meets Chris Martin. Slightly off-key with a tender vulnerability. Which, let's be honest, could be my life's theme song at this point.

They waved me up on stage, and I didn't refuse. I was only going because Hayden was holding Susie.

Sage watched from the table, and part of me wanted to impress her, which made me way more nervous than I cared to admit. I tried not to think too much about it as I walked up, the speakers popping in protest.

We had fun. Hayden swayed to the music while Kristie killed it on the keyboard. I wasn't sure if anything was in tune, especially my voice, but I was getting better at the high notes.

We jammed to "Born to Be Wild" and "Hair of the Dog." The crowd clapped, even when I missed a note. I swear, they were just happy I didn't completely ruin the song. Sage shouted and clapped along, and I hopped off the stage, high-fiving Hayden.

Afterward, Sage asked, "Wanna go for a walk?"

We passed the speakers, and I swear she brushed her hand against mine as we walked toward the kiddie rides. Intentional or not, my heart skipped. We shared an elephant ear. At least she didn't have powdered sugar on her face like Rodney had.

"I'm so glad school's out for the year," she said, taking a bite. "Classes were killing me. You must be glad you're graduating, right?"

I wasn't sure how to answer that. The typical response would be "Hell yeah!" but that wasn't how I felt.

"I'm actually going to miss it," I said, the words slipping out before I realized it. "It was a good run. It was nice knowing what I was going to do every day. Now everything's up in the air. It's weird."

She looked at me, surprised. "No kidding?"

"Change has that effect," I said. "You have any plans?"

"To have an amazing summer and an unforgettable senior year," she said. "I plan on going to Stanford University."

All the way on the other coast? Your parents approve?"

She shrugged. "It's not really up to them, is it? I've wanted to go to California for as long as I can remember. I really like the school. When something feels right, it just feels right."

"It's cool you know what you want," I said.

"Kinda takes a lot of the fear out," she said with a smirk.

"Meaning?"

"Being sure about something . . . gets rid of a lot of excess doubt."

I chewed on that for a while. Sage was smart, and I liked her. I still kept my distance, though, whenever she tried getting too close. It was better that way.

We walked around the kiddie rides, talking about school and hobbies. I knew it wasn't fair to judge anyone by comparison, but I couldn't help it. Sage was sweet and confident, and, yeah, she was definitely pretty. But compared to Leah? It felt like trying to compare a cupcake to a Michelin-star meal. There was no chance.

We ended up back at the stage area. Hayden and Kristie were still going strong, but the noise from the crowd was more of a background noise now.

Although I might never see Sage again, part of me wanted to

spill everything. The mess in my head and why I was still living. Maybe I just didn't want to carry it alone anymore.

She turned to me and asked, "Where are you guys headed after this?"

I watched the stage, knowing nothing was ever planned with Hayden and Kristie. "With these two . . . wherever their hearts lead them," I said.

Sage smiled, a sigh escaping her as she fiddled with her bracelet. "Hey, if you're around tomorrow, wanna get together again? I'll show you around town."

It was now or never. I could either tell the truth or keep leading her on to protect her feelings. Both options felt like I was stuck between a rock and a hard place.

"Sage, I . . . I don't mean to sound all weird and stuff, but I'm in love with someone."

She looked at me, those kind eyes waiting for me to go on.

"Not to get all mushy," I added, "but I'm going to love her for the rest of my life."

Sage's expression didn't waver. No judgment, just that genuine warmth. She tilted her head. "That's sweet."

There was no sarcasm in her voice, just sincerity, and it made me respect her even more.

"It's been nice having someone to talk to," I said. "Means a lot."

Sage nodded. "You going back up there?" she asked, pointing to the stage.

"Nah. It's way more fun just watching them."

We stayed at the table, watching Hayden and Kristie collaborate with their friends on a few more songs. I couldn't figure out where they got all that energy from. The crowd was buzzing, laughing, and clinking beers, but Kristie looked a little drained. She worked last night and didn't get much sleep, but I could tell she loved every minute of it. For them, this wasn't work. It was life.

I looked at Sage, studying her round eyes and pretty rose

cheeks. If Leah hadn't been in the picture, maybe I would've liked to ask her out.

I missed Leah, almost enough to hitchhike back to Tipton County. Almost enough to tell someone what I was planning, so they'd lock me up and put me on suicide watch.

Almost.

The crowd had thickened even more, the stars twinkling above, and the warm night air felt like it was breathing with us.

There was a family with little kids twirling around in front of us. The smell of popcorn and grilled meats hung in the air, mixing with the sweet scent of apple pie nearby. The sound of music washed over us, and the distant crunch of soda cans and happy shouts added to the lively vibe.

I leaned back. Hayden strummed his guitar, Kristie tapped away at the keyboards, and the lead singer had a voice like Bob Seger. Gravelly and rich, but looked more like someone who would ace chemistry, not front a band.

The lights from the stage flickered and swayed with the rhythm of the songs, and for a moment, I let myself feel lighter, the worries and doubts floating away in the comforting night air.

Kristie's face was pale.

"Does she look okay to you?" I asked Sage, loud over the music.

"Who?" Sage glanced at me, brow furrowing.

I pointed at Kristie, her movements sluggish now, her eyes glazed as if she were fighting to stay awake. Something wasn't right.

Sage looked confused, but I couldn't stop staring at Kristie. The music played, but I barely heard it. She looked like she was about to drop any second, and the more I watched, the more I felt like something bad was coming.

I raised my hand, waving frantically to get Hayden's attention, but it was hopeless. My chest tightened. Kristie swayed a little, her gaze unfocused, as if the whole world was drifting away from her.

Panic clawed at my spine.

I stood up and waved harder, desperate now. Finally, Hayden caught my eye. His look shifted from concentration to alarm when I pointed at Kristie. Without hesitation, he dropped Susie. The thud hit the stage like an omen. The band slowly stopped. The crowd fell silent. Every pair of eyes turned toward them.

"Kristie!" Hayden shouted. He ran to her, but in his rush, he slammed his knee into one of the exposed drum legs.

My heart pounded as I pushed through the crowd toward the stage. The music was replaced by whispers of worry.

Hayden was holding Kristie now, cradling her like she was made of glass. She didn't move. Her eyes were wide but unseeing.

"Help!" Hayden's voice cracked.

I jumped onto the stage, my breath catching in my throat. Kristie's face was a ghostly shade, her lips pale. Her body flopped like a ragdoll as Hayden eased her down onto the stage floor. His voice was hoarse now, desperate. "Not again. Not again . . ."

I knelt, my legs like lead, panic crawling under my skin.

"What can I do?" I asked.

Hayden didn't answer. His eyes stayed locked on Kristie, a silent cry for help.

"I called 911!" someone shouted from the crowd.

The festival's emergency crew was there in seconds, pushing through the crowd. They began working on Kristie, checking her vitals, but she remained unresponsive. My stomach twisted with every second that passed.

Hayden sat on his heels, his face crumpled in grief. His sobs shook his chest as he stared at Kristie. "Not again . . ."

The paramedics arrived with an ambulance just as I thought I might lose it. They wheeled Kristie away. Hayden's panicked eyes met mine.

Sage stood by me, her hand on my back. I barely noticed her, my eyes fixed on the scene unfolding before me. The world closed in around us.

They loaded Kristie into the back of the ambulance. Hayden

climbed in beside her, his face a mixture of tears and fear. The doors slammed shut, and I felt the silence hit me like a truck.

"Come on," I said, barely recognizing my own voice. "We're going to the hospital."

Sage didn't hesitate. We were already moving before I could think. I grabbed Susie and ran to Winnie in the workers' parking lot. I jumped into the driver's seat. The engine roared to life, and we shot out of the parking lot, the tires screeching on the pavement.

My hands were slick with sweat as I gripped the wheel, my thighs jittery. The night air was thick, and the heat didn't help calm my nerves.

Sage broke the silence. "She's probably just exhausted. It's hot, and they've been performing all night."

I nodded, but doubt gnawed at me. The way Hayden had reacted, the look in his eyes . . . it didn't add up.

We arrived at the hospital, the tires screeching as I slammed Winnie into park. My heart was pounding. I felt like I might pass out myself.

I ran to the ER desk, noticing the familiar cool, sterile air of the hospital.

"Kristie who?" the receptionist asked, not looking up from her computer.

"I don't know her last name, but she just came in by ambulance. With her boyfriend, Hayden." I couldn't stop my voice from shaking.

The receptionist raised an eyebrow, sensing my panic. She typed something into the computer, but her face stayed unreadable. Then she stood up, lifting a finger.

"Wait here just a moment," she said, and I didn't move. I couldn't. It felt like time was stretching on forever. The ticking of the clock was the only sound I could hear.

Less than a minute passed, but it felt like hours.

The receptionist returned. "Kristie Arnold is with the doctors."

"Can we see her?" I asked, unable to hide my desperation.

"Not yet," she replied. "They're still working on her. Once they've cleared her for visitors, I'll let you know."

"Is she okay?" I forced the words out. They felt wrong in my mouth.

"They're with her. I'm sure they're doing everything they can. But I don't have any information yet." She gave me a tight-lipped smile, but it didn't reassure me.

"How long will it take?" The question felt hollow, like I already knew the answer.

The receptionist glanced at the clock again. "I really can't say. But I'll keep checking and let you know as soon as they give the green light. I promise."

I nodded, my mind racing. Every second stretched out longer than the last. The silence was deafening. I wanted to scream, but I didn't have the strength.

All I could do was wait.

Sage and I walked to the waiting room, the flickering fluorescent lights above us casting a harsh, clinical glow. The buzz of the vending machines in the corner was a constant background noise that didn't drown out the pounding in my chest.

We sat in silence for what felt like hours. The bright pictures on the walls taunted the storm swirling inside me. I kept thinking about Winnie, about what I should do if Kristie came back, about cleaning it up and making the bed for her as if that would somehow fix everything. But there was nothing I could do. Nothing.

Sage, sitting beside me, kept glancing at her phone, tapping her fingers nervously on her lap. She had to leave, I could tell, but she stayed. She stayed out of loyalty. Out of kindness.

I kept asking for updates. The answer never changed. And I

waited. I waited for something to change, for a shift in the air, for a flicker of hope.

The clock ticked on for four hours. The night was slipping away, and still, nothing.

Finally, I offered to drive Sage home, but she waved me off. "You stay here," she said. "In case there's any news." She wrote her number down on a card and handed it to me. I pocketed it without looking at it. She called a friend to come pick her up, giving me a tight hug before she left.

"Hope for the best," she said, but it didn't feel like hope. It felt like a distant whisper, swallowed by the thick, suffocating silence that followed her departure.

The door swung shut behind her, and I was alone. The loneliness hit me like a cold wave, crashing into my chest, leaving an empty hole where the warmth of company had been. I could almost hear the dramatic music swelling. This is it. The moment I finally become a full-blown tragic figure. I rubbed my chest, trying to calm the tightness that felt like it was squeezing the life out of me. There was a coffee machine in the corner, but I couldn't bring myself to drink anything.

I tapped my foot against the floor, the rhythmic sound a desperate attempt to distract myself, but it didn't work. People came and went, checked in, waited, and were called back.

I kept glancing at the receptionist, but she just shook her head each time I caught her eye. I was losing my grip. I paced. The abstract art on the walls displayed swirling colors. Bright yellows, mocking pinks, deep blues swallowing me whole. The longer I stared at it, the more it mirrored how I felt. Lost, unfixable, stuck in the dark, surrounded by the light that wouldn't reach me.

I stopped at the payphone. It was old, its edges scratched and worn. I dug into my pocket and pulled out a couple of quarters, the coins clinking together in my hand like a small, sad reminder of my isolation. I slid them into the slot, my hands trembling as I lifted the receiver to my ear.

This call could change everything. This call could be the end of the numbness I'd been holding onto. It could bring the cops straight to me. It could unravel all the plans I'd been carefully stitching together. But I had no choice. I needed to make it.

I needed someone.

I needed help.

I dialed the number. The ringing stretched the silence. My stomach twisted, my breath shallow. When the voice on the other end answered, I closed my eyes. Tears slipped down my cheeks, warm against cold skin.

"Grandpa," I whispered, voice breaking. "I need you."

Grandpa Norris drove six straight hours from Alabama to Sunflower County.

He was always my hero.

From the time I was a little boy, I wanted to be just like him, and now, as I sat slumped in the emergency room, groggy and disoriented, I was reminded of why. When he shook my shoulder, I felt the steady strength of his presence.

I'd managed to fall asleep across four chairs in the waiting room sleeping like a rock, or at least like someone who could pass out in the most uncomfortable position possible. I woke up with drool stuck to the corner of my mouth, but the first thing I saw was Grandpa Norris standing over me, his grin as bright as it always was, his teeth flashing like headlights in the dark.

The rush of warmth hit me. His presence always had a way of making everything feel okay. No matter how bad things got, no matter how hard the world hit, Grandpa Norris had a way of lightening the load, even if just for a moment.

I sat up, feeling stiff from the hard chairs, and rubbed my eyes. My sore tattoo throbbed, a reminder of my impulsivity. I lifted my shirt sleeve and glanced at the ink.

"That's some nice artwork you've got there," Grandpa Norris said, sitting beside me. His voice was calm, always steady, always exactly what I needed in moments like this.

I pulled my sleeve back down, relieved the tattoo wasn't infected or worse, developing into a mutant disease that would make me bust out of my grave.

I didn't say a word. Instead, I wrapped my arms around Grandpa Norris in a tight hug, squeezing him harder than I probably should have for a man in his seventies. But Grandpa Norris wasn't like other grandfathers.

"Thanks for coming, Grandpa," I said. I didn't bother hiding the relief that rushed through me. "You won't—"

He raised his hand, cutting me off before I could finish.

"Your parents call for updates. But this is your journey, Braden."

I swallowed the lump in my throat. "Thanks, Grandpa."

He kept his arm around my shoulders. "What's going on, young man? What're you doing all the way in Mississippi?"

Where do I even start? I wanted to tell him everything, but I didn't want to make my problems his, even though I knew he'd keep them to himself. That was Grandpa Norris. He never shared my secrets with anyone, but I wasn't sure how much I was ready to reveal, especially the darker stuff. If I said something like "I want to die" out loud, he'd do everything in his power to stop me. He wouldn't be the loving grandpa he was if he didn't.

"I was at a festival last night with my friends," I said finally, not sure how much of the truth I wanted to admit. "One of them passed out on stage. She was playing keyboards, and I saw something wasn't right. Before I knew it, she was down, and an ambulance had to come. I've been waiting here all night."

Grandpa Norris just nodded, no judgment, no questioning. Just the silent understanding that he'd give me space when I needed it, but he'd also be ready to listen when I was ready to speak.

I stood up and walked over to the new receptionist at the counter. She glanced up at me, looking like she was in a hurry but still focused on her work.

"Kristie Arnold?" she asked, her eyes scanning the computer screen in front of her.

"Is she okay?"

She typed something, her fingers quick, her eyes darting across the screen. "Take the elevator to room 203," she said, barely looking up.

I turned back to Grandpa Norris who was already standing, his eyes giving me the push I needed to go.

"Go on ahead," he said, the calm in his voice wrapping around me like a blanket. "I'll be right here when you're done."

I took the elevator to the second floor.

As the doors opened, the noise of laughter and chatter hit me before I even peeked inside. There was something about the joy in the room that seemed out of place, like it didn't belong in the sterile, antiseptic world of a hospital. The room was warm, filled with chatter and coffee. What did I miss while I was sleeping?

"Babe Cakes, look who it is." Hayden pointed in my direction. "Good morning, Starshine!"

The room of eight people turned toward me, and I felt their gazes like a thousand-pound anchor. For a brief moment, I wondered if I was dreaming, caught in some alternate reality where everything was upside down. The people around Kristie laughing, joking, drinking coffee like everything was normal didn't fit into my world of tension and unanswered questions.

"Why didn't you come get me?" I asked, my voice tight, the strain of the last few hours in each word.

"I did, but you looked so comfortable in those chairs, so I let you sleep," Hayden said, his energy easy, unburdened. "I hope you could sleep. I brought you a blanket."

It was hard to breathe in that space, surrounded by smiles that felt like they were mocking me. I kept my arms awkwardly at my sides, stiff with discomfort, trying to hold it all together. The faces, most of them unfamiliar, stared at me like I was a character in a show.

"Braden, these are some good friends of ours," Hayden continued. "You know Waylon and Parker from yesterday. Patty here just drove from Hamilton County to be here. She's known Kristie since grade school. Leonard, Mark, and Zana are from an old bar we used to frequent here in town. I didn't think you lived here anymore, Mark. When I called, I was sure you ended up in Silicon Valley creating the next search engine or something."

They laughed, but I didn't. My stomach churned as I watched them. They kept talking, drifting further into their easy camaraderie, while I stood frozen and distant. Kristie, laughing with them, also seemed so far away. The noise, the movement, all of it felt like a world apart from my own.

"Braden," Kristie said, interrupting my thoughts. She reached for her plate of food and moved it in my direction. "They gave me extra, and I can't eat all of this. You look hungry."

I shook my head. "No, thanks."

I couldn't stay here much longer. It was like I was watching a life I didn't belong to. Everything was too bright, too warm, and I felt like I was suffocating in the contrast.

"Can I talk to Kristie alone?" The question came out louder than I intended, causing the room to fall silent.

The stillness felt heavier than the laughter. Eyes lingered on me like I was a puzzle. One by one, they nodded and left. Hayden was last, his face melting when he caught my eye.

"Thanks for waiting here, buddy," he said, his voice a little strained now. "I won't forget it."

And with that, he left. The door clicked shut, and the room felt emptier. I could breathe again.

I looked at Kristie, her smile no longer innocent. She tried to hold it together, but the situation hung between us. Every step toward her felt deeper into the unknown.

I sat next to her bed, trying to swallow the lump in my throat.

"Nobody stays this long in a hospital for fainting," I said.

Her expression softened, fading into something somber.

"No," she said quietly. "They don't."

The clock read 7:36 a.m., but time felt stretched, every second dragging.

It's sunny outside.

Kristie is *so* happy.

Hayden is back to his old self.

"I don't understand," I whispered.

She took a breath, eyes drifting somewhere beyond the room, as if weighing all the things she'd tucked away.

"Can you imagine if I went ziplining with an oxygen tank?" she asked.

I blinked, caught between awe and disbelief. Her laugh—a little breathless, a little defiant—made my chest ache.

"I'm refusing treatment," she said, the words slow and deliberate.

"What treatment?"

Kristie sighed. "I have advanced lung disease."

The words hit like a punch to the gut, and I could feel the air in the room grow heavier.

"Lung disease?" I thought back on all the gigs we'd done together, the moments of joy, the moments when none of this had even seemed possible.

"If I had treatment, I'd have to stay out," she continued. "I wouldn't be able to do any more shows. I'd have to live a very restricted life. Braden, the adventures we've had since we met you have been unforgettable. None of that would exist."

My heart clenched. "You say advanced . . ."

"I was at a doctor appointment when you and Hayden met. I refused to let him sit in on those appointments anymore because I could see how it was breaking his spirit. That wasn't my Hayden. I'd already been refusing treatment for quite some time at that point. Things had gotten worse. Hayden wanted me to get help, but I knew what it would do to our life, our relationship. I didn't want him to remember us that way."

I wanted to speak, to fix it somehow, but instead I just felt it. All of it. Her truth settling inside me, solid and unmovable.

"I've lost weight. I'm out of breath faster. I'm tired all the time. My immune system is weak, which is probably what's going to get me in the end. Or my lungs will just fail me."

"But you're so young."

"It's genetics, Braden."

I shook my head, trying to push away the dread that was tightening around my chest.

"Since you came into our lives," she said, "you showed us that we were making the right decision. We could really live out our dreams. We could travel, play gigs, laugh, visit friends, eat good food, even zipline. I got to zipline again."

Tears welled in my eyes. "I didn't fix anything, Kristie," I said.

She smiled through her tears. "But Braden," she whispered. "Because of you, I didn't have to stop living my life."

And in that moment, the tears I'd been holding back for so long broke free. I let them fall, each drop carrying everything I was too afraid to say. I cried for all the pain and confusion, for all the guilt I couldn't shake, for the fear of losing someone I'd come to care for.

Kristie reached out and pulled me close, her arms wrapping around me as I let go, breaking down into the comfort of someone who had suffered far more than I ever had.

I cried for her. For Hayden. For myself.

And for the first time, I realized that sometimes, the pressure of life could only be shared with someone who truly understood it.

We sat in silence for a moment before Kristie broke it with a question. "Would you get me something out of my bag over there?" she asked, pointing to the large tote bag next to the recliner. I got up and walked over to it.

"It's the first sketch paper in my folder," Kristie added, as I looked at her.

I found the paper, pulled it out, and held it in my hands. A small laugh escaped my lips. There I was—exaggerated, smiling so wide that my eyes barely fit on the page. My oversized teeth gleamed in a grin that seemed to stretch beyond what should've been humanly possible, and my eyebrows . . . well, they looked like they were ready to launch off the paper entirely. At the bottom was the faint beginning of my yellow-and-red polka dot tie.

"You did this?" I asked, still in awe. The image of myself seemed so far removed from the person I thought I was, yet it was also so perfectly me.

Kristie nodded. "I love it when you smile, so I wanted to draw a smile so big, the world can't miss it."

"Thank you," I said, laughing again, a genuine laugh that felt foreign but welcome. The image of me in that moment, happy and unburdened, made me feel like I could take on anything.

When I left Kristie's room, I half-expected emptiness. Instead, I felt warm and new, like the confusion and hurt had been washed away.

I walked down the hospital hall, clarity settling over me in an unexpected way.

I searched the waiting room for Hayden but didn't see him. My face was still blotchy from crying, and I didn't want him to see me like that. Instead, I turned and headed toward the exit, feeling a pull toward Grandpa Norris.

As I stepped into the sunlight, Grandpa Norris rose from the bench and stretched, as if in no hurry.

We walked together, side by side, taking our time. Grandpa Norris had parked his old, rusty blue truck at the very back of the lot, like always. "We'd miss all this beautiful sunshine if I parked closer," he said, as though it was the most logical thing in the world.

It made me happy because with Grandpa Norris, everything felt simpler.

We passed Winnie on our way to the truck. I placed the caricature in Susie's case and left the keys in the glove compartment for

Hayden. I filled Margaret's food bowl with a can of corned beef hash, and she thanked me with a grunt. When I joined Grandpa Norris, he was waiting for me, his arms folded, standing taller than most people I knew.

"How's your friend?" he asked.

"If you asked Kristie, she'd say she's doing great," I said, still processing what she had told me. "But if you asked her lungs, they might file for divorce."

Grandpa Norris tilted his head. "Then I take it she's doing great."

"She's not going to live long," I said.

Grandpa Norris didn't say anything. Instead, he lifted his face into the sunlight, eyes squinting slightly as if he was considering something far deeper than my words.

"Ah, quantity over quality," he said finally, with a chuckle. "The old fool's priority scale. Don't fall for it, boy."

Kristie's drawing and Grandpa Norris' words made me smile. I realized everything—pain and joy—was part of the journey. And even in the most difficult of times, there was always room for a little bit of light.

In the truck, I asked, "Do you think life's worth living?"

He considered it. "We're here for a reason. If life's not worth living, there wouldn't be life."

We went to a pancake place, and I ordered seconds without hesitation.

After breakfast, I thought of taking him to a spot by the river like I'd done with Sibby, but we ended up somewhere similar. We skipped rocks. The sun was warm, the water calming, and for a moment, I wasn't worried about screwing everything up.

"What would you do if you knew you were dying?" The question tumbled out.

Grandpa tossed a rock, watching it skim. "We all have free will. What we do with it is our responsibility."

Unsatisfied, I opened my mouth to tell him that wasn't fair, but he placed a hand on my chest, making me meet his eyes.

"Nobody's your hero," he said. "You have to find it within yourself."

His words hit hard, but I resisted. Why was it so hard to take responsibility? I knew it was the advice I'd give someone else. Why couldn't I take it?

We sat on the rocky dirt. Grandpa tossed me a sunflower seed. I caught it. A small victory in a life where I was losing battles every day, but hey, at least I wasn't still getting hit in the face with them.

"What are you looking for out here, Braden?" Grandpa asked, his tone gentle, but probing. "Besides the sunshine, food, and music . . . why are you here?"

I smirked. "Free will means I don't have to answer, right?"

He chuckled, but his gaze intensified. I felt it, his focus on me shifting.

I sighed. "I was out here with Aunt Sibby," I confessed.

His expression changed. The amusement faded, replaced by seriousness. "Sibby McGee, huh? But she's up in Memphis."

"We came down here together," I said.

He was quiet for a beat, his fingers working through the rocks. Finally, he looked out at the river. "What'd you all do?"

"Just stuff like this. We hung out by the river, met her parents, some people she knows."

He raised an eyebrow. "You met her folks?"

"Yeah. Real jerks if you ask me."

His lips twitched upward, but he didn't laugh. Instead, he stood, brushing the dirt off his legs. "I figured they'd have croaked by now."

"Where are you going?" I asked.

Grandpa Norris didn't even look back as he made his way toward the truck. "Gonna confront those rat bastards."

I hesitated for a moment, then followed behind him. "Rat bastards?"

"Some of the most arrogant sons of bitches I've ever had the misfortune of knowing."

I climbed into the passenger seat. "But Grandpa, he's got dementia. She's old—"

"There's no excuse for being shitty human beings," he cut me off, his voice hard, unyielding. He started the engine and, for the first time, I saw a fire in him that I didn't know existed.

He drove us in silence, the engine rumbling under his control. I glanced over at him, but he was locked in, his eyes fixed on the road, his fingers tapping a rhythm on the steering wheel. He was pissed, more than I'd ever seen him before, but there was no rush. He was controlled, calculating, like a man who knew exactly what he was doing.

"How do you know where we're going?" I asked.

"I remember where Sibby lived," he replied, eyes still on the road.

"How? You're not gonna hurt anyone, are you?" I asked, though I already knew the answer.

He looked over at me, a half-smile playing at the corner of his lips. "The only antidote to mental suffering is physical pain," he said, quoting Karl Marx like it was a casual observation.

"That doesn't exactly answer my question."

"But it might answer yours from earlier," Grandpa said, pressing harder on the gas. "You're not busy enough, young man. Find sports. Find work. Find something that gets you up every morning. Your mind's too freed up, letting the torment settle in. This too shall pass. Remember that. This too shall pass. In everything we do, good or bad. Nothing lasts forever."

I sat there, absorbing his words.

We pulled up to an upper-class neighborhood, each house more ostentatious than the last. Grandpa Norris parked directly in front of a stone house with dark shutters, a flag proudly waving from the front yard. The kind of house where you don't just walk up to uninvited. But Grandpa Norris didn't give a damn.

He slammed the truck door and I followed, heart pounding.

Without a word, he pounded his fist against the door.

Someone peered through the front curtains, but it took a while before they cracked the door open. It was her. Sibby's mom, Edie. And she looked ready to bite someone's head off.

"What in Sam Hill are you doin' to my door?" she snapped, her eyes narrowing.

"Edie, can't say it's a pleasure to see you after all this time," he said with the slightest smirk. "But if it's all the same to you, I'd like to speak to your husband."

"He's not well, Robert." Edie's voice was shrill with irritation.

"He wasn't well when he kicked his daughter out of the house at seventeen years old either, was he?" Grandpa Norris said.

I heard shouting from inside, followed by the squeaky wheels of an old walker. A frail, wheezing voice bellowed from inside. "What in the name of—"

Edie opened the door fully, revealing Arthur. His face twisted with confusion and anger.

"You get off my damn property now, Robert, before I call the police," Arthur yelled, his voice shaky but full of venom.

Grandpa Norris didn't budge, glaring at Arthur. "You can call whoever you want. I'm not leaving until I know what business you have with my grandson."

Arthur's face turned red with rage. "I didn't call your grandson to town, Robert, and I didn't invite him here now!"

Edie eyeballed me like I was still some bug on her porch.

Arthur sneered. "Where've you been all these years anyhow, Mr. Too Good For Everybody?"

Grandpa Norris didn't flinch. "Where were you when your seventeen-year-old daughter stayed with me and Angela because she had nowhere else to go?"

Arthur's voice cracked. "She was pregnant and unmarried, Rob!"

The words hit like a slap. The air grew thick with silence. I could hear Arthur's wheezing, the rasp of his breath cutting through the quiet. A strange, cold feeling settled in my gut as I thought about Sibby, about the way her parents had treated her. I could still see her face at Charlie Patton's grave, her tears as she walked away.

"We can tolerate a lot of bullshit from people like you," Arthur spat, glaring at Grandpa Norris, "but we live by morals, and she broke damn near every one of them when she came to us with that news."

"Morals, huh," Grandpa Norris said, his voice low, but full of contempt. "Loving your daughter who dared come to you with something like that? And sure enough, your love is conditional."

Arthur's lips twisted in disgust. "We don't have tolerance for bastard children—"

Before he could finish, Grandpa Norris was on him. In one fluid motion, he grabbed Arthur by the collar and lifted him clear off the ground.

Edie gasped, her hands trembling. "That's enough, you two."

"You listen here, old man," Grandpa Norris growled, his jaw clenched. "Nobody on this earth is a mistake. As much as I want to knock your other hip out of place, neither are you, so I suggest you watch your tongue before I shove it all the way down your hissin' throat."

He released Arthur with a hard shove. Arthur clutched his walker, his knees shaking.

"I've never done anything in my life expecting anything in return," Grandpa Norris said. "But the least you could've done is shown your grown daughter the love she deserves."

Edie and Arthur stood there in stunned silence, staring at Grandpa Norris as if they were seeing a man they didn't recognize.

I wished Sibby could see this.

"Edie," Grandpa Norris nodded curtly, his voice thick with finality. He turned and walked back to the truck.

As we headed back, my attitude shifted. It wasn't just Grandpa Norris' confrontation . . . there was something else in his eyes.

When we climbed into the truck, I didn't know where to begin. My head was a storm of questions, but the first thing that escaped my lips was, "You gotta give me something."

"How's Sibby?" he asked.

"She's got a house, a good job. Does that answer your question?"

He leaned back, then said, "When Sibby was seventeen, she called me and your grandmother, asking for a place to stay. Said her parents kicked her out. And you know what? We let her stay with us. Gave her a safe place when she had nowhere else to go." His eyes lowered, but there was something fierce still burning there. "Not everyone has a good family or good friends, Braden."

"Where's her kid?" I asked.

"She gave the baby up for adoption. One of the hardest things I've seen. She didn't talk about it much afterward, but threw herself into school and got her nursing degree."

I didn't know what to say. I was still trying to wrap my mind around everything, and then Grandpa Norris spoke again, his voice quieter but no less serious.

"Boy," he said, glancing over at me. "If you ever need a place to stay, my door's always open. Mum's the word."

And just like that, this man—this unassuming, badass man— was even more of an inspiration to me.

Free will.

Nobody else was going to step in and save me. Nobody was going to be my hero.

I asked him to drop me at Perry's Market. As we pulled up, I met his eyes. "Thanks for coming all this way, Grandpa."

A glint appeared in his eyes, his voice steady. "I'd drive across the ocean for you."

He grabbed my hand with surprising strength and squeezed

until I met his serious, grounded gaze. "Nobody gets to live life backward," he said quietly.

I didn't need to think twice. I finished the quote for him, "Look ahead, that is where your future lies."

He nodded, approval flickering across his face before releasing my hand.

When I stepped out of the truck, the air felt different. Lighter, but clearer too. For the first time, the pressure pressing down on me didn't feel like punishment. It felt like purpose.

It was all in my hands now. No more excuses.

As much as I wanted Grandpa Norris to stay by my side forever, I told him to head back after dropping me off at Perry's Market. He insisted on waiting, but I told him I had things to take care of. He didn't press further. I watched his rusty blue truck drive off, heading back to Alabama, and suddenly the reality of what I had to do hit me full force.

Frederick.

He was key to unlocking the truth, but I didn't know him. Just pieces of what Sibby had shared, and now, he seemed like a stranger with a welcoming smile.

But if he was good enough for Sibby to care about, then maybe he was worth trusting.

I walked into the small market, the earthy scent of dirt and wood filling my nose. There were plants everywhere, a burst of green in an otherwise simple grocery store. My eyes landed on Frederick as he lugged a bag of soil to the front door, his face flushed with effort.

"Hi," I greeted him, the words a little too quiet, like I wasn't sure what I was doing.

He gave me a friendly nod, not recognizing me at first, and I didn't mind. I wasn't here for small talk, anyway. When he returned, wiping his hands on his jeans, his bright smile greeted me. "Braden, right?"

I nodded, still feeling the pressure of everything I was about to ask. "Yeah. I wanted to talk to you about something."

His curiosity piqued, but he didn't press. "Sure. Right this way."

We sat down outside under the warm sun, the air thick with moisture. I fumbled with my words. "I remembered something you said about Sibby's parents."

Frederick's face flickered with something unreadable before he grinned. "They don't make it easy, do they?"

I leaned forward, my mind racing. "They're hard on her. But she still went to them, even after everything."

"Family stuff," he replied, looking away, clearly not interested in digging deeper. "We all have our issues."

"But my grandpa helped her. He took her in when her parents kicked her out."

Frederick's expression hardened. His gaze flicked toward the door, as if he was trying to escape the conversation without outright walking away. But I pushed forward.

"I heard you and Sibby were close," I said. "I figured you might know what happened. Why didn't you let her stay with you?"

He stiffened, the smile slipping from his face. "I don't get involved in family drama. I just do my part and keep my distance."

"But you loved her, right?" I pressed.

"I did. But she left. My part ended there."

There was a flash of guilt in his eyes, followed by a sudden avoidance.

"What happened with the pregnancy?" I asked.

Frederick shifted uncomfortably, his gaze darting away. "She came to me crying. She was pregnant. My parents were okay with her staying with us."

I stood up. "Why didn't she stay with you then?" I demanded.

Frederick stiffened, his face turning red. He mumbled something under his breath, his hand gripping the bench.

"Why didn't she stay with you?" I repeated, louder, my frustration spilling over.

He turned, his eyes darkening. "Why do you need to know?"

"Why didn't she stay with you?"

"Why do you—"

"Why didn't she stay with you?"

"Because it wasn't my baby!" he snapped, the words laced with anger and regret. He stood up. "It wasn't mine, Braden. You're barking up the wrong tree."

I stood frozen for a beat, trying to process what he'd said. The world felt like it was spinning around me. Everything I thought I understood about Sibby, about this whole situation, had just shifted.

Frederick seemed to deflate, his shoulders slumping. "She told me, okay? She told me it wasn't mine. And I didn't want to be some kind of . . . fool."

I felt the honesty of his words, but it still didn't sit right. Sibby had kept this from me, and I couldn't figure out why.

"I didn't even care," Frederick said. "I wanted to stay with her anyway. I would've. I loved her. She could've stayed here with me in Mississippi. We could've done that together. Raised the baby. But she was the one who decided to fall in love with someone else. She was the one who didn't want to be with *me*."

The words cut through me, not out of pity, but because they mirrored the knot of frustration inside me. This wasn't supposed to be how it all played out. I thought I was getting answers, but it felt more like a maze with no exit. I wanted to scream, but instead, I stood there, barely able to speak.

I wondered about Sibby. I wondered about the girl she used to be, the one who seemed so strong yet was capable of so much hurt. I understood making mistakes, I did, but the silence she'd left behind . . . the things she never told me. It felt like a betrayal.

"Why'd she stay with my grandparents?" I asked.

Frederick sighed, his face clouded with regret. "The night she came to my house after her parents kicked her out . . . she told me she'd gotten involved with a married man. Hard to live with, right? Your grandparents took her in."

Frederick turned to me, staring into my helpless eyes.

"I moved on from this, okay?" he had said, his voice calm but resolute. "I love Sibby. She'll always be in my heart, but I moved on. It would be nice if you respected that."

And then he disappeared through the double doors, leaving me to wrestle with everything I'd just heard.

I walked to the payphone, my legs heavy. The more I thought about it, the angrier I got. Grandpa Norris had always seemed like he had all the answers, and I needed him to tell me what to do next, to lay it out straight. I shoved two quarters into the payphone, my hands trembling as I dialed his number. It rang, and I waited, my frustration building with each passing second.

No answer.

I tried again.

Still nothing.

And he wouldn't be home for hours.

I slammed the receiver down, the click punctuating my spiraling thoughts.

I walked away toward the river, more lost than ever.

I clenched my fists, angry at myself and the situation. Memories of Leah, my parents, and Trevor intruded like unwanted thoughts. I grabbed stones from the riverbank and skipped them, trying to erase the thoughts I couldn't control.

But it didn't work.

I squeezed my eyes shut, pressing my palms against them, trying to force the memories out, but it didn't help. I could still see them, could still feel them crashing into me. Like a slow-motion car wreck that I'm too tired to get out of.

I shook my head, unable to escape the power of it all.

I hummed.

I sang.

"Let me take you to a place," I muttered through clenched teeth.

"A place called the tree."

I could hear the defeat in my voice. Not that it mattered. Defeat was kind of my signature flavor these days, like a fine wine that had gone a little off, but you just kept drinking because, hey, what else is there to do? I sat at the water's edge, the cool breeze brushing past me as I stared at the small glistening waves before me.

With a sigh, I pulled out my pen and notepad from my back pocket. I had to make sense of it somehow, even if it was just to clear my mind, even if it didn't fix a damn thing.

And so I wrote.

> *Dear Dad,*
>
> *It's interesting. Life I mean. Have you ever believed in something you thought was true only to find out it wasn't?*
>
> *You never talked much. You never asked many questions aside from, "How was your day?"*
>
> *But for some reason, mom married you. She married you and gave her life away to you. She trusted you. She sacrificed for you. She chose to accept everything about you.*
>
> *Why did you take advantage of that?*
>
> *I understand you stopped drinking, but not after you made one more mistake, right? Just one more mistake, then you would change your ways. Not before you hurt more people though, right? You don't learn until more people have been hurt, more lives affected by your decisions.*

Sure, you aren't the biggest talker, but that doesn't mean you weren't making life altering choices.

You allowed me to believe something that wasn't true.

Grandpa forgave you as he usually does. He's not an enabler, but he believes in people. You kicked him out of our lives, not because he did something wrong, but because you did. You allowed me to believe that he was wrong all these years.

You allowed me to believe it was all mom's fault.

It wasn't, dad. _It_ was yours.

And mom . . . always taking the blame for you. That's real love. The first thing I want to say is that you don't deserve her love. But maybe that's what changed you in the end. You did stop drinking. You did stop coming home late, wasted and stumbling as you once told me. You started getting up early, going to work regularly, coming home for dinner. You might not have known who you were when you weren't drinking, which is why you said you became quiet and bland. But you tried.

I understand that now.

People make mistakes, but love forgives them.

I don't really have a choice because I can't not love you. So I don't want to leave this earth without forgiving you for what you did. I know in hindsight, you would've chosen love, too.

I hope I can forgive you. I really do.

Braden

What the hell was I going to do with all these letters anyway? I wanted to talk to Grandpa Norris, but I didn't even have any more coins for another call. All I had was this letter in my pocket, the song in my head, and the image of my father refusing to leave my mind.

I laid down near the water, the coolness of the tide brushing against my feet before it retreated again. The heat was oppressive, making me wish I could just slip into the river for a swim.

I sat up and gazed over the water. Jeff Buckley died on this day twelve years ago in the Wolf River, just a part of the Mississippi. Maybe it wasn't far from here. I thought about Buckley, about what he must've felt under that water. At some point, he must've known he wasn't coming back. What was he thinking? Who was he thinking of? Was he scared?

I thought about swimming, sinking, letting the water close over me. Would I be scared? Or would it feel like escape? I started singing the words that never seemed to leave me.

"Let me take you to a place, where the world stops for as long as you do . . ."

I lay back, staring at the sky. It was too bright, too blue. Sunlight stabbed at my eyes.

I thought about Tipton High. Teachers, basketball games, working concessions, laughing with friends during lunch. I even missed the dumb stuff like Mr. Hillman's random goatee, musical rehearsals, drama club. The things that made life feel . . . alive.

Maybe Leah didn't say it, but she did see me. I felt it. Maybe it was better to be seen on the inside. Maybe it was everything.

How do you thank someone for saving your life? You don't. You walk away, you let them go, and you don't burden them with your mess.

I thought about suicide more than I should. It's funny how a dark thought can sometimes be like an annoying relative who just won't leave, no matter how many times you politely say, "Not now". Every minute like a constant companion. I'd tried to shut it out, but it always came back, sneaking in when I least expected it. Some people could push their worries away until they had to face them, but depression wasn't like that. It drags you through every little moment, makes you feel everything, even when you don't want to feel at all.

Depression is an invisible torture, a lie. Smiling when you're drowning. Saying "I'm fine" when you're not. Helping everyone else while you're falling apart.

I thought about who I might be in my next life. Would I even like him? Would I see any of these people again? Would I even play guitar?

The sky above me didn't answer. The trees whispered, and the water rippled at the shore, as if everything was too calm to care about what I was feeling. But I imagined myself lying beneath The Tree with Leah next to me.

Would she miss me?

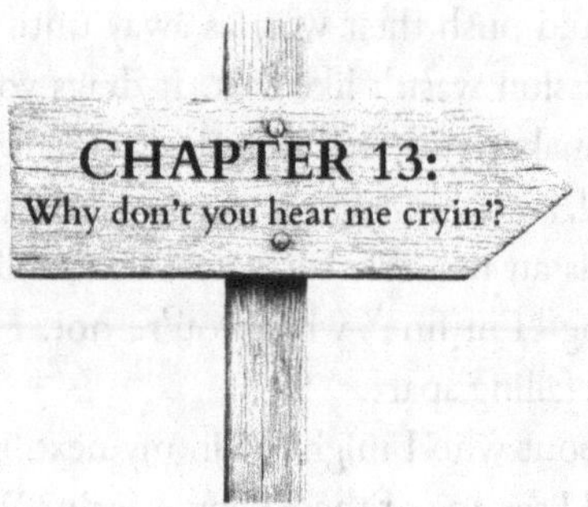

That day I'd spent at the river, I knew I was going to die.

I could've blamed depression, my dad, pressure. Anything, really. But the truth was, this decision wasn't forced on me. It was mine, and mine alone.

I could've blamed Kristie's health too. I'd taken a cab back to the hospital, met them in the cafeteria. Kristie had been ready to go that morning, but they made friends with another couple, and we stayed all day talking. They'd just had a baby, small and perfect, a miracle. It made me think about myself as a baby, but that was a shitty thought. We're all born, and we're all going to die. It's the human version of a one-way ticket to the greatest, most inconvenient show on Earth. And no refunds.

I was about to meet my end, and I was okay with that.

Hayden helped Kristie inside of Winnie. We didn't talk much except when I asked Kristie how she felt.

Kristie smiled, her cheeks flushed. "I'm thankful," she said. If you didn't know her before, you wouldn't guess how sick she was. But I did.

Hayden was Hayden. Cracking jokes, acting like nothing was wrong. He didn't want to believe that the person he loved wouldn't be around forever, and I didn't blame him.

We camped on the riverbank that night. Hayden made a fire. We grilled bratwursts, and music played from Winnie. But the elephant sat between us. I wanted them to acknowledge it, but they didn't. They sang together, and I played Susie, singing along, joining the cast of *Nobody's Fucking Dying*.

I played a tune from the song about The Tree, humming the lyrics, aware they were watching me. I stopped playing. The silence between us stretched. Only the fire crackled.

"Can you guys take me back to Memphis?" I asked.

They both looked at me.

"Memphis?" Hayden asked, disappointment in his voice.

"Yeah," I said.

They were quiet, waiting for me to explain, but I couldn't. I wanted to stay, but I didn't want to watch Kristie get worse. I wanted to leave with the good memories, the ones where everything was still fun songs and happy ziplining screams. You know, the kind of memories that make you feel like you're riding high before life slaps you with a "No Fun Allowed" sign.

And I needed to see Sibby.

Later that night, after they fell asleep, I took the pills from Susie's pocket and walked to the river's edge. Bare feet brushing the cool water, I swirled the pills through my fingers, listening to the quiet sound of finality as they dropped into the river.

Pills . . . this wasn't how I wanted to die.

The next morning on the way back to Memphis, Winnie bounced over the potholes of Highway 61, carrying us to the next marker on the Blues Trail.

Hayden had called ahead to book a recording session for my song at the Delta Blues Museum, but first, we decided to stop at a couple of trail markers on the way there.

Hayden drove while Kristie worked her magic in the tiny kitchen. The comforting sounds of light music swirled around us, a backdrop to the sizzling sounds coming from the stove as she cooked up a corned beef hash recipe she had gotten from a new friend at the hospital.

Margaret guzzled her dish before plopping down for a nap like an overly inflated balloon.

When Kristie handed me a plate, the warmth radiated off it. I dug in, savoring the perfect balance of savory corned beef and crispy, golden potatoes, the richness of the egg yolk breaking as I scooped it up with the rest. The flavors exploded in my mouth. Salty, peppery, with a hint of something tangy from the sauce she had drizzled on top. The potatoes had a satisfying crunch around the edges, soft and creamy on the inside, and the corned beef was tender, almost melting in my mouth. It was everything a good breakfast should be, with a touch of comfort that settled deep in my stomach. I inhaled the meal like it was the first real food I'd eaten in ages, my body and soul desperate for the warmth it provided.

Kristie refilled my plate without a word. I felt guilty for scarfing it down so fast, but the taste was so intoxicating that I couldn't stop. As I chewed, I watched her sipping her coffee slowly, taking her time with each bite, savoring it, as though she was cherishing the very act of eating.

"Are you scared?" I asked quietly.

Kristie paused, her fork hovering near her plate, eyes turning downward as she thought for a moment. She looked up at me, her lips curling into a small, wry smile.

"Of course I am, Braden," she said, her joy fading. "It's my immune system. Catch the wrong thing, and it's over."

"Shouldn't you settle down somewhere then? I mean, life on the road doesn't—"

"But I'm home," she interrupted, her arms spreading wide to gesture around the inside of Winnie, her eyes bright. "Home . . . what could be better for my health?"

I stared at her, trying to understand.

"I love this life, Braden." Her words were soft but resolute. "I would give anything to have more time, but all I have is now. Here, with you and Hayden. Not knowing what's going to happen from one day to the next. That's what's kept me alive so far, hasn't it?"

She took a sip of coffee, staring out the window, her face unreadable, as though she had already made peace with everything.

The road stretched out ahead of us, the music still quietly playing, and Hayden stayed silent, his eyes on the road, his hands steady on the wheel. The world felt small inside of Winnie, and yet, it felt like time was slipping away faster than I could grasp it.

Over the next couple of hours, Kristie worked on a drawing and chatted with Hayden in the front seat while I strummed Susie. I had lyrics and music coming together for a song that made me proud to call myself a musician. The beat was solid, the flow felt effortless, just a voice and an acoustic guitar. All it needed was to be brought to life. So, I strummed and sang it over and over, refining the words, tweaking a few lines, until I knew it was ready.

Kristie took a break from her drawings and whipped up a batch of deep-fried Twinkies in their portable fryer. The oil bubbled loudly, threatening to spill over, but she handled it like a pro. The sweet, greasy scent filled the air, adding a new layer to the experience as we rolled through the countryside.

Our next stop was the Howlin' Wolf, a landmark steeped in musical heritage.

The old town reminded me of Tipton County. Buildings connected, each one a different color. The glass doors of each storefront reflected the golden afternoon light, casting everything in a warm glow. The windows framed the happy faces of locals as Hayden drove by, waving and exchanging southern greetings, "How ya doin'?" as though we were all part of the same big family.

On Main Street, a large mural caught my eye, its vibrant colors depicting scenes of blues musicians who had left their mark on the world. The attached Autograph Wall, painted in a deep blue, invited visitors to leave messages for the Wolf. I couldn't resist, so I took the permanent marker Kristie handed me and wrote: *Why don't you hear me cryin'?*

We wandered over to the statue of Howlin' Wolf, standing tall in the middle of a small green park. The green around me—trees, grass, tall blooming flowers—was so vibrant, almost in contrast with the reverence I felt standing before his likeness. There weren't many tourists here, likely because it wasn't quite summer yet, but the stillness gave me space to reflect, not just on Howlin' Wolf's life, but on my own. His struggles and his rise to fame had brought his music into the world, and I wondered what would happen with my own life if I kept pushing through the pain.

It wasn't about giving up.

It was about knowing when your time had come.

I felt a pang in my chest, an unwilling resistance, but I brushed it off. Just nerves.

At the museum, it felt like I'd stepped back into time. It wasn't as polished as Sun Studio. Pictures, album covers, and paintings of Howlin' Wolf adorned every wall. His hat, his guitars, even the old records were displayed like sacred relics. I grazed my hand over one of his guitars, half-expecting the vibrations of his talent to leap into me.

Kristie moved through the museum, distant in thought. Why did I get to live while someone like her had to accept her fate? My gaze shifted to Hayden. His usual mask of chill had slipped away, replaced by a look that seemed to realize the truth. His favorite person, the one he loved, wouldn't be around much longer.

When we were back on the road, Kristie decided it was her turn to drive. I offered, joking that while I wasn't legally allowed to drink, I did have a driver's license. Still, she insisted on taking the wheel. The open road stretched ahead, somewhere between the music legacy and the reality of our lives, where the past met the present, and the future was still uncertain.

I played a few tunes with Hayden along the way. A distracted gaze took over his face most of the time. I didn't want to push it, so I offered to cook something. The only damn thing I knew how to cook were scrambled eggs and peanut butter and jelly sandwiches.

Gourmet meals? Pfft. I could barely handle the "hot dog and microwave" challenge. I'd have baked some chicken, but the only chicken inside of Winnie was me.

Hayden retreated to the back room, staying there longer than usual. Something in my gut told me he needed space, but I couldn't just leave him alone, not like that.

I knocked before stepping into the room. He was sitting on the edge of the bed, staring down at something in his hands. His shoulders were slumped, and for a brief moment, I saw a side of him I hadn't seen before, a side that wasn't filled with his usual bravado or big smiles.

"Hey," he said, his voice low, almost uncertain.

"Hey."

He handed me a fridge magnet shaped like a fish with "Key West" written on it.

"That was one of our favorite places," Hayden said, his eyes distant. "So easy to find a gig. You could just play on the street, and people would stop and really listen. The best nights were on Duval Street during the heat of summer. I remember laughing so much with people. Everyone was just happy to be there."

I glanced at the magnet, the colors faded and worn from use. "And Kristie?" I asked before I could stop myself. It wasn't just a casual question, and I knew it. It was a question I wasn't ready for, but here I was, asking it anyway.

Hayden nodded slowly, his gaze dropping to the floor. "She got me that souvenir. She said that if things ever got tough, to look at it and remember how beautiful life can be when we stop and embrace the moment. Yeah, if by 'embrace the moment' she meant 'choke down your grief with a side of overpriced trinkets,' then sure."

I looked down at the magnet. I didn't have a memory like that to cling to. The closest thing I had was a trip to Gatlinburg with my family, a night when Trevor and I snuck out to blow all our money at the arcade.

"It's fucked up, isn't it?" Hayden asked, now looking directly at me. His voice cracked slightly, and I knew he was trying to hold himself together. "I keep trying to make sense of it. Keep telling myself this isn't real. But the more time passes, the less we can do . . . Kristie keeps getting weaker."

I stood there as he turned away from me, his shoulders shaking. His weeping filled the room, and my heart tightened. I didn't know what to do, so I just stood there, unsure if I should stay or leave.

Then, instinctively, I walked over and sat beside him, placing a hand on his shoulder. He didn't pull away. Instead, he placed his hand over mine. After a few sniffles, he forced out a weak laugh, shaking his head like he was embarrassed by his own breakdown.

When he looked up, I wiped the tears from his face, my thumb grazing his cheek. For a long moment, we stared at each other . . . too close for just friendship.

Something unexpected stirred in me, a warmth I couldn't name, pulling me in. His vulnerability mirrored something inside me, something I hadn't allowed myself to feel before.

I leaned forward, drawn closer by an unfamiliar longing, and the closer we got, the more I realized how much I cared about him . . . more than I thought I should. My heartbeat picked up, rapid and insistent, and I jerked back, the distance suddenly insurmountable. I stared at the floor, trying to anchor myself.

I wasn't sure what this meant. Was it attraction? Curiosity? Or just empathy twisted into something else? My mind raced with questions. Who am I? What does this make me? Maybe I wasn't thinking straight. Maybe I was letting the moment fool me. But part of me couldn't ignore the pull, no matter how hard I tried.

We both sat there in silence for a long moment, unsure of what had just passed between us. Then, without another word, we both rose from the bed and made our way out of the room. Hayden was back to his usual self as we joined Kristie in the front. He gleamed and grabbed the plate of peanut butter and jelly sandwiches I made.

"Strawberry jelly's my favorite," he announced, trying to make the moment feel normal again.

I passed the time fine-tuning my song, pushing thoughts of Hayden and that moment we shared to the back of my mind. By the time we arrived at the Delta Blues Museum, anticipation was building in my chest like a storm on the verge of breaking.

The museum loomed ahead, a solid structure of red brick, standing proudly amidst the sweltering southern heat. The air was thick with humidity, making the evening feel heavy as we approached the entrance. Small buildings clustered around it like an intimate little village, each a piece of history itself. The museum, though, held the strength of decades of music, sweat, and soul that had poured out of the Delta and into the world.

I followed a well-seasoned gentleman inside, my nerves tingling with excitement and fear as he led me through a narrow hallway. The musty scent of old wood mixed with the earthy tang of the Mississippi air clung to everything. When we reached a small, dimly lit recording room, I felt an unfamiliar lump in my throat. This wasn't just any recording space. It was a room that had held the voices of legends.

I held Susie close, my guitar, my lifeline. She felt heavier in my hands now, but it wasn't the weight of the instrument. It was the weight of what this moment meant.

The gentleman explained the setup, his voice almost drowned out by the sound of my heartbeat. My body was basically a malfunctioning bass drum. Perfect for making sure everyone knows I'm terrified. I nodded along, but all I could focus on was the space—its old wooden floors, the gleam of polished microphones, and the equipment that would soon capture my vocals. He gestured to the chair near the mic, and as I sat down, a fresh wave of nerves washed over me. I was going to record my first song here, in this legendary place.

When he gave me the thumbs up, everything fell silent, and I closed my eyes, bracing myself for what came next.

I strummed the first chords, feeling the room fill with sound. It was just me, Susie, and the words I'd written. I wasn't thinking about the people outside of the room, about Kristie and Hayden, about my past. All I could think about was this moment.

I closed my eyes, lifting my head toward the microphone. Images flashed before my eyes, one after another. Scotty laughing too loud at The Tree, Rachelle's voice cracking on a high note in choir, Sara's studying eyes, and Leah, the one who I let slip away. These memories swirled in my head, blurring as I sang.

"There are times when music fades,
Times when it plays at full blast.
What I learned through it all,
Is that these sounds never last."

The room felt so still, yet I was surrounded by the impact of history. Music that had once been born in these very lands now reverberated in my own song.

"You might think you see it coming,
But it's just a mirage,
Another trick in this world,
A melting collage."

I strummed harder now, closing my eyes, letting the words take me away.

"Let me take you to a place,
Where the world stops for as long as you do.
Where love can't break you into two.
A place where time ceases to exist and all that matters is this.
Let me take you to a place . . . a place called The Tree."

The emotion crept in, warm and overwhelming. I could feel the tears rising, but I held them back.

"For all the memories made,
And all that will come,
I know one thing for sure,

My time in this mirror is done.
Yours should be, too,
Because all that counts is now.
Come with me to The Tree,
And take your well-deserved bow.
Here, you matter.
Here you are seen.
Here, you are worthy.
Here you are clean.
Let me take you to a place where the world stops for as long as you do.
Where love can't break you into two.
A place where time ceases to exist, and all that matters is this.
Let me take you to a place . . . a place called The Tree."

The final chord rang out, and I opened my eyes. Hayden and Kristie were sitting in the control room, their faces lit by the glow of the console, clapping. But the sound didn't reach me right away. The silence between the last note and their applause felt longer than any quiet I'd ever known.

I froze for a heartbeat, lungs burning, heart hammering, as a tidal wave of emotions crashed through me. The song had ripped open something unguarded inside, a spark of truth I hadn't dared to meet before, and now it hit me full force, leaving me exposed and trembling.

I closed my eyes again, and for a brief, impossible moment, I wished I could go back. To The Tree. To the days when things felt simple and full of possibility. But the past was gone, and with it, so were the people I wished I could've saved.

I opened my eyes and allowed myself a small smile. I was here, in this moment. With Hayden, with Kristie, in the heart of the Delta Blues. I could feel the pulse of the land around me, a reminder that even though the past had slipped away, I was still here. My music was still here. My story was still unfolding.

Later, Hayden took me on a tour of the museum. We moved

slowly through the displays, my hand grazing the glass that protected legendary guitars, jackets worn by the greats, and the sculptures of artists who had shaped the very world I now existed in. Their legacy hung in the air, a constant reminder of the lives lived through music. As I read the plaques beside their exhibits, I thought about the question that lingered in my mind. *How do I want to be remembered?*

An hour later, the man who had recorded my song handed me a small flash drive.

"It's all yours," he said.

I looked down at the label: "Braden, a blues trailblazer." Pride and sorrow swelled in my chest as I gripped the flash drive, knowing it was more than just a piece of technology. It was a part of me, now preserved forever in the heart of the Delta.

And for the first time, I felt like I had a story, too.

As we hit the road again, I sat at the little table in Winnie, watching the scenery blur as Hayden and Kristie drove. I'd asked them to stop at the nearest post office.

I stared at the blank piece of paper in front of me, pen in hand. This was the letter I'd been avoiding, the one where I had to face a truth I didn't want to accept.

A quote from Grandpa Norris popped into my head: "In a time of deceit, telling the truth is a revolutionary act," George Orwell once said.

I took a deep breath and began to write.

Dear Mom,

In no way did I want to hurt you with what you probably know by the time you read this. I'm not scared. I'm just in a lot of pain and I don't know how to carry it anymore. It's nothing you did. You did every-thing in love and I know that. You did things you didn't have to do and, knowing what I know now, I see you in an even brighter light than I ever have. I only wish I'd heard the truth from you.

I didn't deserve your love. Dad didn't deserve your love. Really, only Trevor deserves your love and he can be a little shit sometimes, but at least he doesn't go around telling lies and cheating people out of a life they dreamed of.

I'm sorry I couldn't make your dream life happen and I'm sorry for being so difficult.

I didn't know what was going on with me, but now a lot of things make sense. A lot of my questions have been answered and you don't have to live a lie anymore. You can finally be free, too.

I forgive dad. I forgive the whole family for keeping this secret. I hope you can, too.

I guess life wasn't too easy on either you or dad. I was stupid to expect you guys to have life figured out just because you two are my heroes. Sometimes heroes lose their kryptonite.

I won't tell you to forgive dad for cheating on you. I just hope you do.

I will tell you to forgive me though. I need you to forgive me.

Your son,

Braden

I pushed open the post office door, trembling as I placed the letters—one to Scotty, Trevor, my dad, two to my mom, and three to Leah—on the counter.

I slapped stamps on each letter. The woman behind the counter took them, moving them swiftly to the bar behind her.

There they go.

All my letters in Mississippi.

I thought this would feel like relief, but as I watched the letters disappear into the room behind her, all I felt was numbness.

Would they remember me? Scotty, as the friend who failed him? My mom, as the son who kept making her cry? My dad, as the son who reminded him of everything he couldn't fix?

And Leah . . . would she see me as someone who cared, or just the coward who ran?

I stared at the door behind the counter, hoping the letters would come back, hoping the answers would come back with them. But they didn't.

Hayden and Kristie didn't say much during the drive, the air between us thick with unspoken words. As we neared Tennessee, I could feel my time in Mississippi was coming to a close. The road stretched on, but the sense of finality seemed to grow with every passing mile.

We pulled off by the river. The stillness of the water in the moonlight should've relaxed me, but it didn't. I lay restless in bed, staring at the sliver of moon outside the window. My mind kept drifting back to the letters I'd written, who I'd written them for. I'd hoped that by sealing them, I'd finally find some peace. But instead, the words on paper only deepened the ache inside.

I thought avoiding it would keep my mind off Leah, but my hand drifted down my pants as I lay in bed, staring out the window beside me. I hadn't relieved myself since that night with Leah, the first time we'd had sex. I thought about her body as I touched myself. I remembered what her kiss tasted like and how her hair smelled like cashmere when she rested her head against my shoulder. But what turned me on the most was her laugh. I could listen to that laugh forever. I imagined what our life together would've been like. We'd have passionate sex often enough to keep it wild and alive. We would've gone to college together, gotten married, traveled to all the places we ever dreamed of seeing, maybe had a couple kids. Honestly, we would've done whatever made Leah happy. I would've kissed her lips as many times as I could. I would've told her I loved her until I was sure she knew it.

Then I came.

I came with a smile on my face, the tension that had been building for days finally easing. Not long after, sleep took over, the deepest rest I'd had since leaving Tipton County.

"Are we going to see you again?" Hayden's voice broke the silence as Kristie drove through Memphis, uncertainty in his eyes.

"We should do one more show before you leave," Kristie said, almost pleading.

I met their eyes with gratitude, but they saw through it. "Thanks, but I really need to take care of some things." Even as I said it, it felt like betrayal, but they needed to hear it. I needed closure.

I grabbed Susie and stepped out of Winnie, a sigh escaping as I patted its side, watching flakes of paint flutter away. It felt like saying goodbye to more than just a vehicle. It was goodbye to a chapter of my life, the road that had brought me here, to this moment.

Kristie appeared around the corner, her footsteps light. She gazed with quiet fondness, hands on my shoulders as she searched my face. "I'm so glad Hayden found you," she whispered. Her sincerity made the thought of missing her hurt more.

Before I could speak, she hugged me tightly, as if trying to hold me together. I squeezed back, feeling the rawness of everything I was leaving behind.

"We'll miss you," Hayden said, holding Margaret. He patted my back, and for a second, I remembered that quiet moment we shared.

I turned to him, fighting the lump in my throat, and pulled him into a tight embrace. The hug lingered a moment too long, as if holding onto the connection we'd forged. When we pulled away, his grin was forced, a shadow of the real thing. I gave the top of Margaret's bobbing head a pet and said goodbye.

"Call if you change your mind," Kristie said. "We'll be in Knoxville, not far."

I nodded, my throat tight, afraid to speak. They climbed into Winnie, Hayden at the wheel. The loud honk pierced the air.

I watched them drive away, my heart filled with gratitude and regret. What had I done to deserve people like them? I pushed the thought aside, focusing on the house ahead.

Sibby was waiting for me on the porch, her eyes wide, searching for something in mine.

I took a steadying breath as I approached, each step heavier than the last, my mind racing.

I finally stopped in front of her, the silence between us unbearable. Her face was calm, but there was something in the way she stood, a quiet readiness, as if she knew what was coming. She didn't speak, just watched me, her hands resting at her sides.

"Hey, Sibby," I said.

It took a moment for the meaning behind her gaze to sink in. Time stretched, and suddenly everything became clear . . . memories of my childhood, flashes of my mom's love, things I hadn't realized I'd missed. My world was unraveling.

I stared at Sibby, her green eyes staring back at me. Those eyes . . . not my mom's, not my dad's, but hers. And in that moment, I understood. The truth had been here all along, buried deep, hidden in plain sight.

I swallowed, the gravity of my words anchoring me in place. "The baby you gave up . . . it was me."

CHAPTER 14:
It's All Over Now, Braden Blue

G reen.

Green surrounded me as I walked the Wolf River Greenway, the trail barely a whisper beneath my shoes. It had been over an hour of walking. The sky was the deep blue of evening, and the vibrant green grass shimmered in its light, but the beauty felt far away, muted, like something that once mattered but no longer did. It was as though a gray fog hovered just beyond my reach, clouding everything, dragging my mind back to Sibby's words.

Earlier that day, after Hayden and Kristie had driven away, I was left standing in front of Sibby. I'd told her the truth. But she didn't speak. She had only nodded, holding her car keys like a shield. We drove in silence, the sound of the engine filling the space between us. She parked near Beale Street.

I slung Susie over my shoulder and stepped out of the car.

We walked in silence, the neon glow of Beale Street flickering above us. We passed the giant blue sign arching over the street, the music blending with the clattering of the sidewalk beneath our feet. The energy of the place swirled around us, but I felt none of it. We were walking, yes, but it felt like we were standing still, caught in a moment we couldn't escape.

We stopped at the Hard Rock Café corner, waiting for the signal. The tension was thick, neither of us moving, eyes darting, unwilling to face the storm between us.

The horse-drawn carriage trotted by, the sound of hooves thudding off the concrete. The signal flicked green, and we crossed the street, the faint smell of exhaust mixing with something sweeter in the air. The city was alive around us, but our silence felt like a wall, solid and unbreakable.

B.B. King's Blues Club loomed ahead, neon lights glowing. Inside, the smell of greasy, smoky food overwhelmed me. Paintings of blues legends filled the walls. I inhaled, the warmth sinking into my bones.

A waitress with bright blonde hair ushered us to a yellow-painted table, her smile wide but strained. She handed us menus, and I scanned mine absently. The sound of sizzling food drifted from the kitchen, and the air buzzed with conversation, laughter, and the occasional clink of glasses. Everything here was loud, vibrant, alive, except for us.

Sibby's eyes flicked to the menu as she ordered the chicken fried chicken. Her voice sounded steady, but the undercurrent of sorrow she carried seeped through. I ordered a Catfish Po' Boy, never having had catfish before. I was too distracted by everything else to care about the food.

We were stuck in the moment, each second heavier than the last.

"It was eighteen years ago," Sibby said, her voice steady.

I met her gaze. The truth was here, and I had no choice but to face it.

"Your grandparents were vacationing in Mississippi the summer before my senior year of high school," she continued. "Your parents had been dating for a year, so Robert and Angela let your mom come along, too."

The waitress returned with our drinks. Sibby's sweet tea and my Dr Pepper. I downed a big sip, the cold burn of the soda grounding me in the present.

Sibby took a slow sip of her tea, her fingers trembling ever so slightly as she set the glass down. Her eyes met mine again. "My parents are regulars at the American Legion. That's where I met your parents and your grandparents. Your grandmother, Angela, gave me her number in case I ever wanted to take singing lessons with her. She was a heck of a singer. Trish and I hit it off immediately. We spent the evening singing karaoke together."

She paused, gathering herself before going on.

"They all went back to Indiana, but Trish and I stayed in touch. We called each other every day. She was someone I confided in. I ended up having a fight with my parents about Frederick. I called them racist and left for Indiana." Her voice wavered under the burden of that choice. "Trish offered me a place to stay. Your dad was nineteen, already with an apartment near the university, so we all made plans to hang out there. Trish was working at a restaurant, so your dad and I waited for her to get off her shift." She sighed. "That night . . . everything changed. Your dad and I drank. We got drunk. We made a choice we never should've made."

I clenched my jaw, forcing myself to stay still, to listen.

Sibby stared at the table, her fingers fidgeting with the napkin.

"When I found out I was pregnant, I didn't know what to do. I told my parents, but they literally threw me out on the street. That's when I called your grandmother, Angela, and she took me in. Your grandparents didn't hesitate. Trish tried reaching out. She said your dad told her about what happened, and she hated me for it. A few months later, she called again. She had forgiven him, forgiven me . . . on one condition." Sibby's voice cracked, and she wiped a tear away as she looked at me. "She said I had to give you up to them."

I felt my chest tighten. This wasn't just the past anymore. It was me, my life, my family, torn apart in the span of a few selfish decisions.

Sibby swallowed hard, her breath shaky now. "I didn't want to. The last thing I wanted was to give you up. I hung up on her, but the thought kept gnawing at me. The idea of you being with your dad, in a family that could stay together. I didn't want you to grow up without that."

Her gaze filled with sorrow. "Your grandparents, Robert and Angela . . . they told me to think long and hard. I was freshly eighteen, Braden. I was too scared to make the wrong choice. I didn't think I could do it alone. So, I signed the papers. After you were born, I held you. I kept telling myself it was the right choice, but I knew . . . I knew I was letting you go."

She took a breath, her voice trembling as she continued. "I visited you often. I even thought about taking you back. But Trish cut me off when I brought up that idea. I couldn't handle the pain, so I moved here away from family, away from everything that reminded me of my past."

Sibby's words hung in the air. I opened my mouth, but nothing came out. The truth stung and I didn't know what to say anymore.

Her hand trembled as she wiped the tears from her cheek. Neither of us moved for a long moment.

I returned to the present, walking the Greenway path in the warm evening light. A couple passed me, hands entwined, their fingers laced together like they didn't want to forget the connection they shared. I noticed how natural it seemed for them, the easy way they moved through the world together. Maybe life wasn't all fairytales, but sometimes I wondered if I could've had just a fraction of that peace. I wasn't stupid. I knew challenges were part of life. I could overcome anything. But the gray fog that trailed above me made everything else feel like a lie. No matter what I looked at, no matter what I did, it all felt tainted. The beauty around me—the quiet of the Greenway, the gentleness of the trees—seemed distant, like it wasn't meant for me.

I walked deeper into the Greenway, eyes tracing the trees around me. The colors were beautiful. Each leaf a mix of deep green and fresh light green, veins tracing the seasons. The sun was sinking lower now, casting a soft orange-pink glow across the horizon, and for a moment, it almost took my breath away. I could see it, sure, but I couldn't feel it. Not the way I used to. Like a beautiful painting under a layer of glass that kept me from touching it. I used to let the sunset calm me, let it pull a smile from me, reminding me there was something bigger than all of this, something greater than the mess of my life.

But now, I wondered if I had a place there, or if I was too broken for that, too.

I thought about the cross tattoo on my shoulder. The mark of a faith I used to trust without question. Church every Sunday, my mom singing in the choir, me sitting there, believing in the afterlife, in something greater than myself. I used to see the sunset as a sign that something was waiting for me. But now, I wasn't so sure. Was there room for someone like me up there?

I thought about Sibby again. Sitting across from her at B.B. King's. The catfish sandwich I had was surprisingly good, its wild, rich flavor dancing on my tongue. But as I chewed, I realized that the taste of the food was the only thing that really grounded me to the moment. Everything else seemed so . . . disconnected. Sibby talked about what she'd done since moving to Memphis—getting her nursing license, working, even baking cakes and cupcakes on the side. She was doing what she could to stay busy, to move on. She'd made a life for herself, but I could tell it wasn't enough to fill the space I should've occupied. Every day, every decision she made, reminded her of what she'd lost, what she'd given up. It was there in her eyes, in the way her words came slow, weighed down by regret.

After leaving the restaurant, I noticed the pink in her cheeks as we strolled down Beale Street.

"I hadn't dated much since Frederick," Sibby said, biting into her bundt cake. "He asked me out a couple times, but nothing ever went anywhere. Not because of him, but because of me. I never wanted to end up in a situation where I'd have to give up another child."

I paused, taking a bite of my cake. "But he wanted to raise me as his own."

"I know. But it wouldn't have been fair. You had a father who wanted you."

People walked by, laughing, window shopping, while music spilled from every bar and shop on the street. It surrounded us, alive and real.

"For what it's worth," I said. "I'm proud to be your son."

Sibby slowed her steps. Her shoulders straightened, and she pressed both hands lightly to her chest, as if holding her heart in place. Her lips parted, but no sound came out. The noise of Beale Street seemed to fade, leaving just the two of us in a quiet bubble. She blinked rapidly, then looked down, her fingers twisting a strand of hair while a small smile formed. For a long moment, she didn't move, as if she were savoring the feeling, letting it settle in her chest.

We passed Alfred's, then Dyer's Burgers, making our way back across the street. Sibby had gone quiet. I knew she'd said everything she needed to say. Or everything she thought I deserved to hear.

"Thank you," I said, unsure of what I was really thanking her for. Maybe for her sacrifice. Maybe for her truth.

I pulled the flash drive from my pocket and handed it to her.

Sibby stopped walking. "What's this?"

"This is for you. Listen to it when you're feeling down. It'll help."

She took it slowly and looked at me for a long time, her gaze burning with sincerity. "I would've done anything for you, Braden. That hasn't changed."

The way her eyes melted into mine told me she meant it.

I felt that.

The stone path chilled underfoot as I neared the red Wolf River Bridge. The air smelled of damp earth and crisp leaves, like the world was holding its breath. A cyclist in purple zipped past, a fleeting blur.

With each step, the bridge loomed higher, the world below shrinking. The metal groaned beneath my shoes. At the center, I stopped, staring at the dark, swirling water. I'd never felt so small.

The river moved with a slow rhythm. I could almost hear it whisper, urging me to let go. The breeze carried something haunting, something lost. The thoughts weren't mine anymore. They were a dark voice, a pull, gravity shifting, dragging me to the edge.

I stared into the black depths below, imagining the cold embrace of the water as it swallowed me whole. When Hayden and Kristie had taken me ziplining, I'd been terrified, my heart slamming in my chest as I soared high above. But this . . . this was different. There was no thrill here, no release. It was quiet. Solitary. The drop felt certain. The water below promised escape. I thought about floating downstream, the weight of my body taken by the current, forgotten, as if I never existed.

It had to be here. This bridge. This river. Not exactly where Jeff Buckley was found, but close enough. Close enough to disappear. They called it Wolf River. Ghost River. Maybe because it never stopped moving, never let itself be understood. I liked to think it carried spirits with it. That even if I wasn't welcome in the afterlife, I could float, unseen but free.

I gently set Susie against the red railing and pulled out the notepad and pen from my back pocket. I thought I'd said everything I needed to say when I wrote to my mom, but there was one more person who deserved the truth.

The railing was wide enough to rest the notepad on, and I began writing. The words came slowly, each one heavier than the last.

Trevor,

I know I said I wouldn't kill myself, but I have

enough respect for you to tell you the whole truth. The truth is that I have been thinking about killing myself for years now. What started as just some curious thoughts, grew into something that felt good the more I thought about it. I thought about how. Pills. I tried that. Didn't work. Only made things worse. I'm too chicken shit for a gun. I'm too chicken shit for a lot of things, but I don't want to go out a coward. It's funny, you know. Leaving like this is selfish and cowardly. I just don't know what else to do. I don't want to be tortured like this every day for the rest of my life. I can't imagine a life like that and I really don't want to stick around and make everyone else's lives more miserable. I mean, I already know what it's like to be the designated party pooper. I'm not trying to level up.

I knew it had to get done eventually. Now is the time. I'm sorry, Trevor. Whoever finds this will know to give it to you. Just know that I'm not in pain anymore and I really hope you choose not to live in pain either. Please don't miss me. Just remember the good times. Maybe my next time around won't be as painful and maybe my head won't be so fucked up. Maybe I won't fuck up other people's lives either and maybe I will be able to see the colors in the sky again and mean it when I smile.

Sorry, Trevor. I love you, little brother.

And hey . . . be nice to mom and dad. They love you, you know?

Braden

I folded the letter and tucked it into Susie's pocket along with the pen and notepad, zipping it up tight. My hand lingered, pressing against the fabric. The burn in my throat rose to my eyes, pressure building until it threatened to break me.

It was graduation day at Tipton High. Leah and my friends would be celebrating, posing for pictures, laughing about the future. I should've been there. I wanted to be proud of them.

Alone, I let myself cry. First slow, then faster, like the river rushing below. I glanced over the railing. From here, the water seemed closer than it was. Calm, deceptive, unknowable. The fall might not kill me. But I needed it to knock me out. Once I hit the bottom, I'd let the air leave my lungs and just . . . stay. Slow, but peaceful.

"My pain will soon be over," I whispered, clutching my shoulder where the cross tattoo marked my skin. It wasn't a prayer . . . just an echo of emptiness. My tears fell freely, vanishing into the water below.

I climbed onto the guardrail, my knee wobbling while my yellow-and-red polka dot tie flapped in the wind. My arms shook, chest tightening. I couldn't look down. Couldn't look up. My pulse thundered louder than distant traffic, louder than rustling trees. I waited for my breathing to slow, just enough to bring my other leg up, straddling the railing.

I scanned the bridge. Nobody was there.

I was alone.

Every instinct screamed to stop, to climb back over. But why? I'd searched for reasons. None made sense.

Tears blurred my vision, spilling over faster than I could blink them back. I tightened my grip on the railing, my knuckles whitening.

This knot in my gut . . . it wasn't the truth I'd uncovered, or the memories I'd relived, or the goodbyes I'd written. It wasn't the family I'd found or the adventures I'd had.

It was fear.

I was scared.

But fear wouldn't stop me. Not this time.

The air felt heavier as I tried to breathe, the pressure pushing me toward the edge. My legs shook so hard I wasn't sure I'd make it, but I slowly balanced myself, the railing unsteady beneath my shoes.

The river stretched ahead, a path into eternity, framed by towering trees. Gold bled into pink, fading into blue. Beautiful. But not to me.

I thought maybe, in this moment, I'd finally feel something. Relief. Clarity. A flicker of joy or peace. But all I felt was the same crushing emptiness.

I turned facing the bridge, holding onto the railing.

I closed my eyes.

The tune of Bob Dylan's "It's All Over Now, Baby Blue" played in my head. I wanted it to be the last thing I heard. A quiet farewell.

Then I let go.

The wind ripped past me as my feet left the bridge, and for a moment, everything was weightless. But the second my body tipped backward, instinct roared to life. My hands shot out, gripping the lower railing tight. My eyes flew open, the world spinning around me as my palms slipped against the metal.

And then I saw it.

Directly in front of me, taped to the opposite side of the bridge, was my face staring back at me.

MISSING: BRADEN GREGORY

In those fleeting seconds, I saw more than a flyer. I saw me. Trevor laughing, teasing me about music videos. My dad. The tension in his face, then warmth when we made peace. My mom's proud face at my wrestling matches. Leah at The Tree, her face content as she read my letter.

I wasn't Blake. I wasn't invisible. I was *Braden Gregory.*

My grip gave out.

Silence.

Then impact.

The river hit like concrete, stealing my breath. Cold stabbed into every inch of me.

Regret hit harder than the water, sharper than any pain I'd known. I didn't want to die. I wanted to live. I *needed* to live.

I kicked. Clawed. My arms sliced through the water in frantic bursts. The current dragged me deeper, my lungs burning. Please, no. Let me go back.

I wanted to rewind to every ignored lifeline, every moment I believed the pain was unbeatable. I tried to scream, but only swallowed the river.

I kept fighting. My legs burned as they kicked against the force of the water. My arms swung in wide arcs, clawing at nothing, pushing the river away with every ounce of strength I had left. The murky water swallowed me whole, clouding my vision, stealing my breath, but I *fought*.

The surface was closer now. I saw the light flickering above me. I reached for it, my body moving on sheer willpower.

I broke through.

Air hit like fire, searing my throat. I gasped, coughing up water in violent bursts.

I sank again, my limbs too weak to keep me afloat, but I wouldn't stop.

Not like this.

I kicked harder, forcing my way back to the surface. My lungs burned as I inhaled another gulp of air, choking on more water. My arms flailed, desperate to keep my head above the river. I coughed and gagged, my throat raw, my body trembling.

My hand hit mud.

I clawed forward, trembling.

The shore came into view, a blur of green and brown through stinging eyes. I dug my hands into the muck, pulling myself inch by inch until my chest hit grass.

I collapsed.

I rolled onto my side and retched, water and bile spilling from my mouth. The catfish sandwich I'd eaten earlier came up with it, its rancid stench like rotting flesh in the summer heat. My stomach clenched violently, and I gagged again, the smell sticking in my nose as I tried to breathe.

I pushed myself to all fours, my body trembling, my heart hammering so hard it felt like it would tear through my ribs. My vision swam. The world tilted.

The stench forced more vomit up, violent and unrelenting, until I dry-heaved. When it finally stopped, I rolled to the other side, away from the mess, and collapsed onto my back.

I couldn't stop crying. The tears came in waves, hot and unending, streaming down my face, mixing with the cold river water on my skin.

My hands clenched into weak fists, trembling with exhaustion and fury. I punched the ground beside me, the earth dulling the impact but not the ache in my knuckles. Over and over, I pounded the ground, as if I could beat the chaos out of me.

I didn't know what I wanted anymore. My body screamed for rest, but my mind raced, torn between the relief of surviving and the crushing weight of everything else. What I wanted and what I needed blurred together into a storm of frustration and anger.

Regret bled through me.

Regret for jumping.

Regret for wanting to die.

Regret for everything I'd have to face now that I hadn't.

It all came crashing together. The fear, guilt, gratitude, and something darker, something that wouldn't even name itself. They tangled inside me until I couldn't tell one from the other, only that I was still here to feel them all.

Pain rippled through my body in waves, each stronger than the last. My arms throbbed, the muscles burning like they were tearing from the bones beneath. My legs felt like they were on fire, roasting me from the inside out with every twitch, every spasm. My chest felt ready to explode, and my head pounded with a blinding, rhythmic ache.

I let out a guttural scream into the damp air. It wasn't enough, but it was all I had left.

I was alive. Should I be? Would I try again? Regret this tomorrow? What now? Who would care?

"I do," I rasped, the words scraping past my raw throat, torn from me like shrapnel.

"I do," I choked out, coughing until water burned up my throat. I curled to my side, shaking, forcing myself onto all fours. My arms buckled under the strain.

Nobody else had given up on me. Not my mom, not Leah, not even Sibby. Sibby, who thought she was helping, even when it hurt. The truth slammed into me. I was the only one who had given up. I was the one who listened to that voice in my head, the one that told me I wasn't enough, that the world was better without me.

I was supposed to be my own hero.

"Fuck!" I screamed, the word splitting the silence. My voice cracked, breaking into a sob. I pounded the ground, rocks tearing my knuckles raw. Blood smeared the dirt, but I didn't stop.

"Fuck! Fuck! Fuck!" I crumpled, face in my palms, body shaking with sobs.

When the tears slowed, I groaned, pushing myself up. My knees ached. My body sagged. I tilted my head back, eyes hazy with tears and river sting, watching the sunset bleed through the clouds.

I shook my head, exhaling, surrendering to the moment. My gaze still fixed above.

The depression loomed over me, an invisible yet all-encompassing presence. Its voice slithered into my mind like poison. "You are worthless."

I closed my eyes, the temptation to believe it pressing down on me like a tidal wave. But I resisted.

"I disagree." My voice steadier as I opened my eyes. "You are not bigger than me," I said. It was barely audible, but it was mine.

My arms dropped to my sides, trembling, weak, but not defeated.

The depression shifted, circling like a predator that had lost its footing. "Who do you think you are?"

"I get to play *you*," I said, pointing a shaky finger toward the void it occupied. "You don't get to play me."

The depression sneered, dark and venomous. "We are one."

"No," I snapped. "You don't get to define me. You are nothing more than something that needs to be managed. You're nothing more than a string on my guitar."

It tried again, its voice quieter now but still insistent. "I will always be here."

I breathed deep, fighting the knot in my chest. My eyes flickered open, recalibrating. "I'm here." Another shaky inhale. "I'm *here*."

I jabbed my finger toward the depression. "You are *there*." Then I pressed my hand to my chest, feeling the frantic rhythm of my own heart. "But I am *here*."

For the first time, the weight of its presence began to lift. Its voice dulled, its hold faltered.

I was no longer just fighting to survive. I was fighting to live. To believe in myself. To reclaim what was mine.

The depression might always linger, but it wasn't *me*.

And it never would be.

Six months later, I sat on my bed at Hillman's house, a letter in my lap. It then traveled with me from Tipton County to Mississippi. My hands fidgeted as the miles passed, my nerves tightening the closer I drove to my destination.

It's been six months since I walked out of the Wolf River. I wish I could say everything had changed, that I was completely transformed and all my problems had vanished. But life doesn't work that way, and I didn't expect it to. What I told my depression that day still held true. It was something I had to manage, not something that defined me.

Depression loomed like an inescapable shadow, but I saw it for what it was—just a small, tangled part of me. I shrank it down, put it in its place. I was always bigger than it. It just took me too long to realize.

After crawling out of the Wolf River, I spent my last gig money on buses to Tipton County. I walked the rest. With nothing but the clothes on my back and Susie over my shoulder, I knocked on Hillman's door. He didn't ask questions. He just fed me and gave me a bed.

He promised not to tell anyone where I was, on one condition: that as an adult, I'd be the one to tell the people who deserved to know.

I called Grandpa Norris first. Relief filled his voice. He was proud I'd stopped living life backward. Next, I called Trevor. If phones could strangle people, Trevor's would've tried. He cussed me out, then softened, promising not to tell, not even our parents.

But a promise was a promise. Hillman had given me a second chance, and it was time to step up.

A few days later, I dialed my parents. The conversation started with shouting. My mom's voice cracking between fear and joy, my dad's just a low, steady rumble. But when they quieted, we agreed to take things one phone call at a time. They were learning how to meet me halfway rather than pulling me toward their expectations.

On the next call, I told them I knew about Sibby. The silence on the other end was deafening. My dad finally took over, his voice low, careful, and apologetic. Man to man, we talked.

My dad apologized, explained, but never excused. He admitted his mistake, and made sure I knew I wasn't one. He told me he stopped drinking after that night with Sibby. He woke up the next morning and confessed everything to my mom that same day, and promised her he wouldn't touch beer or liquor again. And, to his credit, he never did. I mean, I've seen him stare down a cold beer at a BBQ and he just walked away.

In a phone call with my mom, she told me how she forgave him, even though it wasn't exactly the *cool* thing to do after someone cheats on you. I'm still impressed. When Sibby had called to tell them she was pregnant, my mom said there was no doubt in her mind that they were meant to have me. She called me and Trevor her greatest blessing. Though, she did admit to stressing about Sibby possibly wanting me back. Then Trevor got diagnosed with diabetes, and my mom was convinced the universe was trying to take her two greatest gifts away from her.

A few phone calls later, we agreed to meet with a counselor. She was awesome. Fifty and with the energy of a sugar-high teenager. She bounced in her seat at every breakthrough, fist pumping the air. I half expected her to break into a motivational speech, but hey, it worked.

My parents didn't insist on me coming home right away. They respected that I needed time and were grateful to Hillman for offering me refuge.

The first time I saw Trevor again was in the parking lot after a therapy session. He squeezed me and cried, then without missing a beat, punched my shoulder so hard I wondered if my arm was still attached. "Fuck off," he choked out. Classic Trevor. If emotional breakthroughs had a mascot, it'd be him.

That letter from the Wolf River bridge? Never mailed it. I pulled it from Susie's pocket, tossed it into the water, and watched it float away. Maybe, just maybe, Jeff Buckley would turn it into a song on the other side.

Maybe one day I'll tell Trevor about what I did. Not today, though. For now, it was enough that my parents, Hillman, and this wickedly cool counselor knew about my plunge into the Wolf River.

The day I told my parents, my mom brought her hand to her mouth and started crying. Big, messy tears. But I had to tell her. I had to be honest if there was going to be any real healing. She deserved to know that I'd been at the edge, that I'd fought my way back, and that I was strong enough to walk away from it all.

My parents screwed up, don't get me started, but they got plenty right, too. I hated admitting it, but they did the best they could.

The drive back to Mississippi felt like the final thread between my past and present. I'd spent years running away from my family, my depression, myself. But for the first time, I wasn't running away. I was heading somewhere.

I tapped the letter in my lap, my reminder of why I was here. Susie rested across the back seat, uncased and ready, like even she knew this was an important trip. Before leaving, I told Hillman I'd be back in a few days, packed up my purple minivan with Susie and an actual change of clothes, and set off, feeling lighter than I had in a long time.

The stack of burnt CDs sat untouched. Usually, music filled the silence, but today, anticipation did. The memories of my past visit to Mississippi surfaced now and then, but they no longer pressed down on me like they once had. This wasn't about revisiting pain. It was about moving forward, both for me and for Hayden.

Hayden had been there when I couldn't see a way out, and now I had the chance to return the favor. That thought kept my focus steady, even as the gravel road stretched out before me.

I slowed as the Mississippi River sparkled under the sun, welcoming me back with a clean slate. The navigation ended, and I eased the car into the grass, parking under the shade of a tree. Hayden wasn't in sight yet, so I took the moment to breathe and gather myself.

I glanced down at the letter in my lap and unfolded it, reading the words once more. This time, they didn't feel heavy. They felt like a promise, a reminder of how far I'd come and how much farther I could go.

Hey there, Braden! Hayden here. Greetings from Mississippi. I hope this letter finds you well.

It's been a long six months without you, but we've managed. Kristie and I have traveled as south as Key West and as north as Illinois until she decided she wanted to come back here. There's nothing like it here, buddy. Nothing at all. We've enjoyed playing gigs around town, visiting friends, camping by the river, listening to good music and eating the best southern food around.

Kristie asked about you often. Meeting you let her forget her illness and just live. Thank you, Braden. Thank you for making her final summer the best one yet.

It's with a heavy heart that I have to write you this letter. A few nights ago, Kristie and I were lying by the campfire. Her head rested in my lap as we watched the water and listened to Little Richie playing from the radio. The fire cast a beautiful glow over her face as I slid my fingers across her cheek. She took her final breath that night.

I've lived wild, but life still baffles me. I expected it to feel empty without Kristie, but there is so much of her in my heart and I get to take that with me wherever I go. Sometimes I wonder if this is normal or if I should be sadder than I am. I miss her, but at the same time, it feels like she is still here . . . it's really something, Braden.

Kristie asked that her body be cremated, so that's what we've done. She asked that her ashes be spread in the Mississippi River, so I'm here to honor that. I was wondering if you would be a part of this with me. I understand if it's a lot to ask, so no pressure if you can't or don't want to. But I will be at the address below on November 9 if you decide you want to come.

I really hope to see you soon, Braden. If not, Kristie wanted you to know how much you meant to her. I want you to know that, too.

Your friend,

Hayden

As I stepped out of my purple minivan, the wind greeted me like an old friend, tousling my hair and making me rethink wearing loose shorts. The scent of damp earth and fresh grass mixed with the faint, fishy tang of the Mississippi River. The sun hung low, glinting off the water like a million tiny diamonds, and the sound of the waves gently lapping against the shore was oddly calming.

I kicked off my shoes, letting my toes sink into the cool, slightly squishy grass. Knowing Hayden, this would be more of an "adventure" than a solemn occasion, and, sure enough, I heard him hollering before I even spotted him.

"Braden!"

I turned toward the sound and immediately saw him flying through the air, swinging on a rope tied to a tree. His laughter carried over the breeze as gravity reeled him back, and he landed with an ungraceful hop that only Hayden could make look intentional. He was shirtless, wearing nothing but boxers, his tattoos on full display, and he held a bag to his side like it was a bag of chips.

"Over here!" he called, waving me over with his free hand.

I trudged through the grass to meet him. The bag hit the ground as he grabbed me in a bear hug, squeezing just enough to make me question my lung capacity.

"Nice to see you, buddy," he said, releasing me.

"Yeah, you too. So . . . what are you doing out here?"

"Exactly what I wrote you," he said, his tone matter-of-fact. "We're spreading Kristie's ashes."

I looked at the rope and then at the water, trying to piece it together. "Here?"

"Well, yeah! This is the spot she wanted." He grinned like it was obvious. "Grab the rope, swing out, sprinkle some ashes, swing back. Easy."

I blinked hard at him. "You want me to sprinkle Kristie's ashes mid-air?"

"Don't worry," he said, patting my back. "You'll only snort my girl if you catch a really good wind."

"Wow," I shook my head, amused by his humor.

"Here, I'll show you." He grabbed the rope and backed up a few paces. With a running start, he went full-on Tarzan, launching himself toward the river with a speed that could've earned him a gold medal in Most Dramatic Entrance. One-handed, he clung to the rope like a superhero, while his boxers flapped in the wind like they were waving goodbye to everyone's dignity.

When he swung back to the bank and landed in front of me, he handed me the bag like it was no big deal.

"Your turn," he said.

"Uhhh . . ."

"Come on," he urged. "Do it for Kristie."

I sighed. The old fear crept up like a familiar shadow. The part of me that flinched at risk, that needed certainty before courage. But the Deep South had changed me. Fear no longer felt like the enemy. It felt like a doorway.

Believe in yourself, Braden.

Grabbing the rope and the bag, I took a few deep breaths. "This one's for you, Kristie," I muttered, stepping back as far as I could.

With a running start, I launched myself toward the river. For two glorious seconds, I was airborne, weightless, and free. Then gravity decided I'd had enough fun. I lost my grip and plunged into the water, my splash startling nearby birds.

When I bobbed back to the surface, sputtering and clutching the now semi-soggy bag of ashes, I saw Hayden's wide eyes.

"Let her go, Braden!" he shouted between laughs.

I opened the bag and let Kristie's ashes drift into the current. The water carried them downstream, glittering in the sunlight as if the river itself was welcoming her into its journey.

"Hey, look at you, swimming in the river!" Hayden teased. "Not so monstrous now, is it?"

My feet touched the muddy bottom, and I waded back to shore, dripping wet and feeling strangely at peace. Hayden took the wet, empty bag from my hands, still laughing as he slung an arm around my shoulders.

"Not bad for your first try," he said.

"Yeah, well, next time, maybe I'll stay dry," I replied, shaking water out of my hair.

I looked closer at the tattoos on Hayden's side, the bouquet of flowers intertwined with Kristie's name, and another one I hadn't noticed before. It read, *Inside the impossible.*

"What's that mean?" I asked, pointing.

Hayden glanced down at it, a small smile tugging at the corner of his lips. "We're livin' it. Life, man. We're living inside something that's impossible for us to figure out."

I raised an eyebrow.

He gestured at the river and sky. "We'll never have it all figured out. Might as well let go and enjoy the adventure."

I stood there for a moment, shaking the water out of my hair and letting his words sink in.

"Can I ask you something else, Hayden?"

"Shoot."

"Why here? Why this exact spot?"

His eyes lightened as he glanced out at the river. "This is where Kristie and I used to dream about traveling back when we dropped out of high school."

I nodded, my thoughts drifting to Leah. One day, I'd see her again, explain everything. I didn't know how or when, but I'd win her back.

That evening, Hayden and I set up a small grill by the riverbank and cooked hotdogs, the smoky aroma mingling with the crisp scent of the water. We played music, Susie's strings vibrating in harmony with the croak of frogs and the buzz of cicadas. Hayden shared stories about Kristie and things I'd never known, like how she used to be a ballerina but also had a black belt in karate.

"A ballerina with a black belt?" I laughed. "She could've danced circles around me while kicking my ass."

Hayden chuckled. "She was full of surprises, man."

A snort made me turn. Margaret stood in the doorway, wiggling her nose in greeting.

"Margaret," I said, surprised by the rush of excitement. I stepped forward and scooped her into my arms, her little body thrusting with joy.

"Not afraid of her snot anymore, are you?" Hayden teased.

I laughed, running my hand over Margaret's tough fur.

My mind wandered back to the summer moment in the

Winnebago when I'd wiped the tears from Hayden's face. We'd been too close, too quiet, and for a heartbeat, almost kissed.

It wasn't shameful anymore to think about. Not really. That vulnerability had belonged to both of us, and nothing more. I cared about him now, but not like that. Not in that way. Just as a friend, someone I could trust and laugh with, someone who had been there through chaos, grief, and joy alike.

The memory brought a quiet warmth, like exhaling after holding your breath too long. Hayden laughed at something Margaret did, and I found myself smiling, genuinely, free from the tangle of confusion that had haunted me before.

As the sun dipped below the horizon, the sky exploded into streaks of orange and purple, and fireflies began to blink in the gathering dusk. We crashed next to the fire we'd built, Hayden dozing off almost immediately. But I stayed up, watching the fireflies float like tiny lanterns against the darkened trees.

Margaret snored beside me, satisfied as if she'd conquered an all-you-can-eat buffet.

The next morning, Hayden had plans to meet up with some friends. He invited me to come along, but I knew I wasn't ready for that yet. "One step at a time," I told him, promising we'd meet up again someday.

I patted the top of Margaret's head, and she grunted, a sound I assumed was a heartfelt farewell in teacup pig language, or possibly a demand for more snacks.

Driving down the dirt road, sun on my windshield, Susie in the back seat, I laughed aloud, a light, uncontainable sound that bubbled up from somewhere deep inside me.

Before I left Mississippi, I parked in front of the *Welcome to Mississippi* sign and sat there for a while in my purple minivan. The weathered sign bore the marks of countless travelers before me. I stared at it, grateful for what this journey had given me.

The depression didn't magically disappear. Life doesn't work like that. It wasn't like I walked out of the Wolf River that summer a brand-new man. But I *did* leave a part of myself in that water. The old Braden who thought he couldn't make it, who believed he didn't deserve a second chance. I didn't kill myself that day; I killed the part of me that wanted to give up. And while not every day since had been easy, I made a choice the old Braden wouldn't have. I was going to take it one day at a time, love myself enough to ask for help, and keep moving forward.

I pulled out Kristie's caricature of me, tucked between the seat and console. Her playful lines awakened a version of me I hadn't seen in years. The child within, smiling wide, his eyes gleaming with unfiltered hope. I traced the paper with my fingers and looked back up at the sign. "Thanks, Kristie," I whispered.

Later, as I crossed into Louisville, I made a detour. The little pink house that Hayden and I had wanted to visit during our trip appeared ahead, cheerful with the bright, sunny day.

I parked along the curb and walked up to the small sign out front. It told the story of this place. Muhammad Ali's childhood home, where his values were instilled. I lingered on the words, *"EDUCATION BRINGS SELF-RESPECT."* It hit me hard. Maybe that's why I chose to live. Maybe, deep down, I wanted to learn to respect myself again.

I knocked on the door, half-expecting no one to answer. But before I could talk myself out of it, a lady opened the door. I paid in cash, and she let me roam the house on my own.

Inside, time stood still. The living room, protected by ropes, had an old green couch against a wall of decorative wallpaper. A modest fireplace with a few knickknacks, the air tinged with wood polish and nostalgia. I wandered through the kitchen, its white fridge vibrating quietly like it had in the 1950s. There were vintage stoves, glass bottles, and plain bedrooms that spoke of simpler times. The backyard was small, just a patch of grass and a tree that probably hadn't changed much since Ali's childhood.

Standing there, I felt like I could hear echoes of his dreams, the determination of a boy who refused to let the world dictate his worth. He'd faced challenges I couldn't imagine, yet he never let them stop him. It wasn't that my problems were insignificant. Far from it. But being in that space reminded me to be thankful for the chance to keep going.

When I walked back to my purple minivan, I turned on the CD player and flipped through my burnt discs until I found John Mellencamp's *Pink Houses*. As I pulled onto the road, the opening chords filled the car, their bittersweet optimism wrapping around me like an old friend.

As I drove back toward Tipton County, the wind rushing through the cracked window, I felt it again. That spark. The only person who had ever stood in my way was me. And just like Ali, I was learning to fight back. I was learning to dream big.

CHAPTER 16:
Dream On

It was April 24, 2010, almost six months since the day I'd spread, well, *spilled*, Kristie's ashes into the Mississippi River.

Life had taken a turn for the better. I had my own cozy apartment, just enough space to breathe and grow. Mr. Hillman, always looking out for me, introduced me to the owner of a downtown music store. The deal was I could use the studio apartment upstairs as long as I worked in the shop below. So, I gave guitar lessons during the day, and at night, the studio became my sanctuary. For the first time, I felt independent, responsible, and proud of who I was becoming.

The big news came in an envelope one random Tuesday. An acceptance letter from Ball State University. I jumped so high on my bed I nearly hit my head on the ceiling. I could've gone anywhere, but this school felt like a nod from the universe.

I'd reconnected with Sara, Scotty and Rachelle, too. Scotty had been mad for months, but when I told him I needed to work on myself, he eased up. "Fair enough," he'd said, shrugging like he hadn't been calling me a jerk for months. We picked up where we'd left off. Taco Bell runs, aimless drives through town, and movie nights at my place when they came home from college on weekends. It felt like old times, except now with a side of extra gratitude and probably a couple of extra pounds from all the Taco Bell.

One of the coolest surprises that year came in the mail from Sibby. Inside the envelope was the photo she'd taken of me standing in Sun Studio's legendary recording room, in the exact spot where Elvis Presley had stood. I framed it and hung it on my apartment wall, a daily reminder of how far I'd come.

Therapy became a weekly highlight. After family sessions wrapped up, I kept seeing the super cool counselor on my own. She had this knack for making the complicated feel simple. She taught me to rethink my inner dialogue. Instead of trying to change negative thoughts, she asked me to pause and look at them for what they were. Just thoughts. Were they true? Were they helpful? Most of the time, the answer was no. So now, instead of spiraling into self-doubt, I just roll my eyes at myself and replace those thoughts with something better. It wasn't magic, but it worked. Slowly, my attitude shifted. I noticed the difference in myself, like I was rewiring my own brain, one thought at a time.

"She's the best," I'd tell Scotty and Rachelle whenever they teased me about my "shrink."

She even encouraged me to build a relationship with Sibby, and I'd taken her advice.

That past winter, I'd gone to see Paul McCartney with Grandpa Norris and Sibby, and it was everything I'd ever imagined a Paul McCartney concert could be. From the first chord to the encore, it felt like a dream you didn't want to wake up from. Grandpa Norris cried when he performed "Let It Be," and Sibby screamed louder than anyone else during "Hey Jude." For a while, we were just three people, completely lost in the music. It was one of those nights you'd hold close to your heart forever.

Sibby and I talked often, her visits becoming routine. But nothing compared to seeing her and my parents finally make peace. Sitting at that kitchen table, seeing the warmth in their faces and the respect in their words, was nothing short of incredible. It was like watching a bridge being built after years of separation, and I was standing in the middle, grateful beyond words.

Learning my mom wasn't my biological mother didn't change my love for her or for Sibby. It only deepened. I realized how lucky I was to have two women in my life who loved me so fiercely that they were willing to sacrifice everything for me. Mom, with her endless devotion, and Sibby, with her quiet strength and courage to let me have the life I needed.

It's not every day you get to say you have *two* moms, and I thought that was pretty cool. If love was measured by the sacrifices people made, then I was the richest guy in the world.

That April morning, I left my apartment with Aerosmith blasting, belting Steven Tyler's high notes during "Dream On" like my life depended on it. I wore my yellow-and-red polka dot tie just like old times. I was getting better at singing. My chest voice was stronger, my vibrato was finally on point, and while I wasn't exactly ready to headline a church choir, maybe, just maybe, Aerosmith would give me a call someday.

Mr. Hillman had mentioned Leah was back in town now and then, helping him direct the school play. Today was the big performance, and I'd already decided I was going to show up. But my resolve had wavered more than once in the weeks leading up to the show. Did Leah even want to see me? I hadn't seen her since I left town for the Deep South, the night I thought I was doing her a favor by leaving.

What if Leah had moved on? She might have a boyfriend by now, someone who didn't ghost her before completely disappearing. If she'd forgotten about me, I wouldn't blame her. But even if rejection was waiting for me, I had to take this chance.

I got to the school early, long before anyone else arrived. Walking through the grass between the north wing and the cafeteria, the nostalgia hit me. The place looked the same, yet different somehow, like it had aged without me. Memories floated to the surface, some bittersweet, others filled with quiet laughter.

And now, I was here, hoping for a second chance with the girl I never stopped thinking about.

But . . . where was The Tree?

Where were *all* the trees?

I froze, staring at the empty stretch of grass. The familiar shade, the sprawling branches, the quiet guardian of our lives. It was gone. My heart sank as I scanned the area. Nothing but open space and faint remnants of disturbed dirt.

Construction signs dotted the school grounds, and bright orange fencing surrounded some equipment near the cafeteria. I'd noticed the work going on when I arrived, but I hadn't imagined they'd taken *all* the trees.

I walked to the spot where I knew The Tree had stood, the soles of my shoes crunching faintly over a few dried leaves. My mind raced with memories. Lunches spent sprawled under its shade, Scotty attempting to impress us by kicking The Tree with his already fractured ankle and nearly fracturing it again, and endless conversations that somehow felt more meaningful beneath its branches.

I remembered carving Leah's initials into the trunk one fall afternoon, the way her face lit up with happiness as if I'd just declared some unspoken promise. We kissed there, too. Right here, where I was standing now. I could still picture her lying beside me in the grass, her hair spread like a halo as she stared up at the sky through the leaves.

The Tree had been more than just a tree. It had been our anchor, our meeting spot, a silent witness to all the love, conversations, and growth we shared. And now it was gone. No trunk, no stump. Just an empty patch of grass.

For a moment, I considered calling Hillman to ask about it, but he was inside with Leah and the students. Instead, I stood there, staring at the ground where roots had once run deep, grounding us in ways we didn't even realize.

I remembered telling Leah one evening that The Tree would live on as long as we did, even if it was cut down. You could see how old a tree was by counting the circles in its trunk. But now there wasn't even a trunk left, just the spirit of something we carried in our hearts.

Maybe that was enough. The Tree wasn't really gone, not if we chose to keep it alive in our memories. It was a thought I held onto as I sat down where The Tree used to be, the breeze carrying the faint scent of freshly cut grass and the warmth of spring brushing against my face.

I laid my notepad over Susie, smoothing the page to keep my thoughts from looking rushed.

I began to write.

saturday, april 24, 2010

I was listening to jeff buckley last night. Grace. It reminds me of you every time i hear it. Theres something in his voice, something deeper, more alive than even we are. It reminds me that we all have something to live for. Remember his voice?

I grabbed my guitar and left town. Played music down south for a while because that's what i wanted to do. It felt amazing to play again, so much that i wondered how i could've gone so long without it.

The strings, the sound, the feeling as if i was the music myself.

I stayed at Hillmans house until i was ready to talk to my parents again. Trevor knew. Grandpa Norris knew. Eventually i called my parents and worked things out. I didnt want to say anything to you because i knew youd come looking for me and the last thing i wanted to do was hold you back.

I didnt like the ending, Leah.
So i changed it.
    p.s. I wrote a song about The Tree. Can i play it
for you?
    Braden

I put it in the Ziplock bag, dug a small hole, and buried the letter beneath the dirt and grass. As the audience trickled in, my gaze landed on the back door, where Leah and the cast would eventually walk through. I hoped she knew I'd come back for her.

I grabbed my ticket and sat in the last seat, seventh row from the front. The auditorium was more packed than I'd ever seen for a drama club play. Leah had made it happen, spreading the word, hanging posters. She cared.

She cared enough to travel south and share my flyer, the one that saved my life at the Wolf River Bridge.

I knew it was her. After I returned to town, Trevor told me how she'd organized our friends to put up flyers everywhere. She'd known me better than anyone, knew how much I loved Jeff Buckley and the Mississippi River, knew how deep my despair had run. I imagined her waiting there, hoping to catch me before I made a decision I couldn't take back.

The curtains opened. The play—a perfect mix of comedy, drama, and a tear-jerking ending—was pure Leah. The lines and blocking were technical, but the heart of it? That was all her. Strong, soft, vulnerable, and beautiful.

Ball State was lucky to have her. I'd be attending after summer, planning to study music history and business. I wondered what Leah would think of that, or if she'd want anything to do with me after everything.

When Leah stepped forward for her bow, I froze, then melted. The crowd erupted in applause, and Mr. Hillman pointed to her, clearly proud. She gave a humble wave, still a little nervous in the spotlight, but I thought she was most beautiful when she was just being herself. For a moment, I thought she saw me. I shifted, trying to stay unnoticed, but her eyes searched the crowd.

The curtains wouldn't close on our relationship. Not if I had any say in it.

After the show, the auditorium emptied, chatter fading with the closing doors. I sat alone, remembering four years in this room, the traces of hopes and dreams spoken aloud. It had worked for Leah. She had always dreamed, and look at her now.

I sat there for a while longer before finally getting up, making my way up the side stage steps. I lingered, scanning the script that had her name all over it, remembering our rehearsals for *The Miracle Worker*, thinking of the curtain that had wrapped around us when I kissed her here.

When the noise outside faded, I moved toward the backstage door, stepping into the back hallway. There it was. The back door that led to The Tree.

I paused. Somehow, I knew she'd be there, believing I'd come back.

I walked down the empty hallway, the sound of my footsteps echoing in the stillness. Just as I reached the door, a voice broke the silence.

"Forget something?"

I turned around. Hillman stood there, holding my Chaplin hat I'd left with Leah. He had grown a goatee, and I could see the engagement happiness in his eyes. He'd been dating a woman for a few months before popping the question.

I walked toward him, but his expression was serious, not the smirk I'd been expecting.

"She already left," he said.

I looked at the Chaplin hat in his hands before taking it from him, carefully studying it. It had been with me for so long, symbolizing so much. I placed it on my head with a quiet confidence.

"She'll come back," I said, firm and certain.

Hillman nodded, his gaze thoughtful, and then he turned and walked away, leaving me alone once more.

I stood there for a moment, then made my way to the back door. My hands hovered over the bar, but just before I pushed it open, I stopped.

Through the window, I saw her.

There she was, standing in the very spot where I'd stood, right on top of The Tree.

She was more beautiful than I remembered, her hair falling lightly around her shoulders, longer than before. She wore a light-yellow shirt and a white skirt, a combination that somehow felt both delicate and strong. She carried a book, and for a moment, I couldn't make out what it was. But as she turned, I saw what she was holding—a weathered, well-loved copy of *And To Think That I Saw It On Mulberry Street*.

The memory of reading it to her right there came rushing back. My stomach fluttered as if it had remembered a long-lost song.

She was waiting. Maybe she always had been.

She placed the book beside her, then leaned back on her elbows, settling into the moment. It was then I saw it. The small, quiet gesture that told me everything. She felt the letter from underneath, the one I'd hidden so carefully. She sat up, her hands patting the grass until they uncovered it.

My heart raced. I couldn't breathe.

She was reading it. My letter. The one that carried every ounce of hope, vulnerability, and longing I had for us.

My knees buckled, and excitement surged through me, taking over my body.

I knew it.

I knew she would come back.

I gripped Susie, heart pounding. I opened the door with barely a creak, closing it softly behind me. My yellow-and-red polka dot tie fluttered in the wind. Outside, every sound pierced the quiet. The rustling leaves, distant birds, the crackle of the letter.

I couldn't tear my eyes away. Her face lit up with a quiet laugh, a joyful shake of her head. Was it my words or the possibility of my return?

I stepped closer to Leah, barely a few feet away now. She was still reading, her eyes glued to the page.

I was going to play her the song I'd written. The one about The Tree. The one that held every piece of us. The love, the memories, the promises.

I adjusted my Chaplin hat, my fingers grazing Susie's strap before coming to rest on my shoulder, where my cross tattoo remained.

Mississippi had taught me that life was messy. Seasons came and went, pages turned. But the fleeting, beautiful moments? They made it all worth it.

And in that moment, with the wind swirling around us and the sun spilling warmth over the grass, I thought about Mississippi again, the way the name stretches long, heavy with letters, yet still flows like a river. Life felt the same. Some days moved slow, sagging under reasons to give up. But in the current of it all, it only took one reason—one steady, unwavering reason—to keep moving forward.

Even when life felt impossible. Even when the path ahead was cracked and filled with shadows. Like the tiny pink flower on my cross tattoo rooted in a place it was never meant to grow, yet still, it bloomed. It didn't belong, but it refused to wither. And if something so small could find a way to survive against the odds, maybe I could, too.

With joyful tears streaming down her cheeks, Leah lowered the letter to her lap. Slowly, her gaze drifted up toward me. The world seemed to pause as our eyes met, locking onto each other in a silent connection we had both been waiting for.

The sun bathed us both in its glow, and all the things left unsaid seemed to hang in the air between us.

Because sometimes, all it takes is one reason to keep going. One reason to keep fighting.

And in that moment, Leah's eyes and her smile were all the reason I needed.

THE END

Thank you to the talented Fred Aceves for your thorough edits on this book. Your insights strengthened this story and helped it become what it was always meant to be.

Thank you to Geneva Writers Group for providing countless opportunities for me to grow as a writer. I look forward to visiting as often as I can!

To my readers, and to those who have eagerly anticipated this sequel, your excitement and feedback have guided these stories more than you know.

To my children, thank you for embracing the many worlds that writers live in and for keeping that little girl inside me alive, curious, and inspired. To my husband, Attila, thank you for the weekly flowers, for your unwavering faith in me, and for being my constant reminder to "don't stop believin'."

Above all, I am grateful to God for planting this seed in my heart and lovingly leading it to fruition. Thank you.

While writing this book, I returned to the place that shaped so much of who I am, finding myself there once again—but now as a fuller, more whole version of myself. During one of the most transformative years of my life, when the journey felt difficult, I remembered a painting I made one summer of Peter Pan flying into the stars on a moonlit night. Written on the painting were the words: "To live will be an awfully big adventure."

We are here to live, to experience, to learn. We're here to challenge ourselves, take risks, dream big, pray boldly, and leap even while afraid. Whatever that leap looks like for you, big or small, take it. You might fall. So what? You will rise stronger and wiser. And you might just fly into the stars on a moonlit night, discovering the adventure of a lifetime.

Dream on.

1.) Do you think Braden's discovery about his true
connection to Sibby changed his decision to
end his life?

In what ways did this revelation affect his understanding of himself and his family?

2.) Why do you think Braden's parents chose to
hide the truth from Braden?

Do you believe they were protecting him or
protecting themselves?

3.) What do you think the pink flower on Braden's
cross tattoo represents?

How does its meaning evolve as the story
progresses?

4.) How did Braden's letters to the people he left
behind shape his journey?

What role did writing play in his healing or in his
descent?

5.) What do you think drew Braden to hitchhike
to the Deep South rather than finding another
way to cope?

Was his journey more about escaping or searching?

6.) How do the people Braden meets along the way
influence his outlook on life and death?

Which encounter do you think made the greatest
impact?

7.) The story explores both despair and hope.

At what point do you think Braden begins to truly
want to live and what triggers that change?

8.) Music and the Delta setting are central to
Braden's journey.

How do you think the Southern atmosphere and
blues culture mirror his emotional state?

9.) If you could write one of Braden's letters yourself—to his parents, Sibby, or even to himself
—what would you say?

What message do you think he most needed to
hear?

10.) What will you remember most about this
story and why?

Did any particular scene, line, or image stay with
you after reading?

Step inside the world of *Gray Iris*, Gina's gripping New Adult novel about Darcie Day, a young woman hiding from a dark past, and Gray Iris, a rising Nashville metalcore band on the edge of fame. Visit www.ginamorosey.com now to get a free excerpt. Discover the secrets, danger, and music that spark a reckoning. *Gray Iris*, coming soon.

NERD SQUAD REVOLUTION (*noun, verb, way of life*)

definition: **a proactive approach to ending the stigma on nerdism via unapologetically being yourself.**

Join the Nerd Squad Newsletter for more details! Also, for your chance to:
- be featured as Nerd of the Month
- submit your writing
- win exciting giveaways
- receive special discounts
- access free writing material
- see sneak previews
- and much more!

Visit www.ginamorosey.com to join.
INSTAGRAM @ginamorosey
TIKTOK @ginamorosey
FACEBOOK facebook.com/ginamorosey.author
GOODREADS goodreads.com/gina-morosey

GINA MOROSEY studied Musical Theatre at Ball State University, where she discovered that writing through the night leads to lifelong insomnia. After making it to the finals on Switzerland's Got Talent, she tucked away her theatre dreams to focus on writing—something she's been passionate about since freaking out her elementary school teachers with handwritten horror stories.

Her debut novel, A Place Called The Tree, became a #1 Amazon Bestseller, and her latest release, Letters in Mississippi, continues the story as its highly anticipated sequel. When she's not writing, Gina organizes music festivals and books artists around the world. She lives in Switzerland with her family, still chasing stories (and sleep).

She loves passionate discussions on all topics of creative writing.

To inquire about booking Gina Morosey for a book signing and/or speaking engagement, visit www.ginamorosey.com.

If you or anyone you know is struggling with mental illness or suicidal thoughts, please visit www.suicide.org and www.nami.org for more resources.

www.ginamorosey.com